SAMMY

Working for a Living

SAMMY

Working
for a
Living

Robin Hardy

Westford Press

Sammy: Working for a Living (Book 3 of the Sammy Series)
2nd edition
Contemporary Christian series

ISBN: 978-1-934776-80-3
Copyright © 2003, 2014 Robin Hardy

Cover image copyright Karin Wabro

Westford Press
mail@westfordpress.com

All of the author's characters are "enhanced composites"—fictional creations in fictional circumstances. As fiction, this book is not intended to portray the actual workings of any institution or organization in Dallas.

one

Sammy lay on his back in the middle of the floor listening to his wife, Marni, talk to her mother on the telephone. Six-month-old Sam crawled busily over him, slapping him in the face and drooling. Sammy prevented him from pitching head first off his chest once or twice, but otherwise let him have free run of Gulliver here.

Twenty-two-year-old Marni tucked her legs underneath her on the leather sofa. "He's got that same black hair as Sammy, for sure. And the pediatrician said that if his eyes are still blue at six months, that's their permanent color. Now I'm waiting to see if he inherited that Kidman charisma, as well. I don't know what I'm going to do with *two* men that attract women like flies."

She winked at her husband, who tilted his head back to eye her. "You got nothing to worry about, baby," he murmured. Sammy had relied on that charisma and his drop-dead good looks to get him through some pretty hazardous undercover assignments as a police detective. That charisma was what first attracted Marni to him when she had moved into the apartment next door to his.

But she had found that his smooth exterior covered a

manipulative, disturbed personality. By the time he was through using her, she never wanted to see him again. For his part, Sammy was perturbed to discover that her childlike faith had touched him far deeper than he would have liked. He went way past falling in love, clear down to obsession, and began stalking her. So it wasn't until God hauled him back from the edge of hell that he became suitable for marriage.

And baby Sam? Sammy lowered his chin to watch the baby intently try to pluck out chest hairs from under the t-shirt. Sam was just tangible evidence of God's restorative goodness. As much as Sammy loved children, he had been told not to expect any of his own, not since his first child had died some twelve years before. Yet here was Samuel James Kidman, Jr., a flesh-and-blood miracle. Sammy cradled the perfect little head in fresh wonder and looked back at Sam's mother.

She was a pretty girl, with full brown hair and almond-shaped eyes that gave her a mischievous look. Sammy liked Dallas' long, hot summers because Marni looked so good in shorts. And she had recaptured her prepregnant form quickly.

"Mom, stop whining," Marni said in mock exasperation. "You keep him all the time—I'm afraid he's not going to know which one of us is his mother. . . . Overnight? I don't know about that. Sammy wants him all to himself when he gets home. Yeah, Mike has let him continue to work Auto Theft, but Sammy says he never knows when he'll get called back for a special assignment."

Mike Masterson, Sammy's boss, was the sergeant in charge of the Targeted Activity Section of the Special

Investigations Bureau of the Dallas, Texas, Police Department.

Sammy got up and she glanced over. "Ask Pam to let me talk to Clayton," he said.

"Uh, Mom, Sammy wants to talk to Daddy. Okay. Love you, too," Marni said, giving her a smack over the phone before extending it to Sammy.

He put Sam on one arm and took the receiver. "Hi, Clayton. No kidding. I don't know how Marni keeps up with him—he's got four-wheel drive. Listen, who is that woman you said wanted to talk to me when I was ready to retire from police work? Yeah, I'm ready. Yeah, if you would, call me back after you talk to her. Thanks."

Marni stared at him as he hung up. Sammy had entered the police academy immediately after college twelve years ago, never considering any other type of work. "Sammy?" she asked bemusedly.

He bounced Sam on his arm. "I remember too well what it was like growing up without a father, Marni. It's time I put Sam's security first—time I finished growing up."

"I can't see you happy doing anything else, Sammy," she observed dubiously.

"Give me some credit, Marni," he said, piqued. "I can be flexible."

She held her peace and he answered the telephone when it rang a few minutes later. "Yo. Hi, Clayton. Did you? Good." He handed Sam off to Marni so he could write down a name and address. "Nine o'clock tomorrow? Okay, great. Thanks."

He hung up and folded the sheet with the address, then glanced at her troubled expression. "I thought you

7

would be glad for me to get out of undercover work," he remarked.

"Sammy." She put a gently persuasive hand to his chest. "I wish you would think about this a while. Why don't you talk to Mike about letting you transfer permanently to Auto Theft?"

"I don't *want* to stay in Auto Theft all the time—not for what they're paying me," he declared.

"Oh, Sammy—then you'd never last in a nine-to-five job," she breathed.

Sammy reached out to caress her thick hair. "Let me just go check it out. That's the least I can do."

"What's the job?" she asked cautiously.

"Head of security for FirstPlace Bank Tower," he replied levelly.

Her mouth dropped open. "A security guard?"

"*Head* of security," he clarified.

"Sammy, those are the guys you make fun of!" she said, pained.

He took on his mature tone. "Now, Marni. This is for you and Sam." She shrugged and he added with a gleam, "Call Pam back. We'll let her keep Sam for us tonight." The other member of their family, Marni's cat Smoky, was still in residence at Pam and Clayton Taylor's household.

By the time Sammy had returned from dropping off Sam at his grandparents' house, Marni was dressed and ready. They took off in Sammy's prized '66 Mustang, with the top down, and headed for one of Sammy's old haunts for dinner and dancing. He liked the small, out-of-the-way places that were the antithesis of trendy in serving up plain, homestyle food and earthy blues.

Usually, they were in the poorer parts of town.

The place they went tonight, Mama's Restaurant, looked plenty small and out of the way from the outside. The parking lot comprised weeds interspersed with broken asphalt. Inside, the air was close and smoky, the dim light halved again by layers of grease on the globes.

As Marni and Sammy slipped into a booth with torn vinyl on the seats, she watched the sax player on the tiny stage rip with the most heart-rending version of "Rainy Night in Georgia" she'd ever heard. Sammy was asking the gum-chewing waitress, "What's good tonight?"

"Mama Perkins's cookin' up chicken-fried steak," she replied languidly.

"Mama Perkins is still here?" Sammy exclaimed. "Yeah, get us two, and tell her Sammy says hi."

Marni turned with a half-smile as the waitress left, and Sammy earnestly explained, "I know you don't like heavy food, but you haven't lived till you've tasted Mama Perkins' chicken-fried steak."

"Okay," she smiled in the dim yellow light. Sammy, forever disdainful of dressing up, wore an old favorite tweed sports coat over his jeans—he always wore a jacket, even in summer, to cover the Sig Sauer 226 he always carried. Marni, by contrast, was definitely overdressed in a short halter dress, and Sammy wouldn't have it any other way.

An elderly black woman came out from the back and peered around the room from behind her thick glasses. "Mama Perkins!" Sammy called, rising from the booth. He went over to embrace her with a gentle bear hug. She held his face and patted his shoulder.

Sammy turned to gesture for Marni, who got up and

joined them. "Mama Perkins, this is my wife, Marni," he said in her ear over the music.

"Oh, Sammy, you done went and got married. The girls is gonna cry," she said sorrowfully.

"So?" he laughed. "I've still got you."

"Go 'way. What do you need me for?" she pooh-poohed.

"Mama, nobody on earth can cook like you," he declared.

"Go on, now. You get that pretty girl to dance and let me back at my stove," she said severely, greatly pleased.

Sammy turned Marni around to the ten-by-twelve-foot dance floor. "Did you used to come here as Sax?" she asked, referring to the undercover alias he was using when they first met.

"No," he said, snuggling her close. "Long before Sax. It was my first undercover assignment. I got in trouble right away because a coupla guys didn't like how I looked. I was so green," he shook his head in pity. "They woulda sliced me up for lunch meat but Mama Perkins rescued me. It was the most humiliating experience of my life. I've loved her ever since," he grinned.

Marni sighed as Sammy squeezed her and buried his face in her hair. Like he said, she should be glad that he was getting out of such dangerous work. But this was one fish she couldn't imagine thriving on safe, dry land.

They returned to the booth when the waitress brought out their plates. As Sammy had promised, the chicken-fried steak was so good that Marni ate almost half of it. But better still was the music. There was just

that one sax player—a graying black man named Rosie
—but his songs sank in her heart and stayed there. After
dinner, Marni and Sammy spent an hour slow dancing,
oblivious to everything but each other and the music.

When he finally breathed in her ear that it was time
to go home, Marni laid her head on his chest for one last
dance. Afterwards, Sammy paid their tab and included a
large tip, winking to the waitress, "We'll be back."

She shook her head. "Mama's may not. Ol' Mama
Perkins lost the boy who helped her, and she gettin' so
blind she can't see good enough to clean. The health
department'll be coming 'round in a few days, and if she
ain't got this place spic 'n' span, they'll shut her down."

Dismayed, Sammy pulled out his wallet again. "Tell
her to—"

The waitress shoved his hand away. "She won't take
that. It won't do no good anyway. G'wan."

Reluctantly, they went out to the car. Marni
murmured, "What a shame."

"There must be something I can do," Sammy mused.
"Well, God, since you're the God of widows and
orphans, I guess I'll let You handle this." He started the
car and Marni stretched lazily, arching her back.
Watching her, he promptly forgot all about Mama
Perkins.

The next morning Sammy parked his Mustang in
front of the gleaming FirstPlace Bank Tower downtown
and glanced up at its imposing sixty stories. He entered a
first-floor office and introduced himself to the building
manager's secretary. She showed him a chair, and in a
few moments took him to a large interior office.

He extended his hand to the stiffly suited woman sitting behind a massive desk. "Ms. Bancroft? I'm Sammy Kidman."

"Mr. Kidman." She stood to shake his hand politely. "Clayton spoke very highly of you. You're fortunate to have such a well-connected father-in-law."

Sammy paused. "I'd like to think I earned some of those connections, Ms. Bancroft."

"Of course. Well, let me show you around." She took him out to walk around the ground floor and perimeter of the building before showing him the master controls in the security room. She explained, "Besides FirstPlace Bank, we have Pencor Publishing, DataTree Services, InfoTel, and a number of smaller tenants. There was an attempted robbery three months ago, which led to the installation of the security system you see now. As head of security, you will see that the system is properly operated."

Sammy shook his head slightly, looking over the master panel. "This is state-of-the-art. You don't need anything more than someone to turn it on and off—a button-pusher."

"Perhaps, but management is concerned that this 'button-pusher' be qualified to oversee such a system," she observed carefully.

"Qualified?" Sammy's expressive black brows shot up. "Ms. Bancroft, I was awarded the Medal of Honor."

"That's nice. Does that make you competent to operate a million-dollar system?" she wondered.

"Ma'am," Sammy said, stroking his forehead, "it's the highest award the Dallas Police Department gives. Any lamebrain can learn which buttons to push. In hiring security, you have to first assure yourself that the person you choose won't deliberately shut off your million-dollar system for a cut of the take. It's a question of character."

"I see," she murmured, studying him. He was a character, all right—too casual, too self-assured, too good-looking.

Sammy began, "Look, I appreciate your time, but I think I'm overqualified for what you need—"

"We will pay you an annual salary of ninety thousand, with full benefits," she said.

"Ninety thousand?" Sammy gasped. "You'll pay me ninety thousand dollars a year for throwing switches?"

"Ninety-two thousand. That's my final offer," she said firmly.

"Ninety-two—!" Sammy stared at her. With a salary of $92,000, he could get Marni out of that apartment and buy her a house almost as nice as Pam and Clayton's. "Taken," he said.

"Good. When can you start?" she asked.

"You need to give me at least two weeks to clean up my paperwork," he murmured.

"Today is the seventeenth," she said, looking toward a wall calendar, "so we'll expect you to start on July first."

"Okay. Great," Sammy said, confirming it with a handshake.

He left calculating what his monthly take-home pay would be starting August first. But as he drove toward the Big Building Downtown (the Police and Courts Building), he felt a knot form in his throat. And it wasn't because the department's move to the new, $60-million police complex had been postponed again—this time due to a mysterious outcropping of black mold along the walls. Those poor schmucks working on the construction of the new facility were ripping out huge sections of sheetrock that they had just installed a few months before.

Sammy parked his conspicuous, light green Mustang in the crumbling lot next to the Big Building, lifting his chin to acknowledge the greetings of Officers Brickett and Pierce: "Hey, Sambo!"

Ambling in a side door, he received his lapel ID from Corporal Collins and put it on. This was an unnecessary exercise, as just about everyone here knew him, but one he never failed to perform. "Hi, Dreamboat," winked the pudgy Collins.

Sammy pretended to glare at her to maintain their little game. For some unfathomable reason, it tickled her to think that she was irritating him. Then he went on up to the Targeted Activity office on the third floor and sat at his cluttered, dented, canary-yellow metal desk. He looked up at square-jawed, sandy-haired Dave Pruett on the telephone—Sammy had been Pruett's best man at his wedding.

Sammy's gaze shifted to Garrett. Black, ultra cool, street-smart Garrett, who brought Sammy a hundred solid tips and all his paperwork to go with them. Garrett's wife had brought over a home-smoked ham the week after Sam's birth.

Sammy's heart sank at the thought of leaving all these people—and for what? To be a security guard for a rich corporation. But $92,000 was an inducement he couldn't afford to ignore. Dismally, Sammy inserted a sheet of paper into his old typewriter (on which he had completed a hundred thousand forms, conservatively) and began typing out his resignation letter. The much newer computer sat a few feet away, but he could not bring himself to use it for this letter—not with a printer shared by several sections.

As Sammy typed, Pruett hung up the phone and turned. "Mike called, Sambo. He wants you in his office."

"Will do," Sammy murmured, typing. Sergeant Mike Masterson, Sammy's boss. Who had sheltered him during those dark days of his mental breakdown. Who had been best man at Sammy and Marni's wedding. Who had flown down to San Antonio to keep vigil at Sammy's bedside after that near-fatal shooting. Sammy was now preparing to turn in his resignation to Mike, and he felt lower than a flea on the underside of a dachshund.

Sammy completed the letter, jerked it out of the typewriter and signed it. Rising, he folded it and stuffed it in his coat pocket. On his way out the door, he paused and looked back at Pruett.

Seeing his serious look, Pruett eyed him, then observed, "Sambo, what women see in you when you won't cough up ten bucks for a decent haircut defies all explanation." Sammy turned in sudden pain from the ritual banter. He'd just have to tell Pruett later.

He went down the hall to Mike's office with a sinking feeling. Mike, an African-American, was head of the newly formed Targeted Activity Section. His office should have been closer to the TAS room, preferably in it, but a rookie sergeant got put where there was room for him. He and his section were theoretically supposed to be relocated to an inconspicuous building elsewhere in downtown which already housed Narcotics, Vice, and Criminal Investigations—that is, until the new police offices were made fit for human habitation. But Sammy's gut told him he'd never see the inside of that building. Not as a cop, anyway.

As Sammy appeared at the open door, Mike looked up. "Sammy! Step in. Shut the door, please." Sammy did, so preoccupied with his own stinging conscience that he did not notice Mike's strained manner.

Sammy pulled the letter from his coat pocket as Mike said, "Sit down." He pointed to the chair beside the desk, not the one across from it. Sammy dropped into the chair, formulating the best opening for the bomb he had to drop on his friend and mentor.

"I've got a special assignment for you—no, I can't even call it an assignment. A personal favor. You're the only one I trust enough to ask, and *nobody* can know about this, Sambo," Mike said.

Sticking the letter back into his pocket without a second thought, Sammy asked, "What is it?"

"We've got a—a—a situation at First Metropolitan Church," Mike said.

Sammy stared at him, then started laughing. "The big church downtown here? What are those pesky old ladies up to now?"

"I'm serious, Kidman." At Mike's unamused expression, Sammy wiped the smile off his face.

"Okay, Mike, you wanna tell me about it?" Sammy asked, all professional.

"Here it is. The church wants to buy the historical

building next door to turn it into a gym. The city planners nix it. The church fathers demand a meeting with the mayor and things get heated. Ends up, what the mayor heard in the meeting was a threat that if clearance wasn't granted, the church would release certain documents to the press which reflect poorly on Hizzoner," Mike said.

"Blackmail? You must be joking," Sammy said.

"I wish I were, but I can't say for sure. It was a closed-door meeting and no one other than the Metro people and the mayor heard what was said. This was how he interpreted it, and it worried him enough to go to the chief about it. Obviously, they want it investigated very quietly. You need to get into that church and find out what, if anything, they have on Hizzoner," Mike instructed.

"Oh, man," Sammy muttered, sinking back in his chair.

"Look, Sambo, if we can get this cleared up quietly, the department won't have to fight for any budget requests as long as Hizzoner is in office. I don't need to tell you what that would mean to the chief," Mike advised.

Sammy eyed him dolefully. "Must be nice to have a patsy on the string you can jerk around whenever you need something done."

"I knew I could count on you. Thanks, Sammy," Mike said.

Grousing, Sammy got up and departed. For this job he needed to do several things, one of which was to splurge on a really good haircut—which he didn't bother to do before his interview with Ms. Bancroft.

He walked out of the salon an hour later, eyeing the manicure the girl had insisted he needed while he was insisting he didn't. She had prevailed, and Sammy had to sit there hoping that nobody he knew came in while he was being primped like a Miss America contestant.

He returned to the apartment as Marni was about to feed Sam lunch. She turned in surprise and Sam banged his high chair tray excitedly. "Sammy! You got a haircut. It looks great," Marni said, rising to run her fingers through the feathery layers.

"Thanks," he murmured, bending for a leisurely ice-cream kiss. (That is, he relished ice cream in much the same manner as kisses.)

"You must have been real serious about this interview, to get your hair cut for it," she observed. "So how did it go?"

"Okay," he said. "Actually, I didn't get my hair cut until after the interview. But she made me an offer." Marni watched him and he said, "I'll have to think about it."

"I see. Um, do they have offices in Houston?" Marni asked.

"Houston? I don't know. Why?" he asked, taking off his coat.

"Well, a woman just called and asked for you. I started to tell her you weren't here, and . . . she hung up on me. Caller ID showed a Houston number," Marni said casually.

"I don't know anybody from Houston who would be calling me and hanging up on you," Sammy avowed. Sam, meanwhile, continued to bang the tray and chortle until Sammy came over and sat down. "Hi, guy. What's this? Yum, pulverized carrots. And regurgitated chicken."

Sammy tasted both and grimaced. "Oh boy, this is great stuff. Tell you what. You eat this, and I'll take you out for a junior burger. Deal?" he said, spooning a bite of chicken to Sam, who took it, then slowly pushed it out until it cascaded down his chin.

Marni laughed, "What would you like to eat?"

"Just a sandwich," Sammy murmured. "Look, Sam, I know this is noxious stuff, but your momma won't let me give you ice cream unless you eat it. Be a man, okay?" Sam accepted a few bites of carrots, so Sammy got sneaky and mixed a little chicken in with the carrots. Sam got wise to that after the second spoonful and rejected it.

Marni fixed Sammy's sandwich and set it before him with a cola. "So why did you get the haircut?" she casually asked.

"Could I get a few tomato slices and pickles on the side?" Sammy asked, and Marni nodded. She looked back over her shoulder, waiting for an answer, and he said, "Tell me what you know about First Metro. You took me there when we first met—were you a member?"

"Yes, but only for a while. Then I started going to Grace," Marni replied. This was the little Bible church they now attended, sporadically.

She put a small plate of tomatoes and pickles on the table, and Sammy gave a tomato slice to Sam. He dismantled it with eager, inquisitive fingers, then studiously stuffed all the pieces in his mouth. Sammy gave him another. "What exactly did you want to know?" she asked.

"Give me a rundown of their organizational chart," Sammy said. Sitting with an apple and generous serving of cous cous for herself, Marni told him what she knew about the Metro church structure while he ate and fed Sam bites of this and that.

"What's this about?" she finally asked.

He sighed, "I gotta go see if I can get hired on down there somewhere."

She eyed him. "You thinking of leaving police work for church work?" she asked falteringly.

He looked up quickly. "Now that's a good idea. Yeah," he mused. At her expression, he added, "It's an assignment, baby. Hizzoner the mayor thinks somebody at the church is trying to blackmail him."

"Oh." She stood to rinse off their plates at the sink.

"Don't die of shock, now," he said with gentle sarcasm.

She looked back. "Well, you know, they're just people, and sometimes they can get off track, like anyone can. . . ." She bent to wipe Sam and chair with a dishrag, and Sammy studied her.

"Well," he said, standing, "I'll let you know how it goes."

"Okay," she said distantly. She came out of her preoccupation when he took her in his arms to kiss her goodbye. But after he left, she sank back to the chair, staring off with hollow eyes.

Deliberating, Sammy drove to the downtown conglomerate of buildings from which First Metro ran their operations. "Okay, Lord," he muttered. "I respect this as Your territory, but I've been given an assignment. I'd appreciate it if You could help me get this accomplished with a minimum of deception and sneakiness. You're a God of truth, and all I'm after here is the truth."

He parked and entered the administration building. In the outer office, he paused at a bulletin board that listed job openings at the church. He saw openings for a secretary, a janitor, and parking lot security. "Ah," he said at this last possibility.

A secretary came out from a back office. "May I help you?" she smiled.

"Yes," he said hesitantly, approaching her desk. "My name is—Sammy Kidman. I'm a cop. Currently, that is. But I've got a new baby, and I've been thinking that, for his sake, I need to get out of police work into something less dangerous. I was looking at—"

He started to turn to the bulletin board when a man stepped out from the doorway at which he had been standing and listening. "Sammy," the man said, extending his hand. "I'm Kent Frazier, Director of Youth Programs." Sammy shook his hand. He was about Sammy's age, mid-thirties, with pleasant features and dark brown hair in a trendy cut. He wore a dress shirt and tie. "So you're thinking of church work. Has the Lord called you to preach?" Kent asked.

"Oh no. Nothing so ambitious as that," Sammy said quickly.

"Are you a Christian?" Kent asked.

"Yes," Sammy replied.

"Where do you go to church?" Kent asked.

"Grace Bible Church," Sammy replied.

"I see. Well, what area were you interested in working? Do you like kids?" Kent asked.

"Sure. I like kids a lot," Sammy said.

"Let me tell you what I'm thinking, Sam," Kent said, gesturing, "Come on into my office." Sammy stepped inside the doorway and Kent continued, "I need part-time help with the youth groups—we've got a massive program, you know. The pay isn't much, but it will help you decide if this is the kind of work you want to pursue. What do you think?"

"Sure," Sammy said. "When can I start?"

"Well, today's Wednesday—you can start today. We'll need you to fill out an application and get all the paperwork signed. And, you'll need to apply for church membership here, you know," Kent said.

"Okay," Sammy agreed. Kent said nothing about a background check, so Sammy assumed it was implied. Kent took him out to get the forms from Anna, the secretary.

Sammy paused over her desk. "Since the position is only part-time . . . would you consider my wife for the secretarial position you have open? She has a lot of computer experience."

"Sure thing," Kent said. "Let me talk to our Director of Educational Programs. What's her name?"

"Marni," Sammy replied. "Marni Kidman."

So while Sammy filled out a completely truthful application, Kent went to a back office. In a few minutes he came out and said, "Curtis says he can interview her today. How soon can she get out here?"

"Within the hour, I imagine," Sammy said.

"Okay, let's set her an appointment for three o'clock. How's that?" Kent asked.

"May I use your phone?" Sammy asked the

secretary. (Since the department did not issue TAS phones, Sammy would certainly never pay for one himself, except the ten-year-old car phone in his Mustang.)

"Certainly," she said, turning the base toward him.

Sammy picked up the receiver to dial home. He couldn't believe how smoothly everything was falling into place here—a position for him and for his partner, as well. Marni was an additional set of eyes and ears, an invaluable resource in his undercover assignments. He consistently discouraged her from getting a regular job mainly so that she could be available to help him.

"Hello?" Marni answered.

"Hi, baby. I'm down at First Metro, where they're going to let me intern part-time in youth work. They have an opening for a secretary, as well. I need you to drop Sam off with Pam and come down here for a three o'clock interview," Sammy told her.

There was a long silence. Finally Marni said, "I don't want to."

two

Sammy was flabbergasted. He turned his back to the secretary and said into the telephone, "Uh—I understand that it's short notice, sweetheart, but it's essential, dear."

"For your assignment?" she asked.

"Yes, baby," he said emphatically.

"All right," she said faintly. "I'll try to be there by three."

"Thank you," he said.

He hung up, still shocked. Marni had always been eager to help him on assignments. What was the reason for this sudden mule-headedness? "She didn't know if her mother would be able to keep Sam," he explained to the secretary.

"How old is your son?" she asked.

"Six months," Sammy said, whipping out a wallet photo.

Anna adjusted her glasses and studied the small picture. She was a soft, pink woman, a young grandmother. "How sweet. He looks exactly like you."

"You said exactly the right thing," Sammy replied, and she laughed.

After Sammy had finished the paperwork for his part-time position, Kent took him around to meet some of the other staff and fill him in on his responsibilities. Then they waited for Marni.

At three o'clock, Sammy was studying his watch. "She had to change clothes and take our son to her parents' house in north Dallas. It's a long drive here."

"No problem." Kent returned some phone calls and set up a basketball game with the youth group from the Methodist church several blocks over.

When Kent hung up, Sammy mentioned, "I heard that you needed to build a gym."

"Yeah, we're just outgrowing the one we've got in the activities center. That one is fine for the younger kids' skating parties and such, but we need a professional-quality basketball court. The teens are ashamed to bring visitors to something that's not top-of-the-line," Kent said.

"Oh. What age group will I be working with, now?" Sammy asked.

"Youth—that's thirteen- to seventeen-year-olds."

Sammy nodded in mild disappointment, as he preferred younger children, and then they heard Marni's voice at the receptionist's desk. "That's her," he said in relief, standing. It was ten minutes after three.

Stepping out of the office to greet her, Sammy paused in shock. She was wearing a short skirt and high heels—inappropriate to interview for a church secretarial position. "Thanks for coming, Marni," he said lightly. She nodded and looked away.

Anna said, "Before the interview, I'll need to give you a typing test."

"I'm not taking a typing test," Marni replied curtly. Anna looked at her in surprise and Sammy stared, speechless. Who was this person? It wasn't Marni!

"Well . . . it may not be essential. I'll ask Curtis about waiving it," she said with a glance at Sammy. As she went back to Curtis' office, Sammy stepped around the desk. Kent discreetly withdrew to his office.

Sammy stood very close to Marni, taking her arm. "Do you mind telling me why you're jeopardizing our placement here?" he asked in a low voice.

"I told you I didn't want to do this," she muttered, looking at the wall.

He turned her chin toward him. "I called you because I need you here. But if this is how you're going to be, you might as well go on home." Then he wondered if she was pregnant, the way she was acting.

Marni had turned to leave when Anna came back out. "Curtis says that if you're familiar with word processing, the typing test is unnecessary. His office is second door to your right. Curtis Mayfield, our Director of Educational Programs." Anna pointed behind her.

Marni glanced at Sammy and then went back to Curtis' office. Kent came out and looked at Sammy. "She . . . wasn't prepared for me to leave police work. I guess this is all kind of a shock to her," Sammy mumbled, adding silently, *Not to mention me.*

"I see," Anna said sympathetically. Kent nodded.

Sammy waited beside Anna's desk making small talk while Marni interviewed. Twenty minutes later she came out with the very Curtis behind her—a genial-looking fellow, about fifty, in a dark blue suit and eighties' haircut.

As Sammy stood, Curtis nodded to him and said, "Anna, please give Marni the paperwork to get started today. She'll be working at the desk beside the pastor's secretary."

Sammy breathed in relief, "Thanks, Curtis." The Educational Director acknowledged him and went back to his office. Marni plopped into the chair beside Anna's desk to begin filling out forms with an air of aversion.

After she had completed them and given them to Anna, she went to the back offices without a word to Sammy. He did not see her for the next hour and a half while Kent familiarized him with the youth facilities and schedule of activities.

On Wednesday evenings the church hosted an inexpensive supper, and Kent strongly advised that Sammy be there tonight. Before Marni had a chance to leave for the day, Sammy apprehended her at her desk and took her with him into fellowship hall, where supper was served.

They went through the buffet line and took their trays to a long row of tables covered with white paper tablecloths. This was the youth section. Kids came over with their plates to hover curiously near Sammy and Marni, who were introduced a thousand times. Marni thawed out some, but was not her usual self.

The seats around Sammy filled up quickly as he was subjected to the usual tests inflicted on a new authority. When someone down the table catapulted a dinner roll at him, he caught it with one hand and took a bite while listening to a girl chatter next to him.

Another wag walked up to announce, "As our new assistant youth director, we all agreed you should have the proper tools to execute the duties of your position—" and handed Sammy a plunger wrapped in toilet paper.

"Gee, thanks, Joel." Sammy took it gravely while the kids around snickered. Then he stuck it on the floor next to the table, asking, "But what's your mom going to do when she finds your chair missing?" The kids howled —even Marni smiled—and Sammy was in.

Before the pastor got up to lead the after-dinner program, Marni stood. "I'm going home," she whispered, and escaped before Sammy could stop her.

A girl in braces promptly took the empty seat to begin talking to Sammy in breathy whispers. She continued to talk all through the pastor's short presentation on some budget items. Sammy absently listened to both of them at the same time until the pastor mentioned the gym, whereupon Sammy hushed his conversant with a wink and a nod toward the front.

"I know it seems like a lost cause, but we haven't entirely given up hope. We're continuing negotiations with the historic commission. Now, I understand what having this gym would mean to our young people in terms of outreach, so you just continue to pray with us that the city will see the light and give us clearance to proceed," Senior Pastor Berger said.

When the meeting broke up into smaller groups for choir rehearsal and such, Sammy was still surrounded by a group of young people, many of them female. "Where'd your wife go?" one girl asked.

"To pick up our baby from her mom's," Sammy explained.

"Oh, well, you should bring your baby to our day care here. That's where I'm working during the summer, and I'll make sure to take good care of him," another girl said.

"Thanks," Sammy agreed.

"Somebody said you're a cop. Were you?" one boy asked.

"Still am. I haven't resigned yet," Sammy replied.

"Wow. That's cool," somebody mentioned.

"I think so," Sammy said with a certain pride.

"There goes any fun we woulda had this summer," another boy muttered in disgust.

This prompted someone else to ask, "Is it hard for a cop to be a Christian?"

"Hard?" Sammy thought about that. "I don't know. There are ethical dilemmas, sure. But I don't think it's as hard as it is essential. A cop carries so many lives in his hands, I'd hate to think about trying to do the job without God as my shield. I've been beaten by a group of punks in an alley, straitjacketed in a mental hospital, and wheeled as dead into a morgue. God brought me through every time."

They wanted to hear all about it, of course, so he told them story after story about his work, and Marni figured prominently in several of these episodes. Talking about her, Sammy felt an uneasy tingle. Something was wrong for Marni to be acting this way. There had to be a reason for it.

"Listen, guys," he glanced at his watch. "I'd like to stay longer, but I need to get home."

One blond girl held his arm. "You're coming to the pool party tomorrow, aren't you?"

"Sure," he said. "It's in my job description." They laughed and he waved goodnight. It was after nine.

Pulling into the apartment parking lot, he saw Marni's Miata in her space. He let himself into the dark apartment and trotted up the stairs. First, he opened the nursery door across from their bedroom to check on Sam. The little guy was asleep in his crib. Then Sammy looked in his bedroom. It, too, was dark.

"Marni?" he murmured, sitting on the bed. He stroked her shoulder and turned on the bedside light. She squinted, turning her face away. "Marni, why are you in bed so early?"

"I have to get up early to get Sam over to Mom's before I go to work," Marni said sleepily.

"No, you don't, baby. You can just take him with you. The church has a day care," Sammy said.

Marni sprang up. "I'm not taking my child to a day care!"

"What? Marni," he began in exasperation, "what is the deal? We'll both be right there; we can check on him at any time. What is the matter with you today? This is an assignment; it's important, and you almost blew my placement! What gives?" He began to get angry.

She blinked rapidly a few times. Then she opened her mouth and said, "I'm—sorry, Sammy. I'll do what you ask and not blow it." She sounded sincerely contrite.

Slightly appeased, Sammy got up to undress. "The problem apparently stems from the new gym the church wants to build. The city won't give them clearance to buy the historical building next door for it. So you need to keep your ears open for anything you hear about that, or the mayor."

"Okay," she said faintly.

"I'm supposed to be at a picnic and pool party

tomorrow," he mentioned. She gave him a strange look and he said, "Yeah, I can't believe they pay people to do this. At any rate—" he flopped onto the bed—"we do the job, no matter how demanding. Right, baby?" She did not answer and he leaned over her. "Marni, are you going to help me or not?"

"Of course, Sammy," she whispered.

He studied her masked expression in concern, but she knew just how to distract him. She reached up to caress his hard, delineated shoulders and a certain look came in her eyes. He threw back the sheet and dove in.

The following morning when Marni stepped into the shower, Sammy thought he'd slip quietly downstairs to start coffee and get the paper. Not likely. As soon as Sam heard his father's footsteps on the landing, he raised up in his crib: "Guh? GUNHHH!"

Sammy pushed open the nursery door and went in. Early morning sunlight glowed through the yellow gingham curtains. "Hi, there. You calling me?" The baby chattered and waved as Sammy picked him up. "Whoa, Sam! What have you been doing to smell so bad?" Sammy exclaimed.

He checked the baby's diaper. "What is this, a toxic waste dump? What has your momma been feeding you?" he said in dismay. Then Sammy, possessor of a Medal of Honor, shrank at the thought of changing his son's diaper. He looked back to his bedroom, calculating how long Marni would be mad if he left this mess to her. As strangely as she was acting, he decided not to risk it, and laid Sam on the changing table.

Ten minutes and forty baby wipes later, the job was done. Sammy lifted the miracle child to his shoulder, kissing his head, and they went down to breakfast together. "Okay." Sammy strapped his son in the high chair and paused. "Why, Samuel Junior, I believe I see teeth in there! Hold still and let me look," he said, propping Sam's jaw open with a finger and peering in his mouth.

Sam chomped down and Sammy quickly extracted his finger. "Ow! You have two teeth coming in! That means you can chew the oatmeal instead of just scarfing it down, right, guy? Not that it matters, I guess," Sammy muttered as he fetched the oatmeal box from the cabinet and began reading the microwave instructions on the label.

When Marni came downstairs about half an hour later, she found Sammy bent over the paper with a cup of coffee while Sam happily fingerpainted his tray in oatmeal. "Good morning," she said.

Sammy lifted his face for a kiss, then glanced at her dress. She looked much more professional today. "Are we all okay?" he asked dubiously, feeling that she kept changing the rules without telling him. At that point Sam began slapping his tray to see how far he could splatter oatmeal. "Whoa—okay, pal, that's enough fun. Toss us a dishrag, baby."

Marni wrung out the rag and handed it to him. "I'll take Sam with me to the church nursery today," she said as a concession. Sammy glanced up, wiping the baby's face. "Sammy . . . how long do you think this assignment will last?"

"Marni, you know that I have no way of knowing that," he replied, brows gathering.

She tossed her head slightly. "Yes, I know." She

poured herself cereal and asked, "Where is this pool party?"

"Oh, at one of the kids' houses. I don't remember exactly where. We're meeting at the church," he said. Marni nodded. She sat to eat in silence while Sammy watched her, chin in hand. "I wish you would tell me why you don't like this assignment. Do you feel I'm being disrespectful to the Lord?" he asked.

She looked up. "No, not at all."

"Then what is it?" he pressed.

Marni shrugged, stirring her cereal. "It's just that . . . I grew up in a large church like Metro. I know how things are."

"What things?" he asked.

Defensively, she got up and dumped her cereal down the sink. That told him something. She couldn't eat anything when she was upset. "Oh, no! Look at the time! I've got to hurry or I'll be late!" She grabbed Sam out of his chair and hustled him upstairs while Sammy sat back and looked after her.

He met her at the door to kiss them goodbye. "You're going to have to tell me about it sometime, baby," he said. She nodded quickly and was out the door.

With about three hours to kill, Sammy took his time getting ready. Now that Marni was back in the job market (for however long), he realized that she would be needing help with the housework. So he called the cleaning service he had used for years before he got married.

Then, telephone in hand, he pondered another call. He was good friends with Marni's parents, and Pam had given him vital assistance with Marni's bizarre behavior once before. She might be able to help him again. He dialed.

"Hello?" she answered.

"Hi, Pam. What's going on this morning?"

"Hi, dear. I'll tell you what I would *like* to be going on. I would like for certain people to keep their promise about sitting for a portrait. I have Marni and Sam sketched in, but I've got no photos of the *other* person to work from," she said crisply.

"Eek. Sorry, Pam; I'll get there when I can. I'm working an assignment now. Pam . . . tell me something. Tell me about Marni's experiences growing up in the church," he said.

"Marni's experiences . . . ? I don't know that there was anything unusual. We were always regular attendees, and Marni was heavily involved during her high school years. She was in a special singing group; she attended all the youth meetings and activities and seemed to enjoy it very much. During her last year she did get moody and, for some reason, dropped out altogether. That was about the time she graduated and started community college, so we didn't think much of it. Why, Sammy?"

"Well, to tell you the truth, I don't know. She's— developed this attitude and I was just trying to find the reason for it," Sammy said pensively.

"Oh, dear. Good luck," Pam said.

"Thanks," he laughed. "And I *promise* I'll come sit for you ASAP."

"Yes, you will," she said in a smooth, threatening voice.

"Yipes. Another woman with an attitude. Talk to you later, Pam." He hung up before getting himself in any more trouble.

A while later he rolled up his swim trunks in a towel and tossed it in his Mustang, then set his sunglasses on his nose and drove down to the church. He met Kent in the parking garage by one of the church buses—a fairly new vehicle with air conditioning and seatbelts. Sammy approved. Then they waited for all the kids to arrive.

Arrive they did, in a rowdy mood, with towels and sandals flying through the air. Some kids came already wearing their bathing suits, and Sammy gulped. He would not have let Marni out of the house wearing something as revealing as what most of these girls wore.

Shortly, about thirty young people were gathered, and they all told Sammy hello by jumping on him or yanking his arms. Kent counted heads and then sat in the driver's seat and hollered, "Climb on!" There was a mad scramble for seats.

Sammy stayed out of the way until everyone else was on, then he boarded. "Is it just you and me chaperoning all these kids?" he asked Kent.

"Ooh, don't ever use the word *chaperone* around here," Kent cracked as he started the engine. "And unless you had come on, it would have been just me and all these kids."

While Kent pulled out of the parking garage, Sammy decided to sit in back, where it was most crowded. He plucked a likely troublemaker from a seat and tossed him up the aisle, instructing, "You get to sit up front." Then he took the boy's seat.

The girl who was sitting beside him leaned over and

put her arms around his neck. "You just did that to get next to me."

He glanced through his shades at her, fully developed almost out of her bikini top. "Let go of me, Stacy."

"Yeah, he's *married,*" a boy nearby sneered.

Sammy looked at him in surprise. "You got a problem with that?"

"Not me. That's *your* problem," the boy returned, and there was approving laughter. Stacy, meanwhile, continued to lean into Sammy.

On the very back seat, one guy and his girlfriend were sharing a very demonstrative kiss. Sammy nudged him with his foot. "Cool it, Romeo."

"What?" The boy turned in irritation at the interruption.

"You gotta sneak off to the bushes to do that," Sammy told him, and the kids laughed. The girl blushed, smiling slightly.

"Aw, you're full of it," the guy muttered, turning back to the object of his desire.

She now self-consciously put up the tiniest bit of resistance, so Sammy reached over and pulled him away by the back of his t-shirt. "What's the big idea?" the boy shouted, red in the face.

"I said, cool it," Sammy reiterated in a low voice.

"You gonna make me?" the kid challenged, jaw jutting.

Sammy regarded him: a muscular kid, about seventeen, about his own size less twenty pounds. Deliberately, Sammy removed his sunglasses to stare him down with ice-blue eyes. "You sound like the punks

I used to haul down to juvie for rolling winos. Are you sure you're in the right place?"

The other kids' stares shamed the boy into submission. He sat back sullenly as Sammy coolly replaced his shades and pointed at another boy—a skinny, quiet kid. "What's your name?"

"Keith, sir," the boy replied, and the other kids snickered.

"Keith, what year will you be in the fall?" Sammy asked.

"I'll be a senior, Mr. Kidman," Keith said nervously.

"You call me Sammy. Now, Keith, what do you like to study?"

"Well," Keith began shyly, "Math and science, mostly—"

The other kids groaned and Sammy turned on them irately. "I'm trying to have a conversation here. Do you mind?" Then he asked, "What, specifically, Keith?"

"Well, I'm really excited by communications technologies. Fiber optics may soon be obsolete," Keith offered.

"Yeah? What would they use instead?" Sammy asked.

"Light, Sammy," Keith said, his face lit with a smile.

"Light? How?" Sammy asked. And for the fifteen-minute duration of the ride, the whole busload listened in fascination as Keith gave a spontaneous lesson on laser technology.

He was still talking when the bus stopped at their hosts' home and kids began piling out. Sammy interrupted him for one more question. "Where will you be going to college?"

"Rice," Keith answered.

Sammy regarded him in genuine admiration. "I'll be reading about you someday, Keith."

After being the last to get off the bus, Sammy met the couple who had volunteered their home for this party, then he changed into his trunks and went out to supervise the kids in the pool.

At first he did not get in the water. As Kent was busy helping their host set up the grill, Sammy felt that someone should stay out to watch this group. But the girls came over to his chaise, tugging and insisting, so he finally gave in and knifed the water.

They wanted to play games. He agreed to water volleyball, but not with partners on shoulders. Still, everywhere he turned there was some girl hanging on his arm or climbing on his back—big girls, too, not the little ones to whom climbing was an innocent exercise.

Things got steamy. When one girl approached him underwater and surfaced in his face, brushing every part on her way up, he said, "Enough. I'm getting out." In spite of their protests, he hoisted himself out of the water and took up his towel.

He went over to Kent, who was grilling hot dogs. "Kent, I'm wondering if—if pool parties are such a good idea for this age group."

Kent looked up, puzzled. "Why?"

"Well—the raging hormones, and all . . ." Sammy hinted with difficulty.

Kent shrugged, "They're going to go swimming during the summer. You can't tell them not to."

"But . . . do we have to provide the opportunity for them to get so—worked up?" Sammy asked.

"Look, this is just recreation. We have to provide recreation to get them into the other programs," Kent explained.

"Bible study?" Sammy asked.

"Sure, Sunday school, discussion groups, choir, mission trips, the works," Kent said, turning hot dogs with his tongs.

Sammy thought about this, watching the kids paw each other in the water. "So, we lure them into Bible study with bikinis," he observed.

"That's a strange way of putting it," Kent said with a shade of doubt about his new assistant.

"Just checking to see that I got it right," Sammy flatly replied.

three

When the group returned to the church, Sammy found out about a staff meeting that afternoon and requested to attend. Kent did not see any problem with that. Before the meeting, Sammy stopped by Marni's desk to see how she was doing, but she wasn't there. He nodded to the pastor's secretary and waited a minute to see if Marni would show up.

While waiting, he eyed the security system controls just outside the pastor's office. It was an expensive, sophisticated system, but a few minutes' examination told Sammy all he needed to know to disable it—just in case he might need to, at some point, for some as-yet unknown reason.

Coming out of another office, Marni saw him waiting by her desk. His back was to her. She looked down, away, then turned and went to the women's restroom. When she ventured out five minutes later, he was gone.

Marni put a stack of form letters on her desk and sat to begin stuffing them in envelopes with computer-generated address labels. The pastor's secretary, Mrs.

Wilchester, looked over. She was a tall, thin woman with a commanding presence. "I believe your husband was just here looking for you—a man with black hair, in a sports coat?"

"Yes, that's Sammy," Marni murmured.

"He's a nice-looking man," Mrs. Wilchester said.

"Yes, he is. I love him very much," Marni said, and her eyes began to water.

Another woman suddenly appeared in the office—a very round woman with wild gray hair. "Hello, Ginger," Mrs. Wilchester greeted her.

"Hi there, Iva," Ginger returned. She paused briefly to eye Marni, who was working with her head down, then continued, "Has the pastor found a good date for his book-signing party?"

"Yes." Mrs. Wilchester put on her glasses to look at her calendar. "He can do it right after the late morning worship service this coming Sunday. We'll have a table set up so that people can buy books on their way out of the auditorium. But, Ginger—he said we can't sell them discounted, or he won't get any royalties."

"That's fine," Ginger agreed. Then she asked, "Has Ms. Carlson come in for her 'counseling' today?"

"I understand that Ms. Carlson had her 'counseling' with the pastor after hours last night. I had to get some papers from his office this morning before he got in, and my, what a mess," Mrs. Wilchester observed with arched brow. Marni continued to work with her head down.

Ginger jumped to another topic: "Please be sure to remember Larry's wife in prayer."

"What about Larry's wife?" Mrs. Wilchester asked, leaning over her desk.

"She's started drinking again. Larry had to leave in the middle of choir rehearsal last night when she called, smashed out of her gourd. You could hear him hollering at her over the phone clear down the hall," Ginger said.

"What a shame," Mrs. Wilchester sympathized.

"I'd drink, too, if I were married to him," Ginger noted, lifting a stack of papers from the secretary's desk. "Are these the new schedules?" she asked, and Mrs. Wilchester nodded, opening her mouth, but Ginger plowed ahead: "Oh—Madelyn's biopsy came back negative. It's just a benign tumor."

"I'm so glad," Mrs. Wilchester said.

"Yes, we're all so happy for her. Heaven knows she doesn't have much boob to begin with—it's a good thing she won't have to lose any of it," said Ginger. "Not that it makes any difference. She's not likely to find anybody to marry her at forty-seven."

"Forty-seven?" Mrs. Wilchester asked dubiously.

"Yes," Ginger said emphatically. "She tells everybody she's thirty-nine, but I checked her records and she'll be forty-seven next month. I dropped a hint to her department director to ask her to move on up to the next older group."

"How about that," murmured the secretary.

Ginger shifted the papers under her substantial arm. "Listen, I've got to run. Our women's group is preparing a whole week of activities for Christian Home Awareness Week. We'll have a letter for the pastor to sign telling everybody to be up at church every night that week to celebrate the family. See you later."

"'Bye, Ginger," the pastor's secretary said warmly. As soon as the woman had waddled away, Mrs.

Wilchester muttered, "What a gossip. I can't stand her."

"Mrs. Wilchester, I have a question," Marni said. "With the offering envelopes and this letter about the building fund all going out today, there seems to be some redundancy. I have five separate pieces of mail going to one family. Can we consolidate these to save on postage?"

"That's not necessary. It's in the budget," the secretary answered.

"But—I have computerized offering envelopes going to six-year-olds," Marni murmured. "Is that cost-effective?"

"Don't worry about that. The budget director says send them, so we send them," Mrs. Wilchester said firmly. Shrugging, Marni did as she was told.

A man entered as if to breeze through the office, then drew up at Marni's desk. "Whoa! What have we here?" he asked in pleasant surprise. Marni looked up and he extended his hand over her desk. "Larry Fortune, Minister of Music. Miss—?"

"Mrs. Marni Kidman. Sammy's wife," Marni said, lightly shaking his hand before returning to the envelopes.

"Do you sing, Marni?" he asked, leaning on the desk. He was a good-looking man in his mid-thirties, with a full head of brown hair combed straight back and a well-cut suit. "We'd love to have you in the choir."

"I'm afraid I can't sing a note," Marni replied.

"You should give it a try. We have a lot of fun," he urged.

"I'm sorry, I'm just no good at it. My husband has a nice voice, though," she said.

"Well, we'd welcome both of you any time," he winked in a friendly manner and glanced in a not too friendly manner toward Mrs. Wilchester before moving on.

Meanwhile, Sammy was sitting at a conference table with the other staff as Senior Pastor Ron L. Berger got up to address them. In his late forties, Dr. Berger was an athletic man who projected an aura larger than his five-foot-six-inch stature. He had a pleasant face and the ability to look at people as if he were really listening to them. Today, he apparently did not notice the presence of a new staff member; if he did, Sammy doubted that he would remember him. They had met before.

The pastor slammed a notebook to the table and everybody jumped. "This is the *fourth consecutive week* that First Baptist has gained more new members than we have. People, I'm just not going to put up with that! If we're going to be the preeminent church in Dallas, we are going to *have* to cut into their growth. The fact that we're both large downtown churches should *not* affect our prospects as long as we're doing it right. And that seems to be the problem—we're going about this in a half-ass manner." He leaned forward, fists on the table for emphasis.

Once assured that every pair of eyes in the room was fastened on him, he continued mildly, "Now, our Committee for the Future has come up with some excellent suggestions: One, marketing. We must be more aggressive about getting the First Metro name out to the people.

"Our first line of attack will be mass mailouts, at a cost of twenty-five thousand. Next, we'll purchase lists of new hook-ups from the utilities and hit those people with calls and visits, concentrating on the upper-income areas where we want to draw our membership from. Curtis, you be sure to work into the Sunday school curriculum how important outreach is in our members' daily lives. Remember to impress on them that they're not practicing their Christianity unless they're telling others about our church.

"Oh—I saw those yard signs that First United Methodist is using now, and I really like them. These are professionally done signs that members can just stick in their yards that have the name of the church and a catchy little slogan, like, 'You're welcome any time!' Then members don't have to talk to their neighbors at all, if they're not comfortable with that. Curtis, you want to check on the cost for a couple thousand of those? Thanks.

"Our second area of concern is the level of giving. People, ours stinks. A church our size could have a ten-million-dollar budget if only half the people tithed. As it is, we have to settle for three-point-five million. This is just not enough to pursue a policy of growth. I want one Sunday a month devoted to a lesson on tithing in the Sunday schools, Curtis. I want these people hammered about giving till it hurts.

"Third: facilities. We cannot grow if we do not have the facilities. The importance of this cannot be overstated. So we're going with the vote of the church to hire Belldrop, Associates to conduct a fund-raising campaign for us at a cost of a hundred and twenty-five thousand," Dr. Berger stated.

A white-haired man raised his hand. "Dr. Berger,

there seems to be some resistance among the membership about conducting this campaign. The people that I've talked to want to see their money go toward other things—"

"Dan," the pastor cut him off in a condescending manner, "I appreciate your input, but the average member just doesn't understand the complexities of modern church administration. To survive, we must grow. To grow, we must have larger facilities. To build larger facilities, we must get more money. It's as simple as that."

"Yes, Dr. Berger, I understand that. However, a number of our tithers seem to be concerned about how we will service our present twelve-million-dollar debt, much less take on new debt," Dan said gravely.

"That's what this capital campaign is all about, Dan," the pastor replied patiently.

"Dr. Berger," Dan said uncomfortably, "I don't wish to be a naysayer, but I feel it is my responsibility to let you know what I have been hearing from the membership. The vote to engage these consultants was very close, as you remember. It passed by only fifty votes, with almost three times that many voting against."

"I remember," Dr. Berger said sharply.

"Yes, well, what we have voted to do is pay Belldrop, Associates one hundred and twenty-five thousand dollars to tell us how to hit ourselves up for millions of dollars over and above our regular giving. Frankly, some of our people are appalled," Dan said.

Dr. Berger smiled tightly. "Dan, I'm afraid you've been unduly influenced by people who have no dream, no vision for the future. Sure, some people are content to drift along year after year, accomplishing little, *being* little. But I have to believe that God has called us to greatness—to have an impact that people won't soon forget. In order to do that, we simply must address the stewardship issue. Sure, we could save a few bucks on the front end by going with a cheap, homemade campaign, but to raise the kind of capital required to continue pursuing our dream, we've got to go first-class."

Dan looked resigned and Sammy raised his hand. "Where are we with the prospects for a new gym?"

"Good question," the pastor said. "I've got a follow-up meeting next week with the planning commission, and hopefully they'll have received some new direction from the mayor by that time. We will continue to solicit funds for the construction of the gym, as we've already got thirty thousand invested in architects' fees, anyway. By the way, George, what about our parking situation?"

"We counted eighty-two available spaces during last Sunday's early service and sixty-seven during the later service. That's not enough to encourage visitor attendance, especially as most of those were fourth- and fifth-level garage parking. We've got to build another garage, and in the meantime, encourage our members to park in the upper, less desirable levels," George replied.

"Uh-huh," the pastor acknowledged grimly. "What's the latest on negotiations to buy that warehouse?"

George shook his head. "Word leaked out to the tenants that we were going to raze it for a parking garage, and they got together and appealed to the historic commission. I'm afraid the building qualified, and the city's blocked us on that, too."

The pastor responded with a mild profanity, uttered with feeling, and Sammy glanced around the table. Was he the only one shocked?

The crucial question of parking was put on hold and the meeting progressed to other topics: packing delegates to an upcoming convention, insurance, and clearing up a minor point on the pastor's benefits plan. When Sammy saw that Dr. Berger made almost two hundred thousand a year, not including housing and car allowances and other perqs, he almost dropped his teeth. Then Sammy wondered why he himself ever picked police work over the ministry.

At the conclusion of the meeting, Sammy followed the white-haired man who had spoken up. "Uh—Dan?" The man turned in the hallway, and Sammy extended his hand. "Sammy Kidman. I'm the new youth intern. Aren't you the associate pastor?"

Dan shook his hand warmly. "Yes. Good to meet you, Sammy."

"Likewise. I was wondering—Kent's been telling me how much the young people need a new gym, and I was wondering if you were in on the meeting the pastor had with the mayor about that," Sammy said.

"Yes, I was," Dan sighed, taking off his glasses to rub the bridge of his nose. "I'm afraid it was not a very productive meeting."

"The pastor seemed to think the mayor might come around after that. Do you know why?" Sammy asked encouragingly.

"Son," Dan said, "take my word for it that it was not a productive meeting. Tempers flared and angry words were said that should best be forgotten. I, for one, think that nothing about the project would be honoring to the Lord at this point." He stopped, raised his shoulders as if he had said enough, and then nodded, "Excuse me."

After thoughtfully watching him go, Sammy turned down the hall, intending to stop by Marni's desk again. But being preoccupied with all he had just heard and unfamiliar with the building, he soon found himself in an unknown corridor. There was no one around to guide him, so, hearing music from behind a door that said "Music Resources," he stopped and opened it, aiming to get directions to the pastor's secretary's office.

He saw a guy in a suit locked in a passionate kiss with a girl as orchestral worship music swelled grandly around them. They started at his entrance, looking at him, and Sammy suddenly recognized the girl as a member of the youth group—her name was Lauren, if he remembered right. She had been to the swim party earlier, but she was one of those quiet, withdrawn types who didn't socialize much. "Ah, sorry. Wrong office," Sammy said, studying her. She looked away.

Backing out, he almost bumped into a little round woman with gray hair. "Is Larry in there?" she asked, leaning in the doorway. "Larry, the Power Network called. They want a tape of our Easter presentation to run next week."

"Sure thing," Larry replied. He came out straightening his jacket (with a wedding band conspicuous on his left hand) and barely glanced at Sammy before turning into another office. Pale, with downcast eyes, Lauren hurried out behind him.

Sammy looked at the woman, who sat ponderously behind a desk in the Music Resources room and impatiently switched off the music. "I'm trying to find my way back to the pastor's secretary's office," he said cautiously.

"You go down this hall, turn to the right, make another right at the library and you're there," she said, pointing with a pen.

"Thanks," Sammy muttered, moving off. He half expected to see a white rabbit scurrying along here somewhere.

He had almost reached the library when he heard, "Sammy," and turned around. Lauren came up, glancing warily behind him. "I . . . just wanted to tell you that— it's not what it looks like." He saw that she had beautiful eyes in the few seconds she managed to look up.

"Oh. Then he's not a married man hitting on a teenager," Sammy said, and she winced.

"It's not *like* that. Larry and I . . . I mean, he makes me feel special. You don't know how lonely I am—how miserable I am at home. Nobody else cares anything about me. The time I share with Larry is the only thing in my life that gives me any happiness," she whispered.

Sammy chewed his lip. "Let's take a walk," he suggested, and she nodded. By the library he found a door leading out to a quadrangle. They walked through the grassy spot to another door that led out onto the street.

Here, they found themselves not far from Old City Park, so they walked on over and sat on a bench. It was a typically hot June afternoon, but the old pecan tree that towered above them took the heat instead. And the short walk gave Sammy a chance to think.

"Okay, Lauren," Sammy said. "I'm gonna give you

a hypothetical situation, and you tell me what to do. This involves two people named Lisa and Frank."

She eyed him askance. "You could be more original than that."

"Sorry. Best I could do under the circumstances. Now, here's our situation: Lisa has a diamond ring that's burning a hole in her pocket. She's very anxious to give this ring to somebody, because that's what she's supposed to do with it. But there's a catch: the ring is very valuable, and she doesn't know it. This ring is so valuable, it's worth one hundred pounds of self-esteem. Again, Lisa doesn't have a clue as to the true worth of this ring."

Sammy wiped his mouth and went on, "Okay. Frank comes along one day, and he already has a ring that belongs to someone else. But he tells Lisa, 'You can't wait to give that ring away, so give it to me.' He wants the self-esteem from Lisa's ring. Even though she doesn't know it's there, he does. So Lisa gives him her ring; she's happy and he's very happy.

"But then there's a problem: Frank doesn't take very good care of Lisa's ring. He's already wearing somebody else's ring, and he can't wear two at once, so he puts Lisa's ring in his pocket, where it gathers lint. And Lisa can't see the self-esteem glitter in her ring, 'cause it's tucked out of sight," Sammy explained. Lauren began to blink rapidly.

"After a while," Sammy said, "Frank finds *another* ring he wants, but he can't keep two in one pocket, so he takes Lisa's out. He still wants the self-esteem from it, so he puts it in his shoe. Doesn't smell so good down there." Sammy wrinkled his nose and Lauren laughed.

"Lisa's ring is now really out of sight, getting dirty and stinked up. Pretty soon it starts bothering Frank, too, 'cause it's uncomfortable to walk around with a ring in your shoe. So Frank takes it out and tells Lisa, 'Here. You can have your ring back.' Lisa takes it back and tries to clean it up so it will look nice to give to somebody else. Problem is, there's about fifty pounds of self-esteem missing. Frank stole it, and she can't get it back from him. So, Lauren, what do you think Lisa should do?" Sammy asked.

She dropped her head while the tears ran down her face. "I think," she whispered, "Lisa should get some more esteem by holding on to her ring. And that she should not give it to anybody else unless he promises to wear it on his hand."

"You give very good advice," he said softly.

"But—" she turned to him, "what do I do with the pain?"

"Lauren," Sammy murmured, his own eyes watering, "I don't know what to tell you. I don't know. But I know there's got to be a hundred guys out there who would beg to wear your ring." She leaned into him, crying.

Sammy put his arms around her and breathed, "God, do something about Lauren's pain. You're the only one with a heart big enough to handle it."

She cried her eyes out while Sammy held her, nodding self-consciously to passers-by who stared. Then she sat up, sniffling, and he took out his handkerchief. "Your wife is very lucky," she mumbled.

"That's what I keep telling her," Sammy said, and she laughed wetly.

She took a deep breath and stood. "I think it's time for me to go home now."

Sammy stood as well, asking, "You got a car here?" She nodded. "Okay; I'll walk you."

They amiably strolled across the street to one of the church's parking garages. Sammy glanced at an old stone building nearby. "Is that what they're going to tear down for the gym?"

"Yes. Isn't it awful?" Lauren said in disgust. "We don't *need* another gym; we're just being greedy. I think it would be terrible to lose such a beautiful old building. Some people have no respect for the past."

Sammy grinned at her. "You heretic."

She tossed her head at him. "That's what burns me up. This building program isn't about winning people to the *Lord,* it's about empire-building. It's the pastor wanting to lead the biggest church in the state—in the universe. Nobody stops to realize that the real church doesn't have walls. It exists across time and space, and people who never heard of First Metro can be a part of it," she said vehemently.

Sammy gazed at her as she stopped and unlocked her car door. "That's just about the most profound thing I've ever heard," he said.

Lauren looked at him, then dropped her head. "Listen to me talk, when I'm not worth—"

He cut her off. "Don't let me *ever* hear you saying that again. It's a lie. You have no idea how much you're worth. It would stagger you senseless to find out."

She bit her lip and smiled at him. Reaching up, she kissed him lightly on the cheek. "Thanks, Sammy," she whispered, then got in her car and drove away.

Sammy waved goodbye, then ambled back into the church's administration building. He found his way to the Music Resources office, and, glancing around, knocked on the door. The gray-headed lady was nowhere in sight. "Yeah?" Larry answered from within.

Sammy opened the door to see him sitting behind the nice oak desk surrounded by a lot of expensive electronic equipment. The depth of sound emanating from the Bose speakers was lush and rich—the kind of sound that vibrated your bones even on low volume. "May I talk to you for a moment?" Sammy asked over the music.

Larry switched off a reel-to-reel player. "What is it?" he asked with some impatience. He seemed not to remember Sammy, unfortunately.

Sammy shut the door behind him and stepped forward, tentatively scratching his eyebrow. Then he reached over the desk, seized Larry by the front of his starched shirt and flung him into the wall so hard that two pictures and a diploma came crashing down. Before Larry could recover, Sammy jerked him up and pounded him against the wall a few more times.

"Do I have your attention now?" Sammy breathed, and Larry gazed at him with his mouth hanging open. "Good. I wanted to tell you that if you ever mess with one of my kids again, I'm gonna fix it so that you sing soprano from now on. Are you hearing me?"

Larry dumbly nodded, and Sammy tossed him down to the floor. "Just remember your career, pal, and keep your pants on at work."

With that, Sammy stepped out and shut the door behind him. He smiled and nodded at the gray-haired lady who came bustling toward the office, then he went down the hall whistling.

"It's been a few weeks since I roughed anybody up. That felt good," he reflected, and stopped by the nursery to check on Sam.

four

After work that day, Sammy had just enough time to rush home to grab a bite of dinner with Marni before he had to go back up to the church to lead an evening Bible study. As soon as he entered the apartment, he smelled spaghetti sauce simmering on the stove.

Marni, feeding Sam, looked up: "Hi."

Preoccupied, he began spilling his mind. "Hi, baby. Man, this is so bizarre," he complained, shedding his coat and bending to kiss her. "Hi, Sam. This is a lot different than I thought it would be. You need some help? Want me to fix the salad?"

Without waiting for a reply, he continued, "I went to a staff meeting today—you expect a preacher to open a meeting with a prayer or something, don't you? Or *talk* like a preacher, at least. But this guy comes in pounding the table and cussing—it was unreal." As he talked, he opened the refrigerator to get out lettuce and tomatoes.

"Then I wander into the music wing and stumble onto the Minister of Music locked up tight with one of my girls. I took her out and gave her a fatherly lecture, then came back and knocked him around a little."

Marni started. "You hit him?"

"No, not really. Just threw him around a little. Shook him up pretty good," Sammy said in satisfaction. Marni quietly pondered this, then smiled.

He began preparing the salad by ripping the whole head of iceberg lettuce in half and shredding it by handfuls. "I have to go back up tonight to lead a Bible study. Kent gave me a study guide, but I haven't even had a chance to look at it yet. I'm sure the kids haven't. Man, they seem to think these kids have nothing else to do but go to church . . . then again, it doesn't seem like church at all—more like a country club," he mused disjointedly, filling a large bowl with lettuce. "Is that enough?"

She glanced up. "Yes. I remember someone calling it a 'union,' with a descriptive adjective," she recalled. He looked over, raising a brow, then pulled out a large knife and began hacking up a tomato.

After downing a five-minute meal, Sammy took up his jacket, study guide, and Bible. "For a part-time job, I sure am there a lot," he groused.

"At least you get paid for it. The members don't. Maybe if they had less paid staff, they'd feel less need to have so many programs to justify all those salaries," Marni murmured with an uncharacteristic bitterness.

Sammy paused. She made leading statements like that when she had something on her mind. It was an indication that she was ready to talk—but he had to leave. "I'll be back by nine," he promised, gathering her up for a good, solid kiss.

He arrived at the church in some apprehension, as he would be on his own with this group tonight. He felt woefully inadequate to lead a Bible study or manage an unruly group of teens. "No spanking," he firmly reminded himself. "No matter how much they need it, no spanking."

He found two people waiting for him in the meeting room: Keith and Stacy. The next ten minutes brought Kim, Jacki, and Paul. That was it. Sammy was astonished and relieved. "We had thirty at the swim party this afternoon," he mused. "And according to Kent, that should've brought them all back tonight."

Raising his voice, he ordered, "Okay, guys, Bible study. Pull out those study guides." They sat in a small circle of chairs and dutifully opened their booklets. Stacy yawned.

"Wake up; this is interesting," Sammy insisted, flipping open his book. "The Parable of the Sheep and the Goats. You'd be surprised how relevant it is. Okay, let's read."

Seeing that the Scripture in the study guide was in the archaic King James Version, Sammy amended, "Here—let me read it out of my Bible." He began reading the passage while the kids listened drowsily.

"'Then the King will say to those on his right, "Come, you who are blessed by my Father; take your inheritance, the kingdom prepared for you since the creation of the world. For I was hungry and you gave me something to eat, I was thirsty and you gave me something to drink, I was a stranger and you invited me in, I needed clothes and you clothed me, I was sick and you looked after me, I was in prison and you came to visit me."

"'Then the righteous will answer him, "Lord, when

did we see you hungry and feed you, or thirsty and give you something to drink? When did we see you a stranger and invite you in, or needing clothes and clothe you? When did we see you sick or in prison and go to visit you?"

"'The King will reply, "I tell you the truth, whatever you did for one of the least of these brothers of mine, you did for me."'"

"Right. Let's discuss this, now," Sammy said, looking up the study questions written in the curriculum Curtis had given him. Before reading the questions out loud, he scanned them: "Who is the King? What did the sheep do for the hungry? The thirsty? The naked? The stranger? The prisoner? What does this say about how you should support your church's ministries?"

The kids sat with glazed eyes while Sammy grappled with the questions. He was no scholar, but these questions seemed to miss the point. They reduced a powerful lesson to an ad for the church budget.

Disturbed, Sammy looked up and cleared his throat. "What say we . . . just forget the study guide and talk about the point he's making. A lot of Christians seem to think that what you believe is more important than what you do. I mean, they think faith consists of a batch of ideas, and as long as you agree with these certain ideas, then you can do whatever you want and still be on the inside track to heaven . . ." he trailed off, looking at their vacuous faces.

I'm dying here. There's got to be a better way to cover this, Sammy thought. Then he got an idea. An excellent idea. "Come on," he said, standing and heading for the door.

Five kids sprang up. "What?" "Where are we going?"

"We're going to do some hands-on Bible study," Sammy replied. He led them out through the dark parking garage to his car. "Pile in," he ordered.

Jubilantly, they crammed in: Kim, Keith and Paul sat in the back while Stacy and Jacki squeezed together in the front passenger bucket seat. As Sammy started up the car and put it in gear, Stacy turned on the radio full blast. Sammy turned it down, but the kids made up for the volume by singing along with the latest top-forty hits. Then Stacy picked up his carphone to call one of her girlfriends, but he plucked it out of her hand.

He drove them to a bad part of town and they got quiet. Sammy turned off the radio so as not to draw attention as they crept down dark, potholed streets. Stacy clung to his arm so tightly he could hardly shift gears.

Then he pulled up to Mama Perkins' little restaurant, stopped, and shut off the engine. When he got out, five teens remained huddled in the car. "You going to wait out here?" he asked casually as he turned to the door. They scrambled out. Sammy put his hand on the old brass door handle and pulled, but it was locked.

The kids crowded around him as he banged on the door. "Mama!" he shouted. "Open up!"

"Sammy, nobody's here," Keith said through chattering teeth.

"She's here," Sammy said, still pounding. "Mama!"

From within they heard her frail voice: "We're closed! Go 'way!"

"It's Sammy, Mama! Open up!" he demanded.

They heard the grating of the lock and the door

barely cracked. "Sammy, I ain't cookin' tonight. I's got the health department comin' by tomorrow, and I got to get this place cleaned up."

"That's why we're here, Mama. I brought a clean-up crew and we're gonna do it," he said, gently breaking her grasp on the door to open it. The kids filed into the dim, dingy seating area, looking around.

"You—you're what?" Mama asked weakly.

"We're what?" Jacki repeated weakly, in her fresh red nail polish and crisp designer denims.

"We're cleaning the place for you," Sammy said, stalking back to the kitchen. Mama and the kids followed.

He found Rosie on his knees with a scrub brush and pail of soapy water. "Get outta here and get your sax. We need to hear something like 'K.P. Blues,'" Sammy said. "Mama, you show us what needs to be done."

"Everythin's got to be scrubbed till it shines," she said emphatically.

The kids stared around the kitchen at the old appliances coated with years of grease, and Paul declared, "I'm not doin' this!"

"Fine," said Sammy, turning. "You won't mind watching the car for me then, will you? Let them take the tires if you have to, but *don't* let anybody rip out the phone—I had to pay for that myself."

"I'll clean," Paul decided, dropping to his knees and plunging his hand into the soapy water.

As a matter of fact, all the kids decided they'd help. Mama Perkins set them to work while Rosie pulled out his sax and sat on the counter, producing magical jazz. Sammy found rubber gloves for Jacki and they all started scrubbing to the music, three in the kitchen and three out front.

Sammy and Paul moved the heavy appliances to clean behind them and those kids sweated like they never had before. Being children, they just had to take a break to dance—Rosie's reeds were irresistible—but Sammy cut that short: "We're going to be here ALL NIGHT LONG unless everybody works!" he roared. They fell to.

They scrubbed until their knuckles were raw and bleeding: the stove, the refrigerator, the countertops, the floor, the walls, tables, booths, and chairs—anything that held still got washed down. There were no slackers, either; anybody resting for longer than five minutes caught Sammy's cool glare.

Hours later, Sammy emptied the last of three hundred bucketfuls of dirty water and looked around, panting: Everything shone. The kitchen looked almost new. Ragged, exhausted, and drenched with sweat and soapy water, the kids surveyed their handiwork. "I just dare the health department to find anything wrong with this place," Jacki said defiantly, stripping off her gloves. "I broke two nails," she noted stoically.

"This is what it means to feed the hungry and visit the sick," Sammy muttered, plopping into a chair. "End of lesson."

Brushing damp blond hair out of her face, Stacy came over and dropped into his lap. "You look so sexy when you sweat."

"Stacy," he moaned, "think of me as—as your dad. I can't get romantic over you because I look at you like a daughter. So you have to call me Dad."

She liked that idea. "Okay, Dad," she said happily. She turned to Jacki. "My dad's sexier than your dad."

"Uh-unh. He's my dad, too." Jacki came over and kissed his cheek.

"Can we go now, Dad?" Paul asked.

Sammy pushed Stacy off his lap to stand up, grunting, "Yeah. We're done."

Mama Perkins came over to place her arms lovingly around Sammy while the kids watched quietly. "You done real good. You bring these children back and I'll feed you all," she promised.

"You're on," Sammy said, kissing her head.

They shook hands with Rosie, and Mama kissed each kid goodbye. When they left they were moved and proud and utterly spent.

It was past ten o'clock by the time they got back to the church. Sammy made sure that the weary teens were alert as they climbed in their cars to go home. Then he threw himself behind the wheel to take his aching old body home to bed. He had never realized how strenuous housecleaning was.

Not surprisingly, Marni was asleep. Sammy hung over her a moment, wanting to make her sit up and talk. But he was so exhausted himself that he fell into bed without waking her.

In the morning when he opened his eyes, the first thing he did was look over to her side of the bed. It was empty. Sammy struggled up to blink at the clock: it said 7:30, she was gone, and he had never even heard the alarm go off. Stiff and groaning, Sammy got up and stumbled across the hall. Sam was gone, too.

Sammy went down to breakfast, troubled. He knew she was up at the church where she was supposed to be, but he did not like these long stretches without substantive talking. The growing distance between them was disturbing—he needed her too much to let it progress. Something had to give. He was not due at the church until this afternoon, but he went ahead and got ready to go in this morning. He hoped to pull Marni away from her desk for a few minutes, at least.

As soon as he walked in the door of the administration building, Anna looked up and said, "Kent needs to see you in his office, Sammy."

He paused at her grim tone. "Uh—sure." He opened Kent's door and stuck his head in. "You need me?"

Kent looked up from his desk with a serious expression. "Yes, Sammy. Close the door and have a seat, please."

Sammy shut the door and dropped into a chair. Kent looked uncomfortable, as if he did not know how to begin. "You're pretty new at this, Sammy. Normally, we'd take the time to train you, since I feel confident that your heart's in the right place, but—you've just got no aptitude for working with youth."

Sammy's brows shot up. "What's the problem?"

"You took last night's group out of the building to some—dive?" Kent asked painfully.

"Oh, no. Not at all. Mama's Restaurant. Mama Perkins is very elderly, in her eighties, and she needed help—"

"Sammy, the point is, you weren't supposed to take the kids anywhere. That was supposed to be a Bible study last night," Kent interrupted.

Sammy said, "Yeah, that was the point. You see, we read the Scriptures, but the study guide—"

"Several of the parents called this morning. They were very upset when they heard that their children spent the evening doing degrading, potentially dangerous manual labor in some joint. That's not what these parents send their kids here for," Kent said sternly.

Sammy repressed a sarcastic comment about what the kids actually got when they came and replied, "I understand how it looks, but let me just tell you exactly what happened, and—"

Kent was shaking his head. "I'm afraid it wouldn't do any good, Sammy. Curtis agrees you're not competent in this field of service. I have to fire you."

"Fire me?" Sammy asked, aghast. "Oh, no. Kent, give me another chance. I promise I'll toe the line and do just what I'm supposed to."

"I wish I could, Sammy, but the decision has already been made. Perhaps you could try another church," Kent said.

"Oh, man." Sammy closed his eyes. He had never, ever self-destructed on an assignment like this before. Especially one so simple. "Can Marni keep her job?" he asked.

"I don't see why not. Mrs. Wilchester says she asks too many questions, but other than that, she's doing a good job," Kent said.

"Well, thanks for the opportunity, anyway," Sammy said, standing and offering his hand. Kent shook it and Sammy turned out of the office.

He went back to Marni's desk and found her sorting bulletins. She glanced up as he leaned over her desk and kissed her lightly on the lips. "I forgot you had that dress. You look beautiful," he whispered.

Marni glanced reflexively at Mrs. Wilchester nearby. "Thank you," she smiled.

"I've been fired," Sammy said.

"You *what?*" Marni gasped. "Why?"

"I'll tell you about it tonight. That makes it all the more important that you be here. Okay?" he whispered, and she nodded. "Thanks." He kissed her again and then departed.

Sammy went out to his car and sat, debating his next move. Reporting this unplanned turn of events to Mike was unacceptable. So was giving up. Sammy started the car, put it in gear, then slowly drove around the cluster of buildings, focusing on the administration building. He nodded in sudden resolve, then went home and went back to bed.

When Marni and Sam got home that evening, Sammy was not there. Sighing, Marni put Sam down on the floor and kicked off her shoes. She had just pulled out a pan to start dinner when she heard Sammy come in the door. "Ah ah! No you don't! I'm cooking tonight," he announced, carrying several white sacks to the kitchen table. He began unloading Mexican food takeout. "Hi, Sam. How about a *chili relleno*?"

Marni laughed, "My, aren't we spending freely for someone who just got fired!"

"You bet," he said, then paused to study her. She looked tired. No, more than that. Weary. She looked bone-weary. Sammy opened his arms to her. Tentatively, she put her arms around him and laid her head on his chest.

"You know," he murmured, "sometimes I feel closer to you just holding you than when we make love. When I found Smoky and brought her back, you hugged me. When you came to get me at the mental hospital you held me. And I was told they found you in the morgue holding me. The times when I really understood that you loved me were when you were holding on to me."

Marni burst into tears and let go of him. Weeping violently, she grabbed her purse and started for the door. "What did I say?" he exclaimed. "Marni!" Had he not stopped her, she would have run out to her car. He held her arms, trying to get her to look at him, and Sam began crying.

"Sammy—let go—let me go," Marni pleaded with tears, but Sammy gathered her all the more forcefully in his arms.

"No. No way. Not till you tell me why you have to go." Sam raised his pitch to a bawl now, and Sammy glanced between the two in dismay. "This has gone on long enough." He dragged her to the couch and sat her down, then sat on the coffee table facing her and pinned her in place with his knees.

"You're upsetting Sam," he said quietly. She bit her lip and looked over at the baby still in his carrier on the floor. "It's time for you to talk, Marni. I'm not moving till you do."

She hung her head and looked away miserably. Gulping, she finally admitted, "I didn't want to work at that church because it reminds me so much of my parents' church—it's so big, and rich, it's just a business. Nothing more. Oh, there are a lot of good, sincere people there, but I wasn't one of them."

Marni looked down in profound distress. She had trouble getting out what she had to say next, and Sammy waited in merciless silence. Then she said, "During my junior year of high school I started having an affair with —someone at the church. I knew it was wrong, and I felt like such a hypocrite, since I was one of the Outstanding Young People. Always up at church, in every activity. It was all so meaningless. Finally a deacon got wind of it and threatened to have him fired unless he left the church. He did, and . . . so did I."

Sammy remained silent, and after a few moments Marni said, "I never understood what real faith was until I met you, and suddenly your life depended on my prayers. It was scary to realize all those empty rituals covered something so real and powerful. But I could never go back to my parents' church, what with the hypocrisy I saw there. I had to go some place simpler, purer, where I didn't know what went on behind the scenes. And if there was hypocrisy there as well, I didn't want to know."

She fell silent, sitting slumped on the couch. Sammy opened his mouth and said, "Why didn't you tell me this to begin with?"

She shook her head vaguely. "I was afraid you wouldn't love me anymore. I knew you wouldn't respect me any more."

He studied her so that she had to look away. "Let me guess," he said suddenly. "The guy you had the affair with was the Minister of Music." Marni flushed and nodded. Sammy looked off, thinking. What was it with these guys? Did they think they were rock stars, or something?

Sam began to call for some reassurance, so his daddy came over and picked him up out of the carrier. "One more question," he said as he reseated himself on the coffee table, and Marni could hardly bring herself to look up. "Which of us is better?" he asked.

"What?" she blinked at him.

"Who's the better lover—him or me?" he asked.

"Sammy!" she gasped. "There's—no comparison. I never even had an—I mean, I never knew it could be so good until I had you."

"You never had one until you were with me?" he asked, and she nodded. A self-satisfied grin spread on his face. "Yes!" He got up, striking macho poses while still holding his son. "Sam, she's got herself a coupla *men.*" Marni laughed in relief and disbelief.

Sammy strutted to the table in his inimitable style, pulled out a chair, and winked, "Come eat, baby."

"You're not angry?" she asked, hesitantly coming to the table.

"Angry?" Sammy said, placing Sam in his high chair. "You bet I'm angry. I'm mad as hell at these sickos who abuse their authority for a little on-the-side gratification. But they'll get theirs. Angry at you? Never."

"It was wrong. I knew better. It's haunted me for years. I've prayed for forgiveness a thousand times," she said dully, looking at the floor.

"Time to forget it. You didn't have *me* to take care of you then," he said authoritatively.

"That's right," she admitted. "I didn't." Scooting her chair up to the table, she changed the subject: "So, tell me how you got yourself fired."

"I took the kids to Mama's Restaurant last night, and we cleaned the place for the health department inspection today," he said, opening a carton of aromatic enchiladas.

"And?" she asked.

"And, I wasn't supposed to take them out of the building," he said.

"They fired you for that?" she asked, and he nodded in resignation. She murmured, "What a shame. It had to be a godsend to Mama Perkins."

"She was floored," he said in satisfaction. "And if I had it to do over again, I would do it just the same." She smiled at him as he gave Sam a soft tortilla dipped in *queso* to gum. A moment later he added, "Well . . . at least now I can appreciate what an act of love it is for you to work there for me."

"Funny you should mention it. Suddenly it doesn't bother me at all. I guess keeping all that a secret from you was weighing on me more than anything," she admitted, spooning out guacamole with a chip.

"Good," he said, nodding. "Good. Then you won't be unduly appalled at what I've got to do next."

"What?" she asked apprehensively.

"I've got to break into the church tonight," he replied.

five

Marni stared at him. "Can I go, too?" she asked.

He considered it. "No, not tonight. The way my luck is running, I'm liable to get caught doing something this stupid. I may need you to come bail me out of jail."

"That's encouraging," she murmured.

That evening Sammy went to bed when Marni did, but set his alarm for 2:00 AM. He woke before it went off, got up, and dressed in dark clothes. Taking a pocket pack of burglary tools and a pencil flashlight (standard issue for detectives), he climbed into his Mustang and drove downtown.

He left his car in the parking lot of the bus station and walked twelve blocks to the church. He walked around the dark administration building, scrutinizing it, until he found a certain terminal of hidden wires.

Pulling his tool kit from his pocket, he knelt before the locked box, holding the pencil light in his mouth. First, he used wire cutters to cut the padlock off the box, opening it up to study the array of colored wires. Selecting two, he carefully detached these wires to temporarily disable the system. Then he closed the box and went to an obscure door in the administration building. He picked the lock, slipped inside, and shut the door behind him.

Sammy padded through the building to the pastor's office, which was also locked. Picking that lock took about six seconds. This door he left ajar after he went in. Sweeping the small flashlight around the office, Sammy sat in the leather chair and tried the desk drawers. He whipped out his pick to use on the file drawer that was locked. Then, holding the penlight in his mouth, he began to study the pastor's correspondence.

There was a copy of a letter to his publisher—Dr. Berger was unhappy with the inept marketing of his latest book. There were letters confirming plans for upcoming speaking engagements and the fees for such. Dr. Berger was a popular inspirational speaker whose services did not come cheaply. There were letters from the pulpit committee of an even larger church than First Metro. Apparently, Dr. Berger was about to hear a higher calling.

All these Sammy gave only cursory attention. When he ran across the correspondence with the historic commission, Sammy settled down and began to read in earnest. The commission's first letter explained the building's historical significance and denied the church permission to purchase it. Dr. Berger's reply offered financial inducements to the city for its permission to proceed; that offer was curtly rebuffed. The final letter was Dr. Berger's demand to meet with the mayor. Sammy knew that this meeting had been granted, but there was nothing further in writing about the outcome.

Sighing in frustration, Sammy turned his penlight to a

blank computer screen. Clicking off the light, he turned on the computer and opened the directory. Several files labeled "budget_1stQ" and "pastor_exp" were password-protected, but others labeled "members_A-C," "members_D-F," and so forth were not.

So he opened these files to discover detailed profiles of the church members, including birthdates, incomes, occupations, family members and amounts given to the church. Sammy was momentarily astonished at the range and depth of personal information stored in these unprotected files.

As he was perusing these, he heard something from outside the office. Sammy quickly closed the files and shut down the computer. Someone was in the building. He held still and listened.

Voices and muffled laughter came to his ears. Sammy slipped to the door of the office to peek out. Two hoods had found their way into the building (probably through the door he had left unlocked) and were looking for something to loot. They were picking over Mrs. Wilchester's desk when Sammy creaked open the office door and clicked his penlight on under his chin. "MWA HA HA! I am the angel of the church," he said in a spooky voice.

They jumped out of their shoes and ran yelling out a side door. Sammy had a good laugh, then paused as he realized that their exit might possibly draw somebody's attention. He needed to be going. He left by the rear door, making sure it was locked behind him. Then he returned to undo his work on the wires and reactivate the alarm system.

After the alarm was reset, just as he was putting away

his tools, he heard a car pull up behind him on the street. He froze as a spotlight from a squad car temporarily blinded him. Car doors opened. "Hold it right there, pal. Let's see an ID," one of two police officers ordered.

Shading his eyes from the light, Sammy regarded them as he did some instantaneous calculating. He could not explain to them what he was doing, nor could he let them take him in for questioning—Mike had been adamant about discretion. One officer was a woman, and this was not a K-9 unit.

So Sammy stepped agreeably toward them and suddenly darted into the shadows around the building. "Stop!" the patrolman shouted. Running at top speed, Sammy zigzagged from one building's shadows to another while the pursuing footfalls rang in his ears. Sammy felt it safe to run as long as he heard those footfalls because they meant that the cop had not stopped to shoot.

Knowing that the woman officer would attempt to cut him off with the squad car even as she called for backup, Sammy poured on the speed to make it to the nearest cross street before she did. The cop behind him was not slacking up; if anything, he was gaining. At this point, Sammy regretted having to sit behind a desk as much as he did.

Rounding a corner, Sammy found a dead end straight ahead. To his left was an eight-foot chain-link fence surrounding a parking lot; farther down to his right the alley intersected a major street. He hesitated. The parking lot was most attractive—the fence would slow him down, but after that he was home free. The street, on the other hand, was much too wide open to be safe.

With the cop close on his heels, Sammy was about to turn toward the fence when he felt himself jerked from behind and thrown toward the street. Landing flat on his back on the pavement—"Ooof!"—he looked up and saw no one. The cop on foot came barreling up to the dead end and looked both ways. Fifteen feet away, Sammy lay absolutely still in the middle of the dark alley.

Not seeing him, the cop decided that the parking lot looked good, too, so he gave pursuit in that direction. Sammy waited until the cop had climbed the fence and disappeared, then he got to his feet and walked to the street. He looked up and down, but it was empty. So he casually began walking.

Anybody out this late was automatically suspect, so Sammy flattened himself against the nearest building when the woman officer shot by in the squad car. At the next intersection, Sammy glanced toward the business fronting the parking lot he had almost run for, and broke into a cold sweat. While it was not apparent from the alley, the whole area had been cordoned off as a crime scene, with numerous uniforms and detectives crawling all over the place. In climbing that fence, he would have handed himself over to them gift-wrapped.

How had he been thrown down? He was sure he had not merely slipped. Whatever, it had saved his skin, for sure.

Turning in the opposite direction to walk to his car, he shook his head and muttered, "God, I have mucked this whole thing up unbelievably. What are You trying to tell me? Should I have not taken this assignment in the first place? Should I forget it?" He got into his car and drove home, shaking his head over one bungled endeavor after another. Still, he could not figure out how he managed to evade that cop in the alley.

Sammy climbed into bed and cuddled Marni, but he could not relax enough to go to sleep for a long time. He was just too perturbed over the way this assignment had taken on a life of its own and jumped out of his hands.

As a matter of fact, it made him sullen and moody all weekend. Oh, he wasn't entirely out of options; there were several even more insane measures he could take. But now he was somewhat wary—he felt that he kept getting his hand slapped, and he didn't know why. He pouted until Marni threatened to leave him, so to make amends, he took the family to Pam and Clayton's house for a Saturday afternoon visit. There, he even agreed to sit for the long-delayed family portrait.

"Stop glaring, Sammy," Pam chastised from in front of her canvas. "You won't be sitting for long."

"Sorry," he muttered, shifting on the stool and relaxing his face. A moment later it had settled into the same distrustful gaze. Smoky jumped up in his lap, looking for attention. He started to brush her off as usual, then changed his mind and stroked her silky gray fur. Satisfied, she jumped down.

"It's not the portrait that's bothering him, Mom." Marni came in with a bowl of fresh sliced peaches. Her father, Clayton, sat nearby in his easy chair discussing the Rangers' chances of a berth in the playoffs with his grandson. A televised game was in progress which Sammy watched as he sat. "Sammy's feeling frustrated over this assignment he's on," Marni explained. She fed him a slice of peach and kissed him.

Knowing better than to ask what it was about, Pam

asked, "Did you like the offer at FirstPlace Tower?"

Sammy swallowed and shrugged. "Yeah, sure. But I can't leave the department until this current job is done." Marni took the bowl of peaches over to Clayton and Sam.

Studying his handsome features as she sketched them on to the canvas, Pam murmured, "It must be something important. I've seldom seen you looking so grim."

"My boss asked it as a personal favor, and I couldn't even maintain my placement. I don't know how to proceed," he vented peevishly. Even as he said it, he couldn't believe he was telling her this much.

Pam sketched silently a moment, then said, "I had a dream about you last night, Sammy."

"Yeah?" he regarded her.

"Yes. I dreamed it was Tuesday, and you were very worried about making it Thursday. You weren't *waiting* for Thursday; you felt it was your responsibility to make it Thursday," Pam said, eyes on her canvas.

"What's that supposed to mean?" he asked mildly.

"I have no idea. It was just so vivid, and the expression on your face was just what it is now," she replied.

"That's your way of telling me to lighten up," he said with a hazy smile.

"I would rather not paint you scowling like that," she said testily, and he grinned.

Sunday he did not particularly want to get up and go to church, as he was ticked off at God for not helping him on this assignment. But when Marni began to get ready as if to go without him, he grudgingly showered and dressed.

They went to their little Bible church with its modest auditorium and folding chairs. Sammy refused to sing, and when the pastor got up to speak, Sammy sat back with his arms crossed as if daring him to say something relevant. But at the first reading of the text from Isaiah, Sammy lost his attitude:

> "Why do you say, O Jacob,
> and complain, O Israel,
> 'My way is hidden from the Lord;
> my cause is disregarded by my God'?
>
> Do you not know?
> Have you not heard?
> The Lord is the everlasting God,
> the Creator of the ends of the earth.
> He will not grow tired or weary,
> and his understanding no one can fathom.
> He gives strength to the weary
> and increases the power of the weak.
>
> Even youths grow tired and weary,
> and young men stumble and fall;
> but those who hope in the Lord
> will renew their strength.
> They will soar on wings like eagles;
> they will run and not grow weary,
> they will walk and not be faint."

Monday morning Marni left her boys sleeping while she went in to work. The day started out innocently enough with one of the deacons coming to request a meeting with the pastor. Marni knew him only as Deacon Bob, but she liked him. He had a genuinely cordial bearing and a grave but friendly face.

"Dr. Berger is not in yet," Mrs. Wilchester told him. "You may wait if you like, but I don't really expect him within the hour."

He looked at his watch. "I can't stay—I have another meeting. Please ask him to call me as soon as he comes in."

"Certainly, Brother Bob," she replied.

When the pastor showed up about forty minutes later, Deacon Bob's message was on top of the pile. Dr. Berger glanced at it and put it aside. "I'm too busy to see Bob today," he informed Mrs. Wilchester, then took the rest of his correspondence back to his office and shut the door.

His secretary busily straightened her desk. "My things are in such a mess this morning. It makes me so mad when people wander back here on Sundays. If they don't know where they're going, they should just stay out!" she fumed.

Marni bit her lip, pretending to know nothing about any unauthorized persons who might have been around Mrs. Wilchester's desk recently. "Sorry," she muttered. Marni was stuffing yet another form letter to the membership in computer-addressed envelopes.

As she stuffed, she began to think it rather a shame that the letters were so impersonal—the pastor had not even signed the original. Obviously he didn't have time.

But since Marni had more time, she decided to take it upon herself to sign each one, "Dr. Berger." After the first fifty she decided that was too formal, so she changed it to "Brother Ron," and then creatively, "R ☺ n," or sometimes "R☼n."

She was listening when Mrs. Wilchester's line rang and the secretary answered, "Pastor's office." Then she said, "No, I'm sorry, he's not in yet, Brother Bob. I've left your message for him."

A while later two teenagers, a boy and a girl, walked up to Marni's desk and demanded, "Where was Dad all weekend?"

"Dad?" Marni blinked.

"Sammy told us to call him Dad," the girl explained, "and he wasn't here all weekend. Aren't you his wife?"

"Yes. I'm afraid 'Dad' got fired for taking the Thursday night group to Mama's Restaurant," Marni said.

"What?" the girl exclaimed. She was a blond, rather spoiled-looking girl.

"That's not right! We were feeding the hungry and visiting the sick!" the boy, a straight-A type, said righteously.

"Sammy was very upset about it, but they wouldn't give him a second chance," Marni said, fanning the flames.

"We'll see about that!" the girl huffed, tossing her head. "C'mon, Keith, let's go talk to Curtis!" Marni watched them march back to his office.

Brother Bob called again. Mrs. Wilchester told him the pastor was in his office, but had a full calendar for the day. Then Anna, pale-faced, came back with two men in sports coats. Marni did not know either of them, but one look at them told her they were plain-clothes officers. "Is Larry in yet?" Anna asked tremulously.

Marni glanced at wide-eyed Mrs. Wilchester. "I haven't seen him yet," Marni replied.

"Does he come in this way?" one man asked.

"Yes," Marni said.

"We'll wait," he said, and they sat in a pair of chairs in front of her desk.

Meanwhile, Brother Bob showed up at Mrs. Wilchester's desk again. "I really must insist that Dr. Berger make time for me today. It is quite urgent," he said, looking at the pastor's closed door.

"I'll tell him," Mrs. Wilchester said, brows arched. Unnerved by the presence of the two intimidating men in the office, she put through a call to the pastor in his office five feet away. "Dr. Berger, Brother Bob is here. . . . I'll tell him," she sighed, hanging up. "He's really just too tied up today," she told Bob in a wavering voice. He nodded curtly and left.

The two teenagers emerged from Curtis' office. "I guess that's that. He wouldn't even listen to me or Stacy," the boy told Marni.

Stacy looked up with fiery blue eyes. "The neatest guy we ever had as a youth leader, and they can him! We're not gonna leave it at that, Keith. Come on!" she commanded, and they left talking excitedly.

Before Marni had time to ponder this, Larry breezed in. The detectives stood. Mrs. Wilchester said nothing, so Marni spoke up: "Larry, these two gentlemen need to talk with you."

"You Lawrence G. Fortune?" one asked.

"Yes, I am," he said wonderingly.

They flashed their badges and one handed him a warrant. "Police. You're under arrest for sexual assault."

The first turned him around and handcuffed him while the other read him his rights. Stunned, he was taken out the front door. Mrs. Wilchester bolted from her desk and ran back toward the music department.

Left alone, Marni blinked as something from years past surfaced. Knowing how much money flowed into this church, she knew that they had the means to take care of this little indiscretion so quietly, so efficiently, that no one would ever hear of it. Nothing would come of it, and Larry would be free to continue his career of preying on lonely, alienated, insecure girls.

Glancing around, Marni quickly hauled out the Dallas telephone directory and looked up a number. This she dialed, checking to see that Mrs. Wilchester was not on her way back. "Hello, is this the *Sun-Times?* I thought you'd be interested to know that the Minister of Music at First Metro was just arrested for sexual assault. His name's Larry Fortune." Then Marni hung up and went back to innocently stuffing envelopes.

At that time Deacon Bob returned, accompanied by two other men. They paused in front of Mrs. Wilchester's empty desk, then Bob turned soberly to Marni and said, "If Dr. Berger does not have time to see just me, I thought he might be persuaded to see me and Roger and Harold here."

"He's in his office. Go right on in," Marni said sweetly.

The three deacons went into the pastor's office and shut the door behind them. "My, my," Marni marveled.

A moment later Mrs. Wilchester came back to her desk. Highly agitated, she turned to Marni and said, "Ginger agrees that the first thing we have to do is keep this quiet. We must pray that this gets worked out before too many people hear about it."

"What, Larry getting arrested? I think it would be more profitable to pray for the families involved, and let Larry take his lumps," the cop's wife said. Mrs. Wilchester looked at her in dismay.

Marni went back to signing letters and Mrs. Wilchester wrung her hands. "I suppose we should let the pastor know about this," she murmured, picking up the telephone.

"I wouldn't call right now. Brother Bob and two other deacons are in there with the pastor," Marni warned her.

Mrs. Wilchester looked up fearfully. "Oh, dear. That, too?"

"What's it about?" Marni asked curiously.

"Nothing that concerns you," Mrs. Wilchester said stiffly.

About that time a group of teenagers appeared in the office, led by Keith and Stacy. They crowded in until there was no more room, so they spilled out into both hallways. "We're here to see the pastor," Stacy announced to Mrs. Wilchester.

"He is in a meeting and can't be disturbed," she said shrilly.

"Okay, guys," Stacy turned to the group. "SIT!" And they all sat down right where they were, taking up every square inch of floor space.

Mrs. Wilchester stood, appalled. "What are you doing?"

"We're sitting right here until we get to talk to the pastor about Sammy," Stacy said defiantly, and the other kids supported her with whoops and applause. Marni smiled.

Mrs. Wilchester put through a panicky phone call to Curtis, as Kent was not in yet. Curtis came out, looked around, and said, "Now, young people, if you have a problem, you need to address it in a more mature manner if you expect to resolve anything. Why don't all but two of you go on home, and—"

They interrupted him with boos and hisses. "We already talked to you. You wouldn't listen. Now we're talking to the pastor!" Stacy said, and the others cheered.

Into this mess stepped a man in shirt sleeves. He gazed at the bodies scattered around the floor, then picked his way through them to Marni's desk. He produced a business card that identified him as a reporter for the Dallas *Sun-Times* and asked, "Is it a fact that Larry Fortune was arrested this morning?" The kids became deathly silent while the reporter pulled out his pen and notepad.

"Yes, I'm afraid it is," Marni confirmed reluctantly. "Two detectives were waiting for him when he came in this morning. They arrested him on charges of sexual assault." A gasp went up from several people on the floor. Mrs. Wilchester threw up her hands, fled her desk and did not return.

The reporter began to ask Marni another question when Curtis took control. "We have no comment at this time. I must ask you to leave now." But with all the bodies crowding the place, he could not force the reporter out.

"Do you know who filed the complaint?" the reporter asked Marni.

"Lauren," said one boy from the floor. "That would be Lauren."

"Yeah, everybody knew about them," said a girl.

"I can't believe she had him arrested," said somebody else. "This is so cool."

The reporter asked why they were all there. Stacy declared, "This is a sit-in! We're protesting that our favorite youth leader was fired, and we're not leaving until we talk to the pastor about getting him back."

"What's his name?" the reporter asked, pen poised over his notepad.

"It's—Sammy!" exclaimed Stacy. For lo and behold, who should come to the door but the very Sammy.

With Sam in his arms, he paused as the kids clapped and whistled from their places on the floor. Sammy looked confounded and Sam buried his face on his daddy's shoulder at the noise.

Several kids and the reporter addressed him all at once. Sammy generally replied, "I just . . . came to see if Marni wanted to go to lunch."

"Sammy's a cop," one kid offered.

"What do you know about the arrest of Larry Fortune?" the reporter asked.

"What?" said Sammy.

"Are you coming back to work?" one teen demanded.

"I don't think so," Sammy said, looking at Curtis.

The door to the pastor's office suddenly opened. Deacon Bob came out first, followed by the other two deacons. The pastor remained in his office.

In some surprise, the deacons surveyed the young people all over the place, then Bob handed a letter to Marni, as Mrs. Wilchester was still nowhere to be seen.

"Miss," he said, "please call the *Sun-Times* and inform them of Brother Ron's resignation."

The reporter immediately pulled out a small, voice-activated recorder and introduced himself: "Mark Bowery of the Dallas *Sun-Times*."

"The young lady has a statement to read from the pastor," Brother Bob said, nodding toward Marni.

Hardly anyone in the room was breathing as Marni looked down at the paper in her hands and read out loud: "To the good people of First Metropolitan Church: It is with a full heart that I offer my resignation as senior pastor of this great church. We have had four wonderful years together and I have cherished every moment, but it is time for me to move on. I feel the Lord's call to spend more time with my family and my writing projects; therefore, I am resigning as of today.

"I am confident that I have left the church in good financial condition, and those who accuse me of improprieties in any area of the budget must settle that with their consciences. Yours in faithfulness, Ron L. Berger."

A moment of startled silence followed, then Bob said, "As chairman of the deacons, I regretfully accept Dr. Berger's resignation. We wish him well and speed him on his way with all our prayers. Our associate pastor, Dan Macomber, has agreed to step in as interim until a new pastor is called. Neither I nor Dr. Berger has any further comment."

For an instant no one moved. Then in a sudden surge, the kids and the reporter stampeded out to spread the news. Sammy moved in against the flow to ask Bob, "Where does that leave the plans for the new gym?"

"There will be no new gym. That project has been scrapped," Bob said briefly on his way out.

Sammy turned to Marni. "Write out your resignation and let's go," he said softly.

She did. As they went to the garage for their cars, Sammy said, "You drive on home. Sam and I'll . . . stop and get us a submarine sandwich on the way."

"Okay," she murmured, still in shock.

Sammy arrived back at their apartment with the sandwich just a few minutes behind Marni. As she took Sam from his arms to put him in his chair, she murmured, "Good heavens. I can't believe it. All heck broke loose, all at once."

"I was thinking about that all the way home—that's why I couldn't do anything," Sammy said. "It wasn't up to me to do anything. The Lord was in the process of cleansing the Temple—again."

"Some broom," Marni observed dryly. But Sammy looked perturbed.

six

The headline in the next morning's paper read: "TURMOIL AT FIRST METRO" and the accompanying articles covered half the front page. Sammy hunkered down and read it all word for word.

Fortunately, his name was not mentioned, only his position at the church, and then only in connection with the kids' sit-in. Nor was it mentioned that he was a cop. Ironically, as the reporter had neglected to get Marni's name, he had credited all her statements to "the pastor's secretary, Iva Wilchester."

But all the rest about the pastor's sudden resignation, some questions about his expense accounts, and the arrest of Larry Fortune was there. Lauren was not named in the article, but as far as Sammy could figure it, she had gone straight home after her conversation with him (which also was not mentioned) and had told her parents. They had called first the police and then a lawyer— obviously in preparation for filing a lawsuit against the church.

Sammy was still reading the paper when the telephone rang. Marni answered it, and Mike said,

"Good morning, Marni." He did not sound very cheery. "Is your old man there?"

"Yes, Mike," she said, turning to call him to the phone.

But Mike said, "I need to talk to him in my office. Just tell him to come on in as soon as he can."

"Okay, Mike," she said wonderingly, and he hung up.

Sammy had a strange feeling of oppression driving to the Big Building this morning. The case was cleared and the mayor was off the hook—technically—though Sammy had not discovered what the pastor did or did not have on him.

He parked, greeted his friends, and walked in to receive his ID from Corporal Collins. "Hi, Dreamboat," she said mischievously. Sammy halted, looking at her, then leaned over the counter and kissed her on the lips. She stared after him as he went up the elevator.

Sammy knocked on Mike's closed door. "Come in," the sergeant said in a heavy voice. When Sammy opened the door, he barely looked up. "Sit down, Sammy."

There was no chair beside the desk. Sammy sat in the one opposite it. Mike leaned forward, his hands clenched on the desk. Before him was a copy of that morning's paper. "I asked you to handle it quietly, Sammy."

Sammy gestured at the paper. "None of that was my doing. It was all stewing before I came. The pastor is leaving and the chairman of the deacons said the church will not buy the building, so that takes care of the mayor's problems."

"Maybe so," Mike said, "but he exploded over the publicity. He explicitly told the chief that the press was not to get involved."

"There's nothing about the mayor or even the gym anywhere in there. Besides, I had no control over that," Sammy reiterated.

"I'm sure you didn't," Mike muttered. "But the mayor felt that once the press got wind of the church's doings, they wouldn't stop digging until they found—whatever." For the first time, Sammy began to wonder what the mayor had done that he feared so much being found out.

Mike continued, "The thing that makes it so hard is knowing you weren't responsible for the publicity. But . . . I have orders from the top to fire you, Sammy."

Sammy eyed Mike dispassionately, then pulled off his ID and tossed it on the desk. He stood to place his badge and gun on the desk as well, then turned and walked out. Without a word to anyone, he went out to his car and drove home.

He walked in the door of the apartment and sat on the leather sofa. Marni came down the stairs. "Sammy! I wasn't expecting you back so soon. . . ." Seeing his expression, she asked quietly, "What happened?"

"I got fired," he said blankly.

She stood frozen at the foot of the stairs. "Why?"

"Because of this morning's headlines," he said, leaning back on the couch.

She gulped and looked down at her hands. "That—was my fault, Sammy. I called the newspaper as soon as the cops left with Larry."

"That makes no difference at all," he stated. "They would have found out about that from ten different sources. And that was only part of it."

She came to sit beside him on the couch. "I'm sorry."

He shook his head. "I said I was ready to get out of police work, didn't I? This just confirms that I made the right decision."

Marni saw how shaken he was, how he needed time to come to grips with being so callously skewered, but Sammy refused a pity party. He reached over to the telephone and dialed a number. "Ms. Bancroft, please. Yeah, it's Sammy Kidman."

After a moment of waiting he said, "Ms. Bancroft? Sammy. I finished my last assignment earlier than I expected, so I'm free to start any time now. . . . Sure, I can come in today. Be there in about twenty minutes."

He hung up, then paused, regarding Marni. He leaned over to take her in his arms. Gently he tilted her head back and gave her a deep kiss. "See you tonight," he said in a throaty voice.

"I can't wait," she gasped. A kiss like that usually indicated some pent-up emotions that he expressed best nonverbally.

Sammy drove downtown to the FirstPlace Bank Tower and eyed the gleaming structure almost disdainfully. His one consolation in this jarring turn of events was the $92,000 salary he'd be pulling down. Ambling into the building manager's office, he announced himself to Ms. Bancroft's secretary.

In a moment Ms. Bancroft came out. "Sammy," she nodded cordially, "this way."

He followed her to the security room she had shown him earlier. While he was looking over the monitors and controls, she pointed out a uniform hanging neatly on a rack.

"It should fit," she advised. "You may try it on in this

back room." She opened the door to a small room with a cot and a bathroom.

"A uniform?" he asked with curled lip. "For a ninety-two-thousand-dollar position?"

She amended, "We need to talk about that. The board will only allow me to pay you eighty thousand."

Sammy eyed her. "That's considerably less than what you offered me earlier."

"I am sorry, but I have been informed that it's all I can give you," she said with regret.

This tap dancing was unsettling, but $80,000 was still more than he had been making. Besides, he had no choice, now. Swallowing his pride, he said, "All right," and picked up the uniform. He excused himself to the back room and shut the door to begin undressing.

While he was standing there in his underwear, unbuttoning the uniform shirt, the door suddenly opened. Sammy quickly turned to see Ms. Bancroft come in and shut the door. "I'm not dressed," he pointed out.

Without a word she took off her suit coat, then sat on the cot and kicked off her shoes. "What are you doing?" Sammy asked in alarm.

When she started unbuttoning her blouse, Sammy panicked. He pulled her up off the cot and thrust her out of the room with her coat and shoes. Then he nervously held the door shut for several minutes while fumbling to lock it. Distrusting the flimsy lock, he reached over for the gray slacks and shirt with navy tie and dressed with his back pressed against the door. The uniform fit tolerably well; "But—gee," he muttered.

Cautiously, he opened the door and peeked out. She was gone. Expelling a breath, he sat at the control panel and pulled out the operator's guide to begin monitoring the system.

Several minutes later Ms. Bancroft's secretary opened the door. "Mr. Kidman?" He looked up inquiringly. "I'm very sorry to be the one to tell you this, but Ms. Bancroft says that your résumé did not check out and you do not have the minimum qualifications for this position. She asked you to please hang the uniform back up when you leave," said the secretary.

"Wha—? I didn't even give her a résumé!" Sammy exclaimed.

"I'm sorry, that's all I know," she said, and quickly withdrew from the doorway.

Sammy sat back, stunned and angry. He considered fighting her reversal, then thought about the potential embarrassment to his father-in-law. The job wasn't worth it.

Glumly, he changed and hung the uniform back up. He stuffed his tie in his coat pocket on his way out to his car. The June heat was blistering, so he took off his coat for the drive home. No matter how hot it got, he would never put up the top to turn on the air conditioner. Never. That was for wienies.

He parked at the apartment, walked in and sat on the couch. Marni looked down from the second floor. "Sammy?" She came slowly down the stairs. "Why are you home, Sammy?" she asked.

"I got fired," he said in a mechanical voice. "Actually, I was not hired to begin with."

"Oh, Sammy," she breathed, sitting beside him.

"I've never . . ." he swallowed, "I've never been out of work. I don't know how to look for a job." He looked at her. "Police work has been my whole life. I've given everything for the job. Now what?"

"What about the San Antonio police department?" she asked.

"They wanted me before I got fired. It's going to be a different story now," he muttered.

"Mrs. Threlkeld offered you a job as head of security," she said.

He shook his head. "Dad told us months ago she'd hired somebody, remember?"

"She'd make a position for you, Sammy," Marni argued.

"Please, Marni," he said, stroking his forehead, "leave me a shred of pride." She hung her head and he gathered her in his arms. "I know you're just trying to help," he murmured.

After a moment he squeezed her and stood. "Guess I'd better head to the employment agency."

"Are you going to file for unemployment benefits?" she asked.

"No," he bristled. She bit her lip at his tone and he kissed her repentantly. "I'm sorry. I won't start taking it out on you. I promise."

"Okay," she said softly, then began, "Do you want me to—?"

He cringed, anticipating her next suggestion. "I really would rather you just be here for me."

"Okay, Sammy," she sighed. No, he would rather she didn't get a job. He was the last of the Neanderthals, that dying breed of man who expected to shelter and protect his woman. Then again, remembering how tired and weak she had been in the months surrounding Sam's birth, she wondered: was that so bad? She waved warmly as he got in his car and backed out.

Sammy drove to the unfamiliar Texas Workforce Commission offices and self-consciously filled out an application. He thought about all the different kinds of work he had done as a cover, and how none of it had bothered him. Nothing was demeaning, because it was all done in the line of duty, for a higher purpose. With that reassuring backdrop gone, he felt lost. For a career cop, *this* was demeaning.

He waited about twenty minutes to see an employment counselor. When his name was called, he rose and closed his coat from habit, although there was no gun to conceal anymore. "You'll be interviewing with Mandy Brinker," the secretary told him. Nodding, he stepped through the doorway of the back office that the secretary indicated.

Immediately he felt chafed—the girl sitting behind the desk looked younger than he was. She raised her face and stared at him. "Are you Sammy Kidman?"

"Yes," he said. "And you're Mandy?" Maybe there was a mistake, and the experienced, well-connected job broker Mandy Brinker was in *another* office.

"I don't believe this," she breathed. "You're perfect." Picking up her telephone, she demanded, "What's your waist size?"

His eyebrows shot up. "Thirty-four. Why?"

But she was already talking on the phone. "Allison, I've got one for you. He just walked into my office. No lie! I'll send him right down. His name is Sammy Kidman—isn't that cute?—and Suzy will know him the minute he walks in."

She hung up and wrote an address on a pad. "The Allison Pinella Agency—sixth floor, FirstPlace Bank Tower," she said with authority. "Get down there *right now*."

"What—?" he began, taking the paper, but her telephone rang. She answered and began a long-winded, hyper conversation, so Sammy quietly backed out and drove the few blocks to the bank tower. He ducked stealthily through the lobby (lest Ms. Bancroft see him) and took the elevator up to the sixth floor.

He found the glass doors of the elegant Allison Pinella Agency and walked in. The waiting room was crowded with mostly young, good-looking people. Sammy noted this as he told the receptionist, "I'm—"

"Sammy Kidman," she finished for him, looking him up and down. "I'm Suzy. Ms. Pinella is waiting for you. Last door at the end of the hall." She pointed.

Sammy turned down the hall and approached the open door cautiously. A stylishly dressed woman with sleek brown hair sat behind a desk cluttered with photographs. "Ms. Pinella?" he said. "I'm Sammy Kidman."

She got up from the desk and scrutinized him for several minutes, even from behind. Sammy stood his ground. "Take off your jacket and shirt, please," she said.

"Why?" he asked levelly.

She arched a thin, waxed brow at him. "This is for an underwear spread. I need to see you without your shirt."

"What?" he gasped.

"Oh, don't tell me that Mandy didn't tell you. She is such an airhead. This is a modeling agency, and I'm in desperate straits for male models *today*," Ms. Pinella said. "The client suddenly decided he wanted 'real people' straight off the street—with the shoot scheduled for today. Never mind that he's not pleased with how 'real people' look in underwear," she finished in an exasperated murmur.

"Modeling—underwear?" Sammy croaked. "No way. Absolutely not. Excuse me." He turned to leave.

"It pays five hundred dollars for an afternoon's work," she mentioned.

He paused. "Five hundred dollars?" he asked. She nodded. Then he shook his head. "I still can't. Lady, I've been in undercover work for years, and I can't show my face in photographs."

"They don't need your face. These are torso shots," she said, shutting the door. "Does that make you more comfortable? Come on, sugar; let me see those pecs."

Hesitantly, Sammy stripped to the waist. Maybe he entertained a *little* vanity and curiosity to see if he could pass muster. He eyed her as she surveyed his form.

"Um-hmm. Nice chest hair pattern. Chin up, honey. Flex, now. Okay, you'll do." She sat to fill out a slip while Sammy dressed, then presented him with a contract.

"What's this?" he muttered.

"It just says that you won't take any modeling jobs except through us," Ms. Pinella said casually. "You'll need to sign it before I can send you on the one today."

Sammy read through the contract, shrugged, and signed it. Ms. Pinella took it up with satisfaction. "Excellent. Here." She handed him the slip as he stuffed his tie in his coat pocket. "Take this up to Meinhart

Photography on the twenty-second floor. After the session bring it back signed, and Suzy will have a check for five hundred dollars ready for you."

Still feeling woefully unsure about all this, Sammy took the form with him up the elevator to the photography studio. He walked in and handed the form to the receptionist, mumbling, "Allison Pinella sent me."

The teenaged receptionist with glitzy jewelry and frizzed hair looked over the sheet and popped her gum. "Okay, hon," she said. "My, you are a cutie. Step back here and we'll get you shaved." She stood and swished down the hallway.

Following her, Sammy felt his face. "I shaved this morning," he muttered, "but I guess I've got a shadow by now. My face gets irritated with too much shaving," he warned her.

She opened the door to a brightly lit room with a massage table. "Not your face, sweetie. Your body. Undress and hop up," she said, patting the table.

"My body?" Sammy squeaked in alarm, instinctively raising his arms to his chest. She took out a barber's razor and he backed up to the door. "No way. Uh-unh," he said adamantly.

She laughed, "Don't be such a wienie. I haven't cut anybody yet—not where it counted, anyway."

He opened the door and almost collided with another woman coming in. "Hurry up; we're waiting for you," she chided him.

"He's not shaved," the receptionist objected.

"They want him *au naturel* for this series," the second woman replied, taking him by the hand. She was all business, unglamorous, with straight, dull blond hair.

She dragged him past a set where the photographer stood over his camera. "Get on it, willya?" he demanded. "Models!" he breathed in exasperation.

The woman, evidently the photographer's assistant, stuck something in Sammy's hand and shoved him into a dressing room. "We're looking at an hour's deadline, so you've got thirty seconds to change if you want to get paid today!" she shouted, slamming the door.

Sammy gazed at the skimpy, bright red briefs which barely covered his palm, and he whimpered. "Need help?" the woman shouted through the door.

"No!" he said, dropping off his coat. He undressed quickly and pulled on the underwear. He was trying to adjust them when the door opened and the assistant came back in. He backed away. She surveyed him critically, then reached out to adjust the band. He jumped back skittishly. "I'll do that."

"No, no—you've got it too high," she said in disapproval. "Just relax and let me do this." Sammy winced as she relocated the band and then turned to a makeup table.

She selected a bottle and poured out some base makeup on her fingers. Sammy had a nice tan, but his swim trunks covered a lot more than these briefs. He saw what she was about and took the bottle. "I'll do this," he insisted, and applied the makeup himself.

She scrutinized the effect, then went to the door. "You coming?" she glanced back.

"Sure," he said weakly, sidling out of the room. *Five hundred dollars,* he kept telling himself. *I'm earning five hundred dollars doing this.* It didn't seem as much now as it did 30 minutes ago.

The photographer positioned him like a mannequin in front of a stark white backdrop which extended onto the floor. "You can't take my face," Sammy said seriously.

"No problem," the photographer muttered. "Put your hand on your hip there—lean back—farther. Look back over your shoulder as far as you can. There."

While Sammy held this unnatural position, the photographer adjusted one of the lights so that his face was in the peripheral shadows. "Okay." The shutter clicked several times in rapid succession, then the photographer paused to reposition the model.

Sammy grimaced when the photographer told him to arch his back. "Are you sure you want me to do that?"

"It looks good on paper. The tension's good there. Okay, spread your feet. Good." The photographer clicked away.

When he was done, Sammy let down with a sigh, but they were not through. There were several different styles to be featured, and he was next handed a pair of thong underwear. "Where are you going to print these?" Sammy wondered.

"Friday's paper," the assistant replied.

"The newspaper?" Sammy cried. "The *Sun-Times*?"

"Of course," she said. "Get back there and change!"

"Oh, man, I'll have to leave town," he moaned. They already had him on film, so he might as well go through with it and get his check. Five hundred dollars now seemed a paltry figure.

When he had changed into the thong underwear, he came out feeling totally naked. The assistant handed him a prop: a hair dryer. "I do not use a hair dryer," Sammy said indignantly.

"Great, then nobody'll know it's you," she said, shoving him in front of the camera. Sammy, not entirely trusting the photographer, kept his face turned so far over his shoulder that he developed a crick in his neck.

After those shots he changed again, this time into green boxer shorts. He was so relieved to be wearing these, he did not care that they were covered with what looked like flying rubber chickens. Chicken camouflage gear. More ridiculous poses, one with a pipe and another with a basketball, and the session was complete.

Sammy dressed with unutterable relief and picked up his signed slip from the receptionist. This he took downstairs to present to Suzy, who gave him his check in return. He studied it before leaving: his name, $500, a signature, an in-town bank name and magnetic number —it looked legitimate.

On his way out to his car, he muttered, "That was the most humiliating experience of my life. I'll *never* do that again." He drove home to seek solace in the arms of his wife.

When he opened the apartment door, he smelled something good from the kitchen. Sam, in the middle of the floor with some toys, looked up. "'i!"

"Well, hi yourself!" Sammy exclaimed, bending to sweep up the baby. "Marni, did you hear that? He said hi to me!"

"Hi, too!" she laughed, coming over for a kiss. "Well?" she asked with tentative hopefulness.

"Well . . ." he drew the check from his coat pocket and handed it to her. "That was for a one-time job this afternoon."

She looked at the check. "Five hundred dollars!

Sammy, that's fantastic! What did you do?"

"I, uh—" he tried to say it, but the words would not come out. Marni waited with an expectant face. "I. . . ." He bounced Sam on his arm. "Did you hear him say 'hi' to me?"

"I didn't hear it, but I'm sure he did," she said carefully.

"He did. He said hi," Sammy confirmed. Marni kept looking at him. "Baby, I . . . you won't tell your parents, will you?" he asked anxiously.

"Sammy, what did you do for this money?" she breathed.

"I modeled," he said, wincing.

"You modeled? Modeled what?" she asked.

He looked grievously pained. "Underwear," he whispered.

Marni's eyes got wide. "You modeled *underwear?* Where? For what?"

"For ads coming out in the paper," he moaned.

"Really?" Marni exclaimed with shining eyes. "Sammy, that's *great!* When will the ads run?"

"Friday," he said, evaluating her reaction.

"Wow!" she laughed. "Really?" He nodded and she began jumping up and down like a kid at Christmas. "Wow, wow, wow! *Please* let me call Mom so she can be watching for them."

"No!" he exclaimed. "I don't want *anybody* to know. They just took torso shots. My face won't show."

"Not at all?" she asked skeptically.

"Shouldn't," he replied uncomfortably.

"Sammy," she asked, "how many people have seen you at a pool, or changing clothes?"

"A few," he muttered, eyeing her.

"You have the kind of body people notice. That's what lifting weights will do for you," she purred. His brows drew down and she said, "I bet somebody recognizes you."

"No," he denied it.

"Pruett will," she maintained.

"Oh, no," Sammy groaned. "Not Pruett. Please, not Pruett."

"What's wrong with that? He'll just be jealous. I think it's great," Marni exulted, kissing his cheek. "We'll take this check down to the bank after we eat." She turned to finish fixing dinner.

In spite of Marni's appreciation, Sammy was still so uneasy that all night long he suffered nightmares about showing up for job interviews in his underwear.

seven

The next day Sammy resumed his job quest. With some reluctance, he returned to the Texas Workforce Commission offices, where he firmly told Mandy, "No more modeling jobs."

"Why not?" she wondered. "It's quick, easy money, and Allison said you were a find."

"Look," he said, drawing up a chair to her desk, "for about the last seven years I've been in undercover work, putting some bad-tempered people in prison. Whatever money I earn modeling *might* cover my funeral expenses when one of those people recognizes me from the pictures. No more modeling."

"Okay," she sighed. "Nor police work?" she asked.

"I'm getting out of police work," he said grimly.

"Shame. With your qualifications, I could place you right away in one of the suburbs," she told him. Sammy looked at the floor and was silent.

Searching her computer files, she said, "Here's something—a private investigative agency. That would be a perfect fit."

"Which one?" Sammy asked dubiously.

"Dunbar and Smith," Mandy replied.

"Dunbar and Smith! Those slime-eating, pit-faced, reptilian—" Sammy began in a tirade.

"Okay, not," she said irritably. "Look, it would help a lot if you told me what kind of a job you would settle for." Sammy closed his mouth and looked down at the floor again.

Sighing, she turned back to her computer. After a moment's search, she said, "Wait a minute. Look at this." Sammy raised his face. "Rent-a-Boyfriend," she said.

"Right," Sammy snorted sarcastically.

"No, listen; the name's not great, but it's right up your alley. This is a service company started by a retired cop. He helps single women with things boyfriends or husbands traditionally do—you know, negotiate car prices or repairs, do heavy work or lifting, even provide protection. His business has expanded to the point that he needs additional men. See?" she said encouragingly, and Sammy considered it.

"Why don't you just go talk to him?" she suggested. "I'll set up an interview." She turned to her telephone while Sammy studied the computer listing.

"Okay," she swiveled brightly toward him after a short telephone conversation. "You'll be interviewing with Silas Porter. He wants you to come down right away. Here's the address." She tore off a sheet and handed it to him.

"All right," Sammy said hesitantly, taking the paper. As he left she crossed her fingers and rolled her eyes.

Sammy drove to a brick house in a middle-class neighborhood in Dallas and went up the sidewalk, dodging the sprinkler, to the front door. A woman answered his knock. When he introduced himself she stepped back and said, "Yes, Silas is expecting you. Come on in."

She took him back to a paneled gameroom which had been converted to an office. A big, beefy guy whose appearance screamed *cop* rose from an old desk. "Kidman?" he said, and Sammy nodded, shaking his hand. "Sly Porter. So you're an ex-cop, eh? What department?"

"Dallas, my whole career," Sammy said with a sudden ache in his gut. "Eight years a detective. But I've got a new baby and I decided I'd like to live to see him graduate from high school."

"I hear you," said Sly, settling back to his chair and pointing to another. Sammy sat gingerly. "It's bad for your health to be a cop these days. No respect at all for the uniform. That's one reason business is so good for me." He leaned forward to shove a bulging file at him. "These are just the calls I've received in the past month."

Sammy opened the file and leafed through the call slips jamming it. "A lot of these seem to be women having trouble with stalkers," he observed.

"That's right," Sly said. "And ninety-nine percent of the time the women know who it is—usually an ex-husband or boyfriend.

"Here's what we do with that type of case: we just pay a little personal visit to the party in question and let him know that we resent him bothering our friend. No violence, just a nice little chat. Ninety percent of the time that takes care of the problem—the other ten percent require one follow-up visit. That's it." Sammy nodded.

"The fee is fifty dollars an hour—you get seventy percent of what you earn on your jobs; thirty percent goes back to me," Sly continued.

"Fifty dollars an hour seems kinda steep for a single woman to pay," Sammy muttered.

"Eighty percent of these jobs require two hours or less to complete," Sly said. "And these women are thrilled to pay a hundred dollars to get a stalker off their backs."

Sammy said, "The department's letting these women down. They shouldn't have to pay for private protection. The state and the city both have anti-stalking laws."

Sly threw his head back and laughed. "Spoken like a true cop. Say, how many guys have you put away for stalking?"

Sammy looked uncomfortable. "Well, that wasn't really my area—"

"Then you can see how effective *that's* been," Sly hooted, gesturing at his overflowing file. Sammy nodded unhappily. "As a matter of fact, I got a call this morning from a lady in Plano who's not even covered by the Dallas ordinance," Sly said, leaning aside to pick up a call slip and hand it to him. "This gal's so anxious, she wants somebody to come out to her work. You take that one as a test case. Name and address right there."

"Okay. I'll get right on it," Sammy said, standing.

The woman's name was Beverly Gamble, and she worked as office manager for an accountant off North Central Expressway. Sammy found the address within twenty minutes, despite the typical Dallas traffic. As he parked and entered the building, he noticed a seedy-looking character standing on the sidewalk, looking in the window.

Sammy turned into the accountant's first-floor office, where a woman looked up from behind a desk. She was in her mid-thirties, very slight, with big brown eyes and a rather nervous air, apparently because she was alone in the office most of the time. "My name's Sammy Kidman. Sly Porter sent me," he introduced himself. No way would the words *I'm from Rent-a-Boyfriend* leave his lips.

She expelled a great breath of relief. "I am so glad you're here. There's my problem—right out there." She pointed out the window to the ragged man looking in. "For about two weeks now he's been watching me. He tries to come in every now and then, but when I call building security he leaves. He watches me all day long, wherever I go. If I leave the building, he follows me. Last night he followed me to my car—I thought he was going to grab me. I've never been so frightened in all my life!"

"Did you call the police?" Sammy asked, looking out.

"Numerous times. I think it's getting to be a joke with them. Twice a patrolman has come along and made him leave, but he always comes back. They said there's nothing more they can do because he hasn't made any threats or touched me—he's never said a word. They said it isn't a crime to look, so they can't do anything about him!" she said angrily.

Sammy nodded, then reluctantly asked, "Do you know that we charge fifty dollars an hour?"

"Anything," she said. "I'll pay anything if you can make him leave me alone."

"Gotcha," he said, stepping outside. He had to remind himself that he was not a cop anymore. "Hey, pal," Sammy said, standing in the vagrant's face. He smelled really bad. "Haven't you got something else you need to be doing? My friend in that office is getting tired of looking at you all day long. You ain't exactly romance-novel material, you know."

The vagrant glanced at him and said nothing, but shifted so that he could see into the window. Sammy shifted to block his view. "I mean it, pal. It's time to move on. She's a nice-looking lady, but she doesn't like you."

The vagrant moved the other way, and Sammy moved with him. "I'm trying to explain this as nicely as I can. You're scaring the heck out of her. You've got to leave her alone now, and I'm here to make sure that you do. If you don't leave, I'm gonna cart your tail off to the city dump myself. Are you hearing me?"

After taking a long look at Sammy with his red, watery eyes, the drifter shuffled off. Sammy watched him go up the sidewalk and disappear in the parking lot. Then Sammy came back in and told his client, "He's gone."

"He'll be back," she said flatly. "Would you please stay for a while?"

"Sure," said Sammy, glancing at his watch in some concern.

He drew up a chair and waited with her, conversing lightly as she worked. Gradually she began to relax, and when she asked about his family, he whipped out a picture of Sam. She admired that with all the appropriate remarks, and showed him a framed picture of her eight-year-old daughter in a dance costume. "Her father lives in Fresno," she said. In California. A long way away.

"I see," Sammy murmured.

Suddenly she stiffened and Sammy turned to look out the window. The vagrant was back.

With clenched teeth, Sammy strode out and took the man by his bony arm. "Maybe I didn't make myself clear," Sammy growled as he dragged him unresisting down the sidewalk. "When I say *leave,* that means you *don't come back."* Sammy heaved him into the parking lot. The man rolled on the pavement, then slowly got up and walked away.

When Sammy returned to the office, Beverly was sitting tensely at her desk, trying to resume work. "He'll be back," she said a little desperately, her eyes watering. "He always comes back."

Sammy sagged, looking down at his watch. He had already been here almost forty minutes. But he could think of no other legal method of keeping the man away. "Your boss should pay for this," he suddenly observed. "He's responsible for your safety at work."

"You know, I already asked him about that," she laughed nervously. "He said that's what the building security guard is for. The guard says he just works the building. No one's willing to take responsibility for the sidewalk because it's public property. And meanwhile, there he stands," she said, gesturing angrily. Then she put her face in her hands and began to cry.

"It's okay. It's okay," Sammy said in dismay, reaching out a hand and then withdrawing it without touching her. "Let's just not worry about that right now. We can talk about terms after we take care of the problem, all right?"

"Yes. Thank you," she said, reaching for a tissue. Then she froze, gazing out the window.

Sammy spun to look. Yep, there he was again. Breathing deeply, Sammy stalked out and seized the derelict by his filthy shirt. "Get it through your head that you can't stand here anymore!" he shouted, shaking him. The guy was a limp rag doll in his hands. Sammy dragged him across the access road and threw him on the median. "Go hitch a ride to New York! You'll feel more at home there!"

Sammy strode back to the office and plopped into the chair. "He's about to make me mad," he calmly observed.

"Obviously, he's mentally ill. It's sad," Beverly said quietly.

"Of course," said Sammy, slapping his forehead. "Let me see your phone book, there." Taking the business pages, he looked up the number for the Mental Health-Mental Retardation Center and Beverly handed him the telephone. A long discussion with a woman at that office proved futile: unless the man posed an immediate threat to himself or someone else, or came to MHMR of his own volition, there was nothing they could do. Calls to several other social agencies produced similar results. They would not commit him for standing on the sidewalk and looking.

Beverly regarded Sammy as he hung up in disgust. "At least you can understand my frustration. That makes me feel better," she commented.

"It doesn't take care of the problem," Sammy observed.

"No. There he is again," she said, inclining her head toward the window. Sammy turned, repressing an expletive.

Over the next several hours Sammy expelled the vagrant from the sidewalk three more times. After the third eviction, Sammy accompanied his client to lunch (for which she paid). When they returned, the problem was waiting for them on the sidewalk in front of the window, as usual. He was totally unresponsive to Sammy's threats or rough handling, and just kept coming back like a virus. Yet the longer Sammy stayed, the calmer Beverly became. She saw that he would not give up until the situation was resolved.

Around three-thirty, after hurtling the irritant from in front of the building yet again, Sammy came in and sat to evaluate his progress: zero. He could load the vagrant in his car and deposit him across town, but that would just mean a longer wait before he showed up again. The pest had to be made to leave voluntarily.

While Sammy mulled this over, Beverly was cheerfully working away. But the bill was mounting and he was no closer to a solution. Sammy rested his head on one hand. *Okay, God; I give up. What am I supposed to do about this creep?*

An idea crossed his mind. Sammy considered it dubiously. He could hardly see how that would help, but —after being gone only 15 minutes, the vagrant stood in front of the window again. Beverly hardly noticed, having so completely entrusted the situation to Sammy. He licked his lips in deliberation, then went outside.

Standing at the man's side without blocking his view of the window, Sammy began talking to him in a conversational tone: "You know, you look like a guy who's seen some hard times. I know how that can be—I've been fired from my last three jobs. I was even committed to a mental hospital once. I almost died there, as a matter of fact. But I didn't. Know why? Because I got down on my knees and started praying to Jesus."

The man shifted his hollow gaze to look at him. Sammy continued, "I prayed for Jesus to save me and not let me die, and He did—He saved my life. See, this is what happened: I was plastered out of my gourd, and playing around with a friend's revolver. He wasn't a friend, really, but I had another friend who was praying for me for a long time—"

Abruptly the vagrant turned and started walking away. "Wait," said Sammy, following him, "I wasn't through telling you what happened—okay, forget the details. The upshot is, Jesus not only saved my life, He gave me a new start with a beautiful wife, and a baby. See, I couldn't have any children—it was my fault; I'd been kinda careless—but then my mother-in-law prayed for us to have a baby—"

His captive audience began running off through the parking lot. "Wait!" Sammy called, then watched until he could see him no longer. "Gee, I wish he'd 've hung around until I could finish telling him about Sam," he muttered.

Sammy came back in and sat beside Beverly's desk, but something told him the problem would not come back. He waited until 4:45, when Beverly started closing her files for the day. Suddenly she looked up. "He hasn't come back," she said in awe. "It's been—how long?"

"One hour and seventeen minutes," Sammy said.

"That's—that's miraculous," she said. "He's not coming back, is he?"

"I don't think so," Sammy said.

"You are so wonderful," she breathed, and he shifted. "What does the bill come to?" she asked evenly.

Sammy glanced at his watch and did some mental calculating. "Four hundred dollars," he said.

She nodded slowly. "Do you take MasterCard?" she asked.

Sammy looked at her and shook his head. "No. I'm not taking your money." He got up and started to walk out.

"Wait," she stopped him. "I hired you and I owe you your pay. I deeply appreciate what you did and I want to pay you—if not four hundred dollars, at least something."

"Beverly," he said, "I can't take your money—not four hundred dollars, not a dime. It goes against everything I believe in." He glanced back at her desk. "Are you ready to leave?"

"Yes," she said, taking up her purse. She turned out the light and locked the door. When Sammy walked her out to her car, the vagrant was nowhere in sight. Sammy held the car door open for her and she said, "How am I supposed to thank you?"

"Just . . . say a prayer for me," he shrugged. "Good night." Walking to his car, he added under his breath, "'Cause now I gotta go tell one retired cop that I can do the job, but I can't take the money for it."

When he dragged his tired old body home, Marni met

him at the door with expectant hope. But seeing his face, she didn't even ask. Then she broached, "The woman from Houston called again."

He looked up quickly. "Did she hang up on you again?"

"No, I wasn't here when the call came. But . . . she didn't leave a message, and I felt that if it was about a job, she would have left a message," Marni said hesitantly.

Striding over to the phone, Sammy looked at the Caller ID list, which did not give a name for the Houston caller—only a number. "Well, if they want to talk to me so bad, they're gonna have to leave a message. I'm not calling long distance out of curiosity," he said, peeved, and Marni smiled wryly.

The next morning Sammy was back in Mandy's office. He stared at the floor while she went through her computer listings. "Here's one for a collection agency," she said.

"I may be on the receiving end of that if I don't get a job soon," he said. "No."

A moment's search later: "Store security," she offered.

He looked up. "Okay," he said listlessly.

"It pays minimum wage," she added reluctantly.

"Unacceptable," Sammy said, sinking back.

"Sales?" she ventured, and he gave her a pained look. "How about a nightclub bouncer? The money's good."

"How good?" he asked. When she pointed out the salary he considered it, then shook his head. "I can't see myself doing that for very long."

She looked over her listings a while longer, then said, "Here. A family counseling center needs a therapist to counsel abusive men. You don't have a master's degree, and you'll need to get licensed, but with your experience, that should be easy. Let me call the clinical director and see what we can work out."

Mandy dialed the number from her screen and requested to speak to the director. She began telling him about Sammy, then stopped and listened. "I see," she said, subdued. "Well, thank you anyway." Hanging up, she related with some embarrassment, "He won't consider ex-police officers. He says he has too many of them as clients." Sammy looked stung.

Mandy went back to her listings. "Here's—" she began, then changed her mind and shook her head.

"What is it?" Sammy asked curiously.

"Well, Pinebluff Psychiatric Hospital needs security personnel," she said hesitantly. "Starting salary is thirty-five thousand, plus benefits."

Sammy thought about that. He had worked with a number of mentally ill people, especially when he walked a beat. He thought about Sally, the bag lady who considered him her special friend. The pay at Pinebluff was inadequate, but it was still more than he was making right now. "I might be able to do that," he conceded, so Mandy quickly called the administrator to set up an appointment for him.

The facility was located on several tranquil green acres in north Dallas. Driving through the gates up the long driveway, Sammy noted the pond encompassed by willow trees. One or two people sat on benches at the water's edge, tossing bread crumbs to the ducks.

Sammy parked and walked in through the double glass doors. The similarity of this hospital's layout to Shady Acres gave him a momentary twinge, but he shook it off and introduced himself to the receptionist behind the glass partition.

"Oh, yes, Mr. Kidman. Please fill out this application, and Dr. Arbruster will call you to his office for an interview shortly," she said, thrusting a four-page form through the window at him.

"Thanks," he muttered, taking it to a chair in the waiting area. Pulling a pen from his jacket pocket, he dismally began filling in the numerous blanks.

He glanced up as a middle-aged man in a knit shirt came from a hallway door and sat in a chair. The gentleman nodded at Sammy, who smiled briefly in return. Then the man fastened his gaze expectantly on the parking lot outside. A moment later he moved to a chair that gave him a wider view of the lot. "I'm getting out today," he announced to Sammy.

"Congratulations," Sammy smiled, glancing up as he turned to the second page.

"My daughter will be arriving shortly to pick me up," the man continued. "Phil McGregory," he said, leaning over with outstretched hand.

"Sammy Kidman," Sammy replied, shaking his hand. "That's great. That your daughter's coming, I mean."

Phil nodded contemplatively as he stared out the front doors. "I needed the rest. Had my own business for twenty-two years. Printing supply. But the downturn in the economy, competition up the street, and those desktop printers—technology's a two-edged sword, eh? Well, I was pedalin' twice as hard just to stay in place.

And it got to me. Yeah, I was working too hard. My wife told me, and my daughter told me, but—you do what you have to, don't you?" Phil said. Sammy's pen was idle as he listened.

Phil shifted expectantly as a car passed by out front, then settled back down in his chair. "I guess the last straw was the bank turning me down. Not just any bank, mind you, but the one I'd been doing business with since I first started my shop. Twenty-two years of business— never a missed payment, never a bad loan, then all of a sudden I'm a bad credit risk.

"Yeah, I'll admit that got to me. They tell me I tried to choke the young fella that turned me down. He was new. I don't remember it." Phil wiped his forehead and Sammy twirled his pen thoughtfully. After a moment of silence he returned to the application.

"Twenty-two years of business, and suddenly you're not worth anything anymore. Suddenly you're just— disposable. Is that right?" Phil asked plaintively.

"No," said Sammy, looking up.

"Not hardly," Phil agreed vehemently. He raised up to see past a hedge outside, then settled back in the chair once more. "But what can you do, you know?"

"You . . . can take your experience and apply it to something else," Sammy offered.

"*If* you get the chance. But when everybody sees you as inferior goods, how're you going to get the chance?" Phil asked. Sammy stirred uncomfortably.

At that moment a white-coated attendant came out into the lobby. He spotted Phil with a look of irritation. Taking his arm firmly, the attendant said, "Okay, Phil. Back to your room. Now."

"But—my daughter—" Phil protested.

"Now!" the attendant insisted, dragging him out. Phil's indignant protestations could be heard fading down the hall beyond the door.

Sammy hesitated, then went up to the window and asked the receptionist, "Is Mr. McGregory's daughter coming for him?"

The receptionist glanced up. "No."

"Well, uh, he seems to be expecting her," Sammy mentioned, and she did not reply. "Has anyone told him she's not coming?" he pressed.

Nodding at his application, she asked curtly, "Are you through with that?"

"Almost," he murmured, sitting down to complete it. *They need me here,* he reflected.

The next question on the application was, "Have you ever been committed to a psychiatric hospital?" Sammy chewed his lip as he considered the question, then wrote, "Yes." There was no space given for an explanation.

He finished filling out the application and took it up to the receptionist behind the glass. "Thank you. I will take it right back to Dr. Arbruster," she said coolly. Nodding, Sammy returned to his seat to wait.

He waited an hour, watching the receptionist bustle about her duties. Other than her and himself, the lobby was dead. Finally he got up and requested of her, "Please remind Dr. Arbruster that I'm waiting to be interviewed." She looked momentarily startled, then muttered something and went out.

In a few minutes she returned. "I'm sorry; Dr. Arbruster says your application disqualified you for the position."

Biting back an indignant question about why he was kept waiting an hour to hear that, Sammy said, "May I ask how?"

She was careful to stay back from the window. "Because of your previous incarceration," she said stiffly.

"I would like an opportunity to explain the circumstances to Dr. Arbruster," Sammy said carefully. "I feel the experience gave me some insights that would be useful in handling the patients."

"That's totally immaterial," she sniffed. "You may leave now, or I'll have to call security." She watched suspiciously, hand hovering over the panic button.

Head down, Sammy stood there a moment, then turned and walked out into the bright sunshine.

Back at the TWC, Sammy sat slumped in Mandy's office while she went through her listings over and over again. Finally she pleaded, "Are you *sure* you won't consider one of the suburban police departments?"

After a pause, he said woodenly, "Okay."

"Great!" she said, turning to her telephone. "Now we're in business!"

While she called around, Sammy went out to the waiting area to get a soft drink from the machine and think. He did not want to work for a suburban department—if he was going to be in police work, he wanted to stay in dirty, crime-ridden Dallas. But he had to support his family, and at this point, slapping parking tickets on BMWs looked pretty good.

Sammy regarded the can in his hand. This was hard on Marni, too, and it was not fair or rational of him to ask her to sit around the apartment all day waiting for him to come up with something. He wouldn't even let her tell her parents he had gotten fired. And if she wanted to go to work, he should let her. "Well," he mused, "the 'burbs will just have to do"—though it would be a long time before he could work up to his previous salary level.

When he went back into Mandy's office and sat down, he paused at her pensive expression. Hanging up the telephone, she said, "Well, Richardson, Mesquite and Garland are in a hiring freeze; Plano will look at your application in a month; Carrollton will offer you an entry-level position. . . . The economy's bad and everybody's being squeezed right now."

"Do you mean," Sammy's face was stony, "that I can't even get on in the suburbs?"

"Don't get discouraged, now, we're still looking."

Sammy sat back and closed his eyes. Then he got up, saying, "I'll be back in an hour or so."

He drove out to White Rock Lake and began walking. Bikers and hikers filled up the paths around the lake, but Sammy looked past them to the sun on the water.

It was so easy to take everything for granted when life was rocking along. He could toy with the idea of landing a cushy job and buying Marni a nice house, but all it took was one or two hard jolts of reality to realign his focus. All that really mattered was Marni and Sam, and bringing in enough to provide for them. He hadn't really listened when she said she didn't care about having a house. But now he saw that it was more important to his pride than it was to her to have one.

"God, You know I need a job," Sammy muttered. "I've got to work." The thought came to him, *If you could have any job, what would that be?* Without question, it would be the job he had. The only job he'd ever had, working at the only place he cared to work. That also he had taken for granted.

He considered filing a grievance with the City Service Trial Board over his firing—but he knew such actions were anathema to the supervisors who had to deal with them. If he had to go to such lengths to get his job back, what good would it do? No—Mike could hang him by the toes and flail him, and Sammy still couldn't see inflicting official actions on him. Better to walk away. Sometimes you just had to walk away. Head hanging, he continued to walk around the lake.

As Sammy had realized, Marni was suffering as well. Quietly. She wanted so badly to call her mother and talk it over with her, but not for the world would she go behind Sammy's back to do it. Oh, he hadn't exactly said she couldn't, but she knew quite well how humiliated he would be if she did.

What hurt and baffled her more than anything, however, was the quietness from the other direction. Today was Thursday. Sammy had been fired Tuesday, and in that time they had heard not one word from anyone downtown. No sympathy, no outrage, nothing. These friends of Sammy's whom he had worked with for years, who had been so kind and generous when his son was born, were now inexplicably silent after his dismissal. Marni couldn't understand it, and the hurt went deep.

Sammy, for his part, walked the lake just long enough to shed sufficient pride to return to Mandy's office and see what she had.

eight

When Sammy returned to the TWC, Mandy was with another client. Sitting to wait, Sammy picked up a newspaper and opened it to the employment section. There was an ad from a loan company looking for people to repossess cars.

An as indication of how low he felt, Sammy actually considered it. That was truly dangerous work, which amounted to stealing the cars in the middle of the night under threat of gunfire. He wondered how much they paid.

Mandy's other client came out, and when she saw Sammy waiting, she waved him back. "I've got the perfect thing. Come here," she ordered.

Sammy followed her back to her office. "What is it?" he asked listlessly.

"A local community college desperately needs qualified instructors for their Law Enforcement classes," Mandy said, handing him a sheet. "They have a summer session which starts after the Fourth, and a full range of course offerings in the fall. I've set up an interview for you with the executive director at one o'clock today.

Meanwhile, we'll go ahead and prepare your application to the Plano Police Department."

Sammy read over the sheet of required qualifications for instructors, which he met easily. "That's great," he said quietly. "Thanks, Mandy."

She handed him a slip with a name and office number. "Richland Community College, one o'clock today."

"Okay," he said. "Thanks." And he turned out. Mandy pumped the air with a victorious fist.

Sammy loitered, walking and thinking, until his scheduled appointment. Then he drove to the college, met the director overseeing Law Enforcement, and had a look around. It was a beautiful campus with burgeoning enrollment figures and ambitious programs. The director was impressed with Sammy's experience and quickly added him to the instructor lineup, pending completion of all the paperwork. After a cordial, productive hour, Sammy shook his hand and left.

He drove home, walked in the door, and sat on the couch. When Marni did not show right away, he went to the foot of the stairs. "Marni?"

She hurried down the stairs, whispering, "I just put Sam down for his nap."

"I can't tell you how much I appreciate your willingness to stay home with him," Sammy said. "It makes me feel good to know he's in your care during the day."

Marni smiled slightly, a question in her eyes. Since he knew what she wanted to ask, he said, "I'll be teaching classes in Law Enforcement at a community college while I'm waiting to get on at the Plano department. They have a class starting after the Fourth of July holiday." As he talked, he turned to sit on the couch.

"Great, Sammy!" she said, coming to sit beside him. "That's great—!" He leaned over to take her tightly in his arms. As he squeezed her, burying his face in her hair, she murmured, "Sammy . . . ?" Something about his breathing was strange.

She pulled back and saw the tears dripping from his long eyelashes. "It's like—" he whispered with shame, "like I've been sidelined, unfit to play anymore. So I have to stand on the sidelines and watch others do what I should be doing."

She opened her mouth, wanting to comfort him, but saw that this was one of those times she should not say anything. So she let him rest his head on her shoulder and caressed his hair. "You can call your parents and tell them anything you like," he mumbled. "They ought to know."

"Later," she murmured. Then they heard a restless wail from upstairs; it was wishful thinking that Sam was down for a nap.

"Go get him," Sammy said, sitting up. "Let's blow outta here." So while Marni put a t-shirt and cap on Sam and packed his bag, Sammy moved his car seat from her Miata to his Mustang, and off they went to the Dallas Zoo. It had been newly renovated, with huge, naturalistic exhibits that were comfortable for the animals and accessible to visitors.

Sam fell asleep as soon as the car hit the freeway, of course, and he slept right up to the zoo's parking lot. But Marni put him in the stroller anyway and they wheeled him up the curved paths past the lions and hippos and zebras.

As the zoo was crowded with children's groups today, Sammy was in his element. He had a good time entertaining them all. He leaned over the railing to make obnoxious noises at the elephants. One stuck its trunk in the pond and sprayed in Sammy's direction, causing gleeful shrieks from the kids around him who got wet.

They moved on to the next spacious, landscaped pen. Watching two big cats loll in the shade, Sammy improvised a stream of chatter between them: "'Hey, Maude, get up and bat my flies.' 'Get up and bat your own flies, ya lazy bum. Sixty miles an hour, right. You couldn't get to the bathroom and back during a ten-minute commercial.'" When one cat suddenly leapt up and snarled at the other, the kids around Sammy howled and pointed.

He had collected quite a following by the time they got to the monkey cages, which housed all sorts of comedic possibilities. Sammy chattered at them and they chattered right back. And when he mimicked the baboons, one mimicked him back. It was astounding to watch Sammy and the baboon sway in unison. Several people pulled out phones to record it, and Sammy didn't even care that his face would shortly be all over the internet.

A zoo employee came down the path in a zebrine golf cart, honking the horn, so Sammy decided his son would enjoy a similar ride. He pushed the stroller with revving engine noises, making it pop wheelies and take curves on two wheels. Safely strapped in, Sam blissfully slept through it all.

They stopped to rest and sip a soft drink in the shade, where Sammy watched a strutting peacock roam the path up ahead. The bird had gotten himself into a few scrapes, for when he ostentatiously spread his tail, it revealed a number of missing and damaged feathers. "That's me," Sammy said, studying the bird.

Marni glanced at the peacock. "He's beautiful."

"He's making an ass of himself," Sammy said spitefully, and tossed his cup in the trash to go see the gazelles.

The zoo proved to be only a temporary diversion. Sammy manfully fought the depression and self-pity, but when they went to bed that night, he only wanted to hold her—nothing more.

The next morning, Friday, Marni got up early, quietly, so as not to wake either of her boys. She crept outside and retrieved the morning paper. Ignoring the headlines, she opened it up to look at the ads.

When she found the one she was looking for, she drew in a breath. It was a half-page of three shots—a large one flanked by two smaller ones. They were gorgeous black and white studies, very arty and quite provocative. The two smaller shots were indeed torso only, but the large center one showed his neck, part of his jaw and hairline—marginally recognizable to anyone who knew Sammy well. Marni sank down to the couch.

"Is it in there?" At his question, Marni's head shot up toward Sammy standing sleepily on the stairway in his underwear. He yawned and scratched, then came on down the stairs. "Does it look okay?" he asked.

"It's beautiful," Marni said cautiously as he leaned over to look at the paper.

Sammy looked at the ad, blinking, then sat beside her on the couch. "Only one thing left to do," he said. "Kill myself. I am going to kill myself."

Marni choked back a laugh, getting up to fetch the kitchen scissors. "You were only trying to earn an honest buck. You don't mind if I tape them to the dresser mirror, do you?"

He eyed her narrowly. "Not at all, unless you'd like me to sleep in the same room." She sat to cut them out and he protested, "Marni, you're not really going to keep them, are you?"

"You bet I am!" she said firmly, and he groaned.

"Well, that's it. That's the last straw. There's no point in getting out of bed today. Wake me next Tuesday." He dragged himself up the stairs in abject humiliation and despair.

A little while later, as Marni was feeding Sam breakfast, the telephone rang. When she answered it, her mother said, "Marni? Um, how are you today, dear?"

"Fine," Marni answered, giggling. Her mother's careful tone was a dead giveaway.

"How is my precious grandbaby?" Pam asked.

"Oh, just having breakfast. He sends you an oatmeal kiss," Marni said, smiling.

"Good. And how is Sammy?" Pam wondered.

"Not taking it too well, Mother," Marni said. "He did it for a quick five hundred dollars, but they showed a little more of him than he would have liked."

"I guess so," Pam observed. "They were very nicely done, but Clayton almost fainted when he saw it."

"Sammy doesn't want me to, but I'm going to keep them. I'll have to hide them," Marni whispered.

Pam laughed. "I'm tempted to keep them too, for a portrait study. But Sammy would never forgive me."

"Never," Marni affirmed.

"Dear, we were wondering what happened with the FirstPlace Bank Tower job," Pam asked seriously.

"It never materialized, Mom. When Sammy went up there to start, they reneged on the offer they'd made to him," Marni told her.

"Oh, no! Why?" Pam asked.

"I don't really know. He didn't want to talk about it," Marni said, stretching the cord to reach Sam's face with a dishrag.

"Oh, dear. Did he quit his job to take that one?" Pam asked.

"I'm afraid so. But he's got something else lined up. Don't worry, Mom," Marni reassured her.

"Still, Clayton wanted to know what happened. And —we'll just pretend we didn't see the ad," Pam said.

"I'd appreciate that, Mom. I'll have Sammy call Daddy a little later," Marni said.

"Thanks, dear. 'Bye-'bye." Pam hung up and Marni studied the pictures, grinning, until she found a safe place to stash them for the time being.

The doorbell rang. Marni, in her bathrobe, hesitated. She looked out the peephole to see Pruett and Garrett standing on her front step. *It's about time,* she thought sternly, opening the door. "Hello, boys." She offered a cool smile.

They grinned at her like little devils. "Hello, Marni," said Pruett smoothly. "Your husband's late for work today. We're here to bring him in."

"What?" Marni exclaimed, stepping back to let them

enter. "He's—still in bed," she said, gesturing upstairs.

"Really? That's too bad," grinned Pruett as he and Garrett headed for the stairs.

Taking out a pair of handcuffs, Garrett said, "You'd better stay down here, Marni. This won't be pretty. Just get on down to the Big Building as soon as you can."

Marni nodded bemusedly but wouldn't hear of staying downstairs. She followed them up to the bedroom.

Sammy, lying on his front, quickly raised up from his pillow as they entered, but he was a half second too late. Pruett jumped on his back and clapped cuffs on his wrists while Garrett held him in a headlock. Sammy struggled and called them despicable names as they calmly discussed whether to take him in wearing boxers or let him dress.

Their discussion seemed to tilt quickly in favor of utmost humiliation, so Marni pulled out a pair of Sammy's jeans and slipped them on him while the men held him by the arms. "Pruett—you're dead meat. You'll never walk the street safely again," Sammy vowed as Marni took a t-shirt from the closet.

"Shaddup, you sectional coelenterate," Pruett snarled. "That's good enough," he said when Marni had the t-shirt around his neck. They yanked him out and down the stairs in this disheveled state, then tossed him in the back seat of Pruett's car.

While they drove him downtown, Sammy climbed through the cuffs to at least get his hands in front of him. But he couldn't get the cuffs off, so he took the t-shirt off from around his neck and sat back for the ride.

They parked in the Big Building's lot and opened

the car door for him, smirking. Sammy climbed out in his bare feet and presented his wrists. "Okay, dweeb, I'm here. Take the cuffs off."

Pruett and Garrett studied him, considering it, then Garrett advised, "Better, so he can get his shirt on. You don't know what the women might do if they see Dreamboat here without his shirt."

Pruett snickered, "You're right," and uncuffed Sammy so he could pull on his t-shirt. Rubbing his sore wrists, Sammy walked between them to the building's side door.

He started at the mass of people who greeted his entrance with cheers and applause. There was a crude banner hanging from the ceiling that read, "Welcome back, Sammy." He gaped at it, and around at the smiling faces of all the people he had worked with over the years —Collins and Pierce and Brickett and—Mike, making his way forward with a threatening scowl.

The crowd hushed as Mike drew up in Sammy's face and yelled, "You're late! You look like crap! What kind of a cop are you?" Sammy just stood there, speechless, while Mike dressed him down as only a sergeant could, the many spectators nodding and applauding at certain points.

Finally, Mike crossed his arms and stepped back. "I guess you want to know why you're here," he said. Sammy could only blink in reply. "It's because of the cretins you work with. When they found out about your dismissal, they all came down with stomach flu—every last one of 'em. The next day we had a mysterious outbreak of migraines that knocked out almost everybody in Targeted Offenders.

"And then Thursday, with the others still out, Auto Theft and Special Services got blitzed by an attack of—get this—'sleeping sickness.' They were dropping like flies, Kidman. The deputy chief had a cow. So when I suggested to him that we call the chief, the mayor and the press for a little tour of The Bureau That Wasn't, he agreed that maybe we should reinstate you." Mike held out Sammy's badge.

Sammy, dazed, took the badge, then threw his arms around Mike for a bear hug. "Cut that out," Mike chided, embarrassed.

The division personnel applauded and pushed forward to pat Sammy on the back. Grinning, he shook everybody's hand and hugged anybody else who came within range. "C'm here, you," Corporal Collins growled, advancing, and Sammy paled. Then she repaid his goodbye kiss with a lusty smack of her own, and for only the second time in his life, Sammy blushed.

At that point Pruett leaned down in his ear and advised, "You've got a little work piled up on your desk, Sambo."

"Yeah, I guess so," Sammy mumbled, still grinning as he pocketed the badge. He turned toward the elevator and everyone went expectantly silent, parting like the Red Sea.

Sammy looked up and froze solid. There, taped to the elevator door, was the center picture from this morning's ad. The large, hand-lettered caption underneath proclaimed, "OUR MAN SAMMY."

"ARRRGHH!" With a strangled cry, Sammy lunged forward and tore down the picture, shredding it. The coworkers behind him fell over each other in laughter.

The elevator door opened and there, taped up to the back wall, was another copy of the same picture. This one was captioned, "Medal of Honor," with the date it had been awarded. An artist had decorated the model's bare chest with a facsimile of the medal. Gritting his teeth, Sammy ripped that ad down and mangled it.

Of course, the door to the TAS room sported another one, this one captioned with his home phone number. Sammy, followed by numerous friends, ripped it down and swore, "One more and I'm taking the job in Plano anyway!"

Opening the door, he almost had heart failure. The ads, sixty or seventy of them, were taped up *everywhere* around the room—the walls, support columns, bulletin board, desks—the front of his desk was laminated with them. And sitting on his desk was one horrendous, disorderly pile of forms two feet deep. They overflowed his desk onto the floor around it.

Pruett slapped him on the back. "To show your appreciation for our support, you get to fill out all of the bureau's paperwork that went undone while we were out 'sick' this week. Do type neatly, Sambo." The others expressed their genuine pleasure to have him back, then returned to their work areas.

When Marni arrived at the Building a bare twenty minutes later with Sam, she was thrilled to hear of their show of support and Sammy's reinstatement. But no one remembered to tell her about Pruett's fortuitous discovery of the visual aids in this morning's newspaper.

Upon entering the Targeted Activity office, she found Sammy standing over a huge pile of paperwork on his desk. His trash can was crammed full of crumpled newspaper. Seeing her, Sammy hastily dragged the trash can out of sight behind his desk. "Look at this!" he exclaimed. "They're not joking! They expect me to do all of their paperwork!" Reports were usually entered on computer and filed directly on disk, eliminating the paperwork, but for this special occasion everyone found the appropriate hard copies to increase the workload thereby.

"Well," she tried not to laugh, "come home and get showered and dressed—"

He didn't want to leave. "Let me at least sort through this and see what all's here," he said gravely, looking happier than she had seen him in weeks.

After thirty minutes she forcibly dragged him out to the car. He climbed behind the wheel talking about all the indignities they heaped on him and scheming to revenge himself on Pruett while Marni just smiled and listened.

Once home he got ready in record time. He kissed Marni goodbye in a very businesslike manner: "I'm going to be working late tonight, so I'll just eat whatever's left over when I get home—" The telephone rang and he paused as Marni answered it.

She turned. "It's Daddy, for you."

Sammy took the telephone. "Yeah. Hi, Clayton." He hesitated. "Well, no, once I got there, Ms. Bancroft's secretary came in and told me that I wasn't qualified for the job after all. Listen, it doesn't make any difference now. I just got reinstated in my old position, and there's no doubt at all that's where I need to be. . . . What?" He listened for a long time, then his eyes got big. Marni edged closer to the phone.

Sammy laughed in astonishment. "Well, how about that. No, I'm not filing any complaint—they can do whatever they want. Thanks for the offer, Clayton. I've got to get to work now—you wouldn't believe the pile they left for me on my desk. Right. 'Bye."

When he hung up, Marni asked, "Was that about the FirstPlace Bank Tower job?"

"Yeah," he said with a quick nod. Then he glanced up guiltily at her. "Uh, there was a little more I didn't tell you. This lady had a uniform for me to wear, and while I was changing, she came in like she wanted to, uh, get intimate, you know," he said and her look changed slightly. "I got rattled and just kind of shoved her out of the room—I wasn't dressed and all my clothes were in there. Well, after that her secretary came in and told me I didn't have the job after all.

"I should have realized it—I don't know why I didn't think of it—but the security room is monitored as well! Somebody got that whole episode on videotape, though part of it was sound only. Clayton was just asking whether I wanted to file a sexual harassment complaint against her! I told him no; it didn't matter now. She's in plenty enough trouble anyway. Clayton also told me that if I still wanted the job, I could have it." Sammy paused awkwardly. "I—didn't realize that your dad is on the building management's board."

She nodded absently. "Daddy seems to be involved in more things now than before he retired." She was wondering how many of these little incidents Sammy neglected to tell her about.

"Well," he said thoughtfully, "I appreciate that he's willing to pull strings for me, but this ol' peacock's learned to stay where it belongs. See you tonight." He leaned over to kiss her full-heartedly.

Sammy worked until nine o'clock that night, and most of that weekend. But Sunday morning he was to be found in church worshiping with a sincere heart of gratitude.

nine

"Actually, Sammy, as much as we were all impressed by the division's support of you, there was another reason you were brought back on." Sammy sat in Mike's office the following Monday and the sergeant closed the door. *I should've known*, Sammy groaned inwardly. *Drudge detail. They reinstated me just for an assignment that nobody else would touch.* But he was so grateful to be back at work, he kept his mouth shut.

"Assistant Chief Groebel at the north central substation requested you for special detail in his sector. He's got a young hotdog—a detective—who's made inroads into some gang activity up there, and needs a partner experienced in undercover work to assist in concluding the assignment," Mike said.

Sammy looked confused. "Why isn't this being handled by the regular gang unit?"

Mike raised his brows. "Apparently, it's a new gang they had no previous knowledge of. Groebel indicated that his detective stumbled across them while investigating area burglaries, went undercover to learn more,—"

"—And having gotten that far, wanted to see the assignment through to completion," Sammy finished for him, nodding. "Yeah, I can understand that."

"I know how you prefer to work alone, or with Marni, but on a high-risk assignment such as this, you're going to have to cooperate with the more knowledgeable operative," Mike lectured.

Sammy shrugged. "What's more important is trusting your partner. If this other guy's anything like me, then he doesn't like working with a stranger on a high-risk assignment either."

"You ever hear of Canton Reese?" Mike asked. Sammy shook his head. "She said she's never heard of you, either," Mike allowed.

Sammy's defenses sprang up. "I do not want to work undercover with a woman," he stated flatly.

His objection went unheeded. "You meet with her and Groebel at ten o'clock this morning to hammer out the particulars. Since you're representing me and the entire Targeted Activity Section, I expect total professionalism, Kidman," Mike said, and that concluded the discussion. As Sammy rose to leave, Mike did add: "Nice to have you back, Sambo." Sammy regarded him dolefully.

By ten o'clock, Sammy was pulling into the north central police substation. Generally, the farther north one got from downtown, the cleaner and newer one's surroundings became. Sammy was having a hard time understanding what gang activity could be plaguing this area to such an extent as to befuddle an extremely competent gang unit out of downtown. Perhaps he felt a smidgen of superiority toward the junior detectives working out of the substations—all the plum detective assignments originated out of the Big Building, where the action was. So Sammy may be excused for a tiny swagger as he entered Assistant Chief Groebel's airy office.

"Chief," Sammy shook his hand and then paused at his first glimpse of Canton Reese. She was a knockout, simply, even wearing a shapeless suit. She had very pale blond, shoulder-length hair, seductive eyes and pouty lips. As he regarded her, he got the distinct impression that she hated him right off the bat.

"Detective Kidman, Detective Reese," Groebel nodded and the two briefly shook hands before sitting across the desk from the assistant chief. "Okay," he began, "this is a departure from our normal operating procedure, but with the intelligence Reese has already gathered on this gang, we feel that we're in the best position to quash it quickly. I'll be frank with you, Kidman—we've felt some public heat on this. Even though they're not as violent or entrenched as any of the southside gangs, there are certain, ah, unsavory aspects surrounding this one that makes for splashy headlines and lots of letters to the editor—that, plus the fact that a number of civic leaders live in this sector," Groebel admitted. Sammy covered a knowing smirk with two fingers.

"As senior partner, Kidman, you'll be given a great deal of freedom in addressing the problem. Detective Reese can brief you on the one solid contact we have within the gang. How to proceed will be totally at your discretion, and you will report straight to me. I know I don't have to impress upon you the responsibility that goes with this kind of latitude," Groebel said gravely. "Suffice it to say that if you bring so much as a shadow of disrepute over the department, it'll mean your badge. I will approve a reasonable amount of expenditure, but the less you ask for, the fewer questions I'll have to ask." Groebel paused to eye Sammy as an unknown quantity. "So get after it."

Canton got up and briskly left the office. With a nod to Groebel, Sammy followed. Catching up with her in the hall, Sammy asked, "You got a file?"

She glanced at him and continued walking, tight-lipped. Sammy followed her to the detectives' room. He was momentarily irked by how spacious and well-equipped it was, far nicer than the TAS room downtown. Sammy repressed an urge to spit in it somewhere. Canton went to her orderly desk and took out a manila file folder to hand to him. Sammy pulled up a chair from another desk and sat to study the documentation on the gang.

While he was looking through it, a woman officer came in with a vase of roses. "These just came for you," she said, putting them on Canton's desk. The officer paused to glance at Sammy and he nodded. Canton straightened and, without looking at the card, picked up the vase and dropped it into her trash can with a resounding bang. Unfazed, the officer walked off.

"Some poor schmuck is out forty dollars for those," Sammy observed.

"Then he should send them to someone who wants them," she replied. Sammy evaluated her for a moment, then returned to the file. It chronicled the usual gang activities: burglary, vandalism, assault, and so on. No homicides. This trivial stuff would hardly merit special operatives downtown, but Sammy supposed it was enough to unnerve a division used to corralling dangerous jaywalkers.

"Is this it?" he asked. "Is this all?"

"Chief Groebel laid it out for you—we're of the opinion that this activity needs to be controlled now, before it becomes a serious problem like it is in *other* sectors," Canton replied sneeringly.

"So who's your contact?" he asked with a slight yawn.

"His name is Jobs. I leave a signal for him when I want to meet him," she said, leaning back in her chair.

"He's in the gang?" Sammy asked, and she nodded. "He knows you're a cop?"

"Yes," she said shortly.

"Why's he helping you take down his buddies?" Sammy asked.

"Get real," she said, with a look of contempt.

"You need to get real, baby. A pretty woman's just property, and he's not risking his hide for love. Ten to one they know all about you," Sammy returned with aplomb.

She looked unperturbed. "He'll do anything for me. When you meet him, you'll see what I mean."

He shook his head. "No way am I going to put my neck in your noose. As far as I'm concerned, this investigation is already tainted."

She sat up, glaring. "You s.o.b., who do you think you are, coming in here and just dismissing six months' worth of work?" Two other detectives in the room were trying not to listen too obviously.

"All I'm saying is that I'm not going in trusting your contact," Sammy said. "You set up the signal, and I'll go meet them on my own terms."

"Which are?" she asked.

"I go tell them you're a cop," he replied.

The other two detectives looked over quickly as Canton sprang forward. "Don't you *dare* try to set up a cover by blowing mine! You're in *my* territory!"

Sammy laughed. "Look who's talking territory when your boss is talking about getting the job done. I'm telling you, this gang *already knows* you're a cop. The only way for us to salvage this operation is for me to play the wild card. At least then we find out just how trustworthy this guy is. Now what do you want, Canton, funerary honors or the chance to pull this off?"

She was infuriated to the point of speechlessness that he could waltz in and establish his dominance just like that. He grinned at her like the Cheshire cat, and she sat back, masked. "Suit yourself," she said.

"You can count on it," he said. "Now tell me what you know."

Leaning over the file, Canton covered with him the first signs of the gang's emergence in north Dallas two years ago. They called themselves the Doors, and had various internal levels such as Doorman, Doorbell, Doorknob which were highly secret and mystical. They were implicated in numerous burglaries, drug dealing, and possibly prostitution, but it wasn't until they made their presence felt on the high school campuses that public outcry became sufficient to merit stronger police action against them.

"Then the chief decided that I should be assisted by

somebody more experienced, so they made a search for their most successful undercover officers. They showed me the list of candidates. *I* asked for Geoff Stanislaw, but *they* decided on you. Even though your record is spotty, they seemed to be *really* impressed by your Medal of Honor," Canton related with a slight sneer.

Sammy regarded her, then said without expression, "Cheer up. It could just mean that I'm the most expendable. Since they already paid out my death benefits once, they won't have to do it again." She glanced down. Bending over the file, he began, "Now, these names—"

"Those are verified gang members. Some have records, some don't," she volunteered with a shade more professionalism.

Sammy pored over the list of eight names. "Miles Craddock," he muttered.

"He's the leader," Canton informed him.

Sammy glanced up at her as he thought, *Craddock, Craddock. I know that name. Where have I heard that name?* "What was your cover?" he asked as a diversion.

"Prostitute by the name of Angie," she replied. Sammy glanced up at her and she waited for some crack about entrapment, but he cagily said it all with that one look.

"Okay," he said, closing the file. "I'll go get ready, then you send Jobs your signal. What's his rank in the organization?"

"He's a Doorknob," she replied.

"And do you have any idea what that means?" he asked.

"No," she said. "He's very close about it."

"How did you make contact with him to begin with?" Sammy asked.

"He approached me on duty in decoy," she said.

"As a prostitute," Sammy said, and she nodded. "Okay then, I'll meet you back here at one o'clock," he said. As Sammy started to stand, her telephone rang. She turned away from him to answer it.

On impulse, Sammy sat back down and reached into the trash can beside her desk to retrieve the card attached to the flowers. He took note of the name on the card before dropping it back into the trash can, all without her seeing. When she hung up, he resumed standing with an innocent face. "Oh, Sammy," she said, and he glanced back at her. "Don't forget to take off your wedding ring."

He glanced at his hand and smiled. "I have another for undercover assignments. I wear it through my nose. *Ciao.*"

When Sammy got home, he met up with Marni at the door as she was just about to leave on some errands. "Oh, good, baby. Glad I caught you. Come on back in for a minute." He took Sam off her arm to nuzzle his tummy, and the baby screeched.

He trotted up the stairs, loosening his tie. "Mike put me on another assignment, this one out of the north central station. It requires infiltrating gang activity, which'll mean odd hours." He handed her Sam as he took off his coat and reached for his biking jeans in the closet.

"Sounds dangerous," she murmured.

He shrugged, shedding his slacks to climb into the tight jeans. "Not really. The only thing that bothers me is that they've assigned me to partner a woman, and it was loathe at first sight." He zipped the jeans and hoisted the waistband. "Am I putting on weight?"

She eyed his taut waist and slender hips. "Not that I can tell." She wanted to ask about this woman but refrained, determined not to complicate the assignment with petty displays of jealousy.

Sammy jerked on a tattered, sleeveless gray undershirt and stuck a dangly silver earring in his earlobe (the mate of which rested in Marni's jewelry box). He tried to muss up his short hair, but it fell in perfect feathery layers—it was hard to hide a good cut. "Might have to shave my head," he muttered, and Marni winced. "Or maybe not," he smiled at her reaction.

"Do what you need to do to get through this safely," Marni insisted.

Sammy took the baby from her arms and placed him on the floor, then put his arms around her in a good solid squeeze. "I remember not too long ago," he said, "when I'd come home to get ready for an assignment, and no one was there to tell me to be careful. The first time *anyone* outside the department ever told me that was when you came over to my apartment to wash your clothes. You ate all my *moo goo gai pan*, remember?" he grinned, and she nodded.

"When I saw you really meant it, and you really cared—it was like an angel whispering to me. I still feel that way. No one will make me feel differently, Marni." She understood the subtle reassurance.

He turned to pilfer her bathroom cabinet for a can of little-used mousse to spike his hair. And when he nailed her with a good hard kiss she did not want to let him to go. So she all the more deliberately released him and said, "So be careful." He grinned at her.

Turning, he said, "'Bye, Sam," and trotted down the stairs. Marni sighed.

Sammy dropped off his Mustang downtown and signed out the black Harley-Davidson. But before picking up the hog, he went up to the TAS room and accessed the computer files of known felons. "Craddock, Craddock," he murmured, searching.

He was so intent on his search that he did not look up when the door opened. Mike, with Lieutenant Kerr and his captain, was giving some City Council dignitaries a tour of the new Targeted Activity Section. When Mike saw Sammy sitting at the computer dressed as he was, he dismally put his face in one hand, then explained, "The officers dress appropriate to their assignments." That was as close as Mike could come to explaining that Sammy was undercover.

"Hi there," Sammy said breezily, without looking up. Lieutenant Kerr's eyebrows gathered ominously, but the City Council members were quite impressed, so he said nothing. After a moment's inspection, the group filed out.

"Bingo," Sammy muttered. He hunched over the computer screen, digesting what he had found, and a plan began to form in his mind. He skipped to another felon's file and memorized every tiny bit of information in it.

Closing the file, he then went downstairs to check out a handgun from the equipment room. (Carrying his department-issue Sig Sauer would be a dead giveaway to anyone familiar with Dallas Police small arms.) He debated trying to requisition a phone, but the department was so stingy with them, he'd probably have the assignment completed before it came through. With his plan hardening into shape, he went down to the garage to claim the Harley-Davidson FXR.

He stood over the bike, tinkering with it happily. This good ol' hog was the best partner he'd ever had, next to Marni. Sammy paused, wondering if he'd ever feel free to use his son's mother on an assignment again. Not this one, that's for sure. Sammy slapped on a helmet and jacket, sitting on the bike to start it up.

After stopping for a burger, he roared into the north central station's lot, parked the bike, and ambled in to meet Canton. Inwardly, he smiled at the eyes which followed him in the station. These people had seen him this morning, but he assumed an attitude when he had the hog that transformed him into a different person. They didn't recognize him. It was only when Canton came to the lobby in a short denim skirt and high heels that they realized who he was.

He and she looked each other over. "You're too clean," she said.

"A few minutes on the hog in this heat will take care of that," he said. "Your clothes are too new. Your hair is too big. Your makeup is too thick. You look like a Cowboys cheerleader."

A uniformed officer passing them barely contained a laugh and Canton did a slow burn. "Obviously, you're not familiar with the look in this part of town. This get-up has been very successful for me," she said crisply.

"Yeah, but what your johns are really after is free tickets to a game," Sammy said, donning his shades, and the sergeant behind the desk guffawed. Canton turned on her spiked heel and Sammy followed her out, flashing a grin at the desk sergeant.

Out on the parking lot, Sammy asked, "When and where do you meet your contact?"

"In thirty minutes, in front of the drugstore on the northwest corner of Coit and Arapaho," she replied, looking at the motorcycle.

He shook his head. "That's too public. Get him to go back to the alley."

"Why?" she asked suspiciously. "Look, I've been working too long and hard on this to let you blow my cover. I want to know what you're going to do."

"I won't blow your cover. I got a better idea," he assured her. "It's a surprise. Just remember that you've never seen me before. You don't know anything about me."

"Right," she said warily as he climbed on the bike.

"*Ciao.*" He flashed his teeth and started off.

Half an hour later, Sammy was sitting on his motorcycle watching the shopfronts in the strip shopping mall. He saw Canton meet up with a guy a few inches shorter than she, then take him around to the rear of the stores. Sammy surveyed the area around the shops for a few minutes to satisfy himself that the guy was alone, then he throttled up and drove to one end of the alley. He parked the bike, peering around the edge of the brick at the lone couple in the alley.

Glancing about, he put his hand to the loaded pistol in his belt and quickly approached Canton and Jobs. They were passionately kissing, unaware of his stealthy advance until he was on top of them. Sammy yanked

Canton's purse off her shoulder and simultaneously pointed the pistol at Jobs' head. "Hand over your wallet real quick," Sammy instructed. Canton dropped back with a gasp. Young Jobs started.

"You're gonna regret this," Jobs promised as Sammy opened Canton's purse with one hand, took out the money, and flung the bag away. The boy, probably seventeen, had a curious manner of holding his mouth that gave his delicate features a perverse look.

"I'm the one with the gun, Shorty, and I ain't big on debates. You got five seconds to hand over your money before I splatter you across this here wall," Sammy uttered convincingly.

As he reached for his back pocket, Jobs warned, "I'm in the Doors, you fool."

"Yeah? Sing 'The End' then," Sammy laughed, then suddenly went silent with the shock of recognition. "Craddock's gang?" he whispered eagerly.

"Yeah, Craddock heads it up. What's it to you?" Jobs said suspiciously.

Sammy's face lit with a megawatt smile. "Wow! Awesome. Just totally awesome." He stuffed the gun back in his belt. "I'm Todd! Todd Stripling!"

"So?" Jobs asked with narrowed eyes.

"Oh, man." Sammy ran over to fetch Canton's purse and stuff the money back in it. He handed it to her. "Sorry 'bout that, baby."

Turning back to Jobs, he demanded, "Miles never said nothing 'bout me? Does he know where Ben is? I been tryin' to find Ben ever since I's paroled, man."

"Wait, now." Jobs motioned him down as a parent would an excited child. "How do you know Miles?"

"I only know what his brother Ben told me about him. Ben and me were cellmates at Huntsville, man—Wynne unit. I was paroled 'bout three years ago, and then I heard he got out, but I lost track of 'im. Is he with you guys?" Sammy asked.

"No. He's not," Jobs said, and Sammy's face fell.

"Does Miles know where he is?" Sammy asked hopefully.

"I dunno," Jobs shrugged. Sammy looked so despondent that Jobs had to add, "I'll ask him."

"Tell him, see, it's real important that I find him. Ben had asked me to—to look up some people for him. I did, and Ben's got to know what I found, but I swore I'd tell him in person," Sammy said earnestly.

Jobs looked thoughtful, and Sammy waited for him to suggest the next move. "Maybe I could call him," Jobs finally said.

"That would be great, man," Sammy said, all humbleness.

So Job took his cell phone out of his belt holder. He turned his back to Sammy to place the call, and talked in a low voice. Finally, Jobs handed the phone to him and said, "Okay. Miles is on the line."

Sammy took the phone and demanded, "Miles? Miles Craddock?"

"Who's this?" the other asked.

"It's Todd Stripling. Ben's bunkmate from Huntsville," Sammy said.

"What was your number?" Miles asked, testing.

"Seven nine four three six two two four," Sammy said promptly.

"Say again?" Miles said, and Sammy repeated it.

"Say it backward," Miles demanded—a good test to see if the number was really ingrained in the mind or just quickly memorized.

Sammy closed his eyes to envision the number in writing, and simply read it backward: "Four two two six three four nine seven."

"Who was your warden?" Miles asked.

"Fishbreath," Sammy replied promptly with the inmates' sobriquet for the man.

Miles chuckled. "Yeah, okay. Guess Jobs had better bring you in. Put him back on."

Sammy handed the receiver back to Jobs, who listened and nodded. "Right. Sure thing." He hung up and told Sammy, "Miles wants to meet you. You got any wheels?"

"Yeah, I got my hog." Sammy nodded toward the bike sitting at the corner of the building.

"Smooth," Jobs approved. He turned toward his Pathfinder and Canton quickly hopped in. "Follow me, then," he instructed.

Sammy got on his bike and started it up, following Jobs and Canton out of the shopping center. Putting his hand to the gun in his waistband, Sammy slowed. The last thing he wanted was for a juvenile gang to get hold of another weapon. Passing a dumpster, he tossed the pistol inside it, making a mental note of the time and location for yet another form that would have to be filled out.

They went north on Coit several miles, then pulled into the parking lot of a beautiful pink granite office building. The newly constructed building had been vacant for several months, and showed some vandalism despite the eight-foot fence around it. Jobs parked and slipped through a hole in the fence. Canton and Sammy followed.

Jobs opened an unlocked glass door which sported several bullet holes, then took Canton by the hand and told Sammy, "You wait here." Those two then disappeared up a flight of stairs. Sammy uneasily waited in the close, empty lobby. He took off his jacket as he waited. The jacket was a necessary piece of motorcycle safety equipment in any season, but wearing it off the bike in summer was intolerable.

Some long minutes later Jobs returned alone. "Okay," he said, glancing slyly at Sammy. "Come with me." Jobs started out of the building.

"What's the deal?" Sammy asked impatiently as he followed Jobs out. "I thought I was gonna meet Miles."

"You will, if you pass the entrance exam," Jobs replied. He and Sammy slipped back out through the chain-link fence and Jobs pointed to his Pathfinder. "You ride with me."

Sammy tossed his jacket onto his bike and climbed in the truck. He braced himself with one hand while Jobs started the engine and lurched into gear. He drove a few minutes to a convenience store on a busy intersection. With the motor running, Jobs leaned over and opened Sammy's door. "Okay. Here's your test. You go in and get us two six-packs and at least fifty dollars."

Sammy glanced in dismay at the mom-and-pop store, then turned back to hiss, "Not here! I just hit this place three days ago. This old man keeps a sawed-off shotgun behind the counter." He hopped out and trotted around to the driver's side. "Move over and let me drive.

I'll pick the place," Sammy said. Hesitantly, Jobs moved over to the passenger seat and Sammy roared away from the convenience store.

He drove south, deep into Dallas, pretending to scope out likely targets on the way. After twenty minutes Jobs became impatient: "I'm gonna die of old age waiting for you to find a place, man. Why're you so picky?"

"Because I've hit most of these so many times, they'll shoot me on sight!" Sammy snapped back.

Then he slowed in front of a Quik Mart and peered inside. "Okay. This place'll do. Keep the engine running," he instructed as he slipped out of the seat. Jobs scooted over to the driver's side, watching as Sammy sauntered into the store.

Sammy went to the back and took two six-packs from the refrigerator units, taking his time until the solitary customer left. Then he took the six-packs to the counter, glancing outside. Jobs was watching. The clerk turned from his cash register. "Hey, Sammy! What's up?"

"I'm robbing you, Dwight," Sammy said apologetically. "Would you please throw your hands up and give me all the twenties from the cash register?"

Dwight obligingly raised his hands. "Cool. Are we on tape?" he asked, turning his good side slightly toward the window.

"Not this time. Don't look out, dweeb; look at me. You're in fear of your life," Sammy reminded him.

"Oh, yeah, right," Dwight said, opening the cash register and counting out twenties with one hand.

"Willya please just grab it and hand it over? Gee,

Dwight, you're makin' this look like a bank transaction!" Sammy complained.

"I have to know how much to bill Mike," Dwight insisted. "Here. A hundred twenty."

"Thanks," Sammy said, grabbing it. "Plus two six-packs."

Dwight looked at the brand. "Those are on sale for three-sixty-nine each, plus tax."

"Great. See ya later." Sammy scooped up the six-packs and ran out. "Move it!" he shouted, jumping in beside Jobs, who gunned the Pathfinder out into traffic.

When they were out of sight of the store, Jobs looked over. "Smooth. How much did you get?"

Sammy counted it. "A hundred twenty. Man, he was slow. I'm afraid he mighta recognized me."

"Got a reputation, huh?" Jobs looked over at Sammy in something approaching admiration.

They returned to the vacant building, where Jobs led him up the flight of stairs to the second floor. With no air conditioning, the close air was hot and stifling. Jobs stopped at a door on the second floor and knocked. "Round one!" he called.

He was answered, "Okay." Jobs opened the door, leading Sammy into an office devoid of furniture. Two windows had been broken out for ventilation. There were six or seven teenaged boys lounging around smoking or eating. Sammy was momentarily dismayed at how young they were, averaging about fifteen, from what he could see.

The guy who stepped forward to meet them with Canton on his arm was unmistakably Miles. He was about ten years older than the others, with a beach-boy look and bodybuilder's shape—prison buff. He wore a black t-shirt and worn jeans. "You got it?" he asked. Sammy handed over the money and the beers. The boys quickly divided up the six-packs while Miles took the money to count it.

"He's loaded," Jobs warned. Miles gestured at Jobs, who stepped forward to frisk Sammy. Finding no weapon, Jobs asked suspiciously, "Where's your piece?"

"I lost it goin' around a corner on my bike. I wasn't gonna stop and pick it up. I can always lift another," Sammy replied without concern.

"Then how did you rob that guy?" Jobs asked in astonishment.

Sammy looked down on him disdainfully. "With the right look, you don't need a weapon. Then they can't nail you for aggravated robbery."

This answer gratified Miles. Stuffing the money in his jeans pocket, he said, "So tell me how you knew Ben."

"We were assigned together when he first got to Wynne," Sammy replied. "I was up on assault and he got nailed for delivery. We hit it off right away—we both just wanted to get our time done and get out. So we watched each other's back and promised we'd look up certain people for each other when we got out. I got paroled first, and I kept my promise, but I hadn't been able to track Ben down to tell him."

Miles, his dark blond hair hanging in his eyes, listened. Then he said, "Ben's dead. He was killed in a car crash about a year ago. But I know who he wanted you to look up—the cop who put him in prison. He's an undercover cop named Samuel J. Kidman."

ten

Sammy looked down at the floor. "Dead," he muttered. "What a cryin' pity. He was a real class act." Appearing believably shaken, he waited a few seconds to see if Miles knew undercover cop Kidman by sight. During those few seconds his mind combed his recollections from the trial years ago, trying to recall what family members had been present. But too much testimony in too many trials intervened and ran together.

"Yeah," Sammy finally sighed, raising his face, "Kidman was one of 'em. I was able to find out just last week that he'd left the department—word was that he'd gotten fired. But then he dropped outta sight."

"He's still around," Miles coolly observed. Sammy met his gaze. "If he got fired just last week, then he's still around. He can be found. We got our own snitches in the department, and we can find him."

"Good," Sammy nodded approvingly. "I'd consider it a favor if you'd let me in on it, outta respect for Ben." As critical as it was to know who these snitches were, Sammy could not just come out and ask. That would be fatal.

"Sure," Miles said hazily. Partly turning, he added, "I suppose you'll be wantin' a tattoo like Ben had on his chest."

A tattoo? Sammy smelled a test. Miles had turned away from him to the window, but Sammy had been observant enough to note no tattoos on his arms. Sammy glanced at a shirtless boy sitting on the floor smoking, and saw no tattoos. But many of the men in the Wynne unit were tattooed, considering it a mark of honor. What kind of tattoo did Ben have? Having claimed to have known him well, Sammy would expose himself promptly with a wrong answer about something as obvious as a tattoo.

He breathed a prayer for enlightenment, and suddenly recalled Ben's fear of needles which prevented him from becoming seriously addicted to the heroin which Sammy helped convict him of selling. Taking a bold risk, Sammy said, "Ben didn't have no tattoo."

Miles turned from the window with a lopsided smile. "Actually, he did. But it was badly done 'cause he just couldn't sit still for it, and anybody who asked, he told them it was a bruise."

"Them blue marks? He told me he got those in a fight, that liar!" Sammy exclaimed, and they had a thigh-slapping laugh over Ben's stories.

"Did he tell you about the time we ran away from home?" demanded Miles.

"Which time? He had you both runnin' away from home once a week," said Sammy.

This provoked fresh laughter and a touching story about how the brothers at seven and five ran away after the death of a beloved dog. Sammy then related a story allegedly from the lips of Ben about the two brothers' first car theft, which Miles corrected on many points. As it turned out, both brothers were such habitual liars that Sammy could safely make up anything as having been straight from Ben and Miles would never doubt it.

This bonding progressed very satisfactorily until Miles said with magnanimity, "Todd, you're okay. I like you. So tell you what—I'm gonna let you have Angie first today."

Sammy's face registered his surprise as Canton came up and put her arms around his neck. The other boys sat up in renewed interest, and Jobs barely sighed. "Why, thanks—" Sammy said, cut off as Canton pressed her mouth to his.

"C'mon, Todd, don't be so stingy with the tongue," she chided, and the boys rolled in laughter. In retaliation, Sammy pulled her head back sharply by her hair to kiss her, but Canton only laughed. While the boys watched expectantly, she pulled him down to the floor. This situation was unacceptable to Sammy. Knowledge of that flashed in Canton's wicked green eyes even while she stroked him: *Who's in charge now, Hot Shot?*

But Sammy was too much the proud professional to give up control through anger or lust. As he raised up on his knees to unzip his pants, he glanced down out the window. "Cripes—somebody's coming!" he hissed. In a flash he had jerked Canton up and was heading out the door and down the stairs with her.

As they burst out of the building and ran to his bike, someone actually did drive up. He did not see them until Sammy had put on his helmet and started the bike, losing his jacket in the process. The driver shouted at them to stop, but Sammy throttled up and peeled out of the overgrown lot with Canton on the seat behind him.

He drove to a shopping center a safe distance away, then yanked off his helmet and hopped off the bike. "Are you crazy?" he exploded. "What do you think you're doing?"

She laughed until she was breathless. "You should've seen your face when I kissed you! Some tough con!"

He tossed down the helmet and put his hands on his hips to compose himself. "Okay, you just had to have a little fun. Great. But it's bad for business, baby. Didn't anybody ever tell you that you don't sleep with somebody you're going to arrest? You'll jeopardize the conviction."

"Don't tell me how to do my job, scuzzball. I'm not arresting him for solicitation. This is much bigger," she spat.

Sammy regarded her quietly. "Canton, how many trials have you testified in?"

"Several," she said defensively.

"Any in which you were up against a hired gun? Not a court-appointed attorney?" Sammy pressed.

"Make your point," she said impatiently.

"The point is, a really good attorney will use any inconsistencies in the case against you. He'll wrap them around your neck and hang you with them. You can't sleep with Miles and then haul him into court, because then you're regarded as an accomplice—you're seen as aiding and abetting, and the case gets thrown out of court. Don't you see, Canton? Your objectivity is lost. The case is tainted," Sammy argued calmly.

Canton folded her arms, glaring at him, but her shallow breathing indicated she had heard him. "I had no choice," she said in a low voice. "I had to submit to get into the gang. It was the only way I had of getting in."

Sammy sat heavily on his bike. Then he asked, "How long have you been undercover? Not just for this assignment, but total?"

"Six months," she replied.

"Six months?" he repeated in wonderment. "You mean they put you on deep cover as your *first* assignment with no backup? Whose asinine idea was that?"

She looked uncomfortable. "I . . . talked Lieutenant Peters into letting me do it my way, since I had already made contact. . . ."

Suddenly the situation became crystal clear to Sammy. *Peters* was the name on the card that came with the flowers. This was a favor granted her in hopes of reciprocation. But to save her hide, get her an experienced partner—one they could bury with honors.

Sammy looked across the sea of cars in the parking lot. Craddock's vendetta against undercover cop Kidman was an additional unforeseen complication. But who better to keep tabs on a vendetta than Kidman himself? Sure, it could blow up in his face at any time—such risks came with the job. And having come this far, he was loathe to walk away from it. That much he shared with Canton. "We might be able to salvage something yet," Sammy mused. "First thing, absolutely, is to find out who their sources are in the department."

"Oh, that's no problem. That's someone we set up, who feeds them what we want them to know," she said.

"Great. Who is it?" Sammy asked, relieved.

She lowered her delicate chin in condescension. "That's on a need-to-know basis only."

Sammy just about lost it. He grabbed her upper arm, breathing between clenched teeth, "Baby, I *need to know.*"

Wincing, she set her lips stubbornly, then replied, "Gib McRoy. He's on car patrol."

"Good," he said slowly, leaning down to pick up his helmet. "Let's go have a talk with good ol' Gib." He threw a leg over the bike, then held out his hand to her. She took it with some suspicion to climb on the bike behind him.

In the parking lot, Clayton Taylor was heading toward his car after several errands at this shopping center when he saw the man and woman arguing beside the motorcycle. He paused. Was that Sammy? It sure looked like Sammy. The woman was not Marni. Was he working an undercover assignment, then? If he was, then Clayton knew better than to interrupt. With a dubious glance at the two, Clayton went on to his car.

Sammy took Canton back to the north central substation, where she paged Officer McRoy. When he called, Sammy took the phone, asking, "McRoy, how did you make contact with the Doors gang?"

"Well, uh, sir, Detective Reese set it up so that they were watching while I busted her and then let her go for a cut. So then they've called me a few times to get one of their buddies off the hook—nothing we hadn't cleared first with the DA," he said quickly. He sounded green and eager to please.

"Okay," Sammy said slowly. There was something a

little too pat about the setup, but since he was unable to pinpoint what bothered him, he went on, "They're going to call you about one Samuel J. Kidman. This is what you know about the guy. . . ." And Sammy briefed him on everything he should tell Miles.

When that was covered to Sammy's satisfaction, he hung up and turned back to Canton. "Now—can you call Miles directly, or do you have to go through Jobs?"

"I have to call Jobs," she admitted.

"Okay, you do that. I want to get back with Miles," Sammy instructed. Canton pulled out her cell phone and he said, "Not here." They went out to his bike, and he drove several miles to a service station. While Canton dialed, he suddenly asked, "Is that yours, or the department's?"

She glanced up at him, the phone to her ear. "The department's. What, is your section not important enough to get phones?"

Sammy looked away without answering. No, the department issued cell phones to janitors but not TAS, and he refused to buy one that he'd use for work ninety percent of the time. "Never mind. By the way, we just jimmied the door to a room at the EconoLodge where I took Miles up on his offer."

"And I slept through it," she said snidely. Into the phone, she said, "Hi, baby, it's me. Yeah. Yeah, we— jimmied a room door at EconoLodge." She glanced at Sammy, who perceived that Jobs was the jealous sort. "He wants to get back with Miles now. Okay. Will you be there? Good." She terminated the call. "There's a vacant house on a street off Preston next to a field. He'll meet us there."

"Right," Sammy said, climbing on his bike. Canton climbed on behind him to direct him to the house in question. En route, Sammy kept an eye out for traffic cops. He knew that he looked suspicious enough, but that did not concern him nearly as much as the fact that Canton was not wearing a helmet. With her blond hair and long legs, they'd be sure to be stopped for a lecture, and he was carrying no license, no identification at all. Fortunately, the meeting place was not too far away.

Driving up to the house, Sammy felt a twinge of alarm: this was a quiet residential area with children on the block. He and Marni had actually looked at a house for sale on this block only two months ago.

Sammy parked his bike behind a pair of trees in the lot next to the house and took Canton around to the back door, which had been forced open. One back window was raised—not enough to cool the room any. Miles, Jobs, and three other boys were there. Two of the boys were older, but the third could not have been more than twelve.

"Hey," Sammy said, slapping Miles' hand casually. "Anybody get caught?"

"Just a coupla Doormats," Miles said. "They'll get a talking-to, then get let go."

"Right," Sammy nodded. "Uh—what are Doormats?"

Miles folded his muscled arms. "Doormats are the newest members. They got the most to prove. If they do what they're told, then they get to move up to Doorbells. Doorbells can carry heat and make buys—but you'll find out about that as you go. Doorbells that do a good job become Doorknobs. They assign duties to the other two levels. Beyond that is the highest position, that's Doorman. Only me and Fos are Doormen. We're the only ones who can set up the Doors."

"That's cool," Sammy agreed without the least comprehension of what Miles meant.

"So you wanna be in," Miles said as a statement.

"Yeah, while I'm in town. I got some rounds to make—people to see in LA, you know. But for Ben's sake, yeah, I want to be in," Sammy replied.

"You gotta be initiated," Miles said, settling down on the floor with a beer.

Sammy sat, too, his back to the wall. "Sure. Whaddya want me to do?"

"Kill a cop," Miles said with a lopsided smile.

Sammy eyed him. "That's a capital offense, man."

"You chicken?" one kid popped off.

Sammy barely glanced at the boy. "It had better be someone worthwhile."

"Kidman," Miles said. "You kill Kidman."

Sammy locked eyes with the languid Miles. For a brief, heart-stopping moment, Sammy was sure Miles knew who he was. The setup was just too perfect. But there was no way out but to play it through. "Sure," said Sammy. "For Ben. I can do that. But it had better land me up higher than a Doormat."

Miles smiled in a superficially charming way. He had a habit of hanging his mouth open that made him look either boyish or idiotic, depending on one's point of view. The look made Sammy queasy, as it signaled Miles' indifference to little things, like living. "Sure— you knock off Kidman, that'll get you in as a Doorknob," Miles conceded.

On hearing this, Jobs glanced quickly at Miles in displeasure. "First, you gotta take a little trip. Fos," Miles said, jerking his head toward a young accomplice.

Sammy tensed, expecting the requisite drugs to appear. But the boy pulled a candle and a knife out of a wrinkled paper sack. Then he began drawing on the carpet with a black marker. Sammy shot a questioning look to Miles, who said, "You're goin' through the Doors, man. You're gonna go Outside."

Sammy glanced toward the back door. "Outside? What do I need to go for?"

The boys snickered and Miles grinned with a superior air. "Not out *there,* man. Out *here.*" He pointed to the floor, where the boy had drawn a series of concentric rectangles.

Sammy eyed the design with skepticism bordering on derision. "How much paint you been sniffing, Miles?"

"It's part of the initiation. To be in, you go out, and you get the Outsiders to help you kill Kidman," Miles said in all seriousness.

Sammy scoffed, "You're jiving me. I don't need nobody's help."

Ignoring him, Miles said, "This is what you do," and knelt before the design on the floor as he extended a knife (handle first) toward Sammy. "You cut your hand right here, enough to draw good blood, and drip it on the Doorways. That's the key to open the Doors. Then you stand in it and call for the Outsiders. I'll tell you the words to say."

Spiritually, Sammy was not particularly alarmed. He knew that several of the gangs played occult games to enhance their self-image, but he considered it all empty verbiage, performed just for effect. He started to shrug acquiescence, but then something within him reared up in resistance. When in doubt, he always followed his gut feelings.

"I ain't givin' nobody else credit for what I do," Sammy sniffed. "You can tell the ol' boys outside I said thanks but no thanks."

Miles insisted, "You have to walk through the Doors to be one of us."

"Then I'll be, like, an adjunct member," Sammy returned dryly. "I'll kill Kidman, but I ain't calling up no outsiders—"

"Watch this," Miles ordered. He placed the candle in the center rectangle and lit it. He held the knife blade over the candle flame while the other boys knelt around him, then he closed his eyes and began mumbling words. It sounded like nonsense to Sammy, who rolled his eyes toward Canton. She returned a warning look.

Something unusual began to happen. The room grew darker by degrees, as if clouds were passing over the sun. Sammy glanced outside to see the sunshine bright still. But the room, without electric lights, darkened to a twilight.

Sammy's skin crawled. Not a breath of air came through the one open window. The closeness of the room in the summertime heat became suffocating. As sweat trickled down the side of Sammy's face, Miles said, "Now you repeat the words."

"I wasn't listening," Sammy sneered. But his heartrate began to escalate.

Miles pointed the blade of the knife at him. "I don't

think you get it," Miles said softly. "You've seen too much to walk away. You're either in, or dead."

The others grinned maliciously as Sammy stared tensely at Miles. *Okay, God!* Sammy inwardly exclaimed, *You can send the calvary any time now! Calvary? Cavalry*? He was momentarily perplexed as to which word was appropriate. *Whatever!*

When Sammy did not respond, Miles ordered, "Hold him." The two larger youths caught Sammy's arms. While he twisted in their grip, Miles slashed a two-inch gash in Sammy's forearm. They held his arm forward, forcing it to drip great drops of blood within the rectangles. Then they grasped Sammy by the back of the neck and thrust his forehead down to the carpet in front of the candle. "Now this is what you say," said Miles in a gritted whisper, repeating the chant.

Summoning all his strength against the three sets of hands holding him down, Sammy lunged forward, knocking over the candle. It extinguished in the carpet, and the room was filled with eerie, unnatural shadows.

As the shadows began to move, the boys let go of him. Cradling his arm, trying to stanch the bleeding, Sammy sat back and watched in a stupor as the rectangles on the floor began to slowly spin in front of him. *Great—I'm about to pass out,* he thought. But he remained conscious to watch the rectangles spin faster and faster, forming a circular vortex into which the shadows merged and spun around them.

It began spinning so rapidly that Sammy lay down for dizziness. He felt as though he were in the grip of a maelstrom at sea, and when he opened his eyes he saw a black opening in the center where the rectangles spun.

The whirling of the vortex was drawing them all toward this yawning hole.

Sammy watched in consternation as one boy rolled toward the opening and disappeared through it. Then Canton and the youngest boy began slipping toward the doorway.

Sammy reached out both hands and caught the kid by his ankle and Canton by her elbow. Pain shot up his arm from the laceration, and Canton slipped through his fingers until he caught her hand in a last-ditch effort. Both she and the boy seemed unconscious, dead weights, and could not help him hold on.

Straining against the suction, Sammy closed his eyes for strength and saw instead nightmarish, grasping images. Taloned fingers clawed his arms, trying to make him let go, and hazy, grotesque figures invaded his mind to distract him.

Ten-thirteen! Assist! Assist! Where's the cavalry? Sammy cried inwardly. Fighting for control of his own mind, he deliberately pictured Calvary—three stark crosses on a skull-shaped hill. As he intently looked, he became aware of a torrent rushing toward him from that hill. He braced for the impact, and the torrent met him. In a rush of power it lifted him and those he grasped to ride on a crest, obliterating the vortex.

A moment later the flood had gently deposited him on a still, level floor. Weaving slightly, Sammy sat up and looked around. The unnatural darkness had lifted. The others were rising up groggily. Sammy let go of the boy's ankle and Canton's hand. They blinked at him, seeming to realize something unusual had happened.

"What a trip," Miles muttered, pushing up from a

sprawl. "That's never happened before. Did we make some waves, or what?" he grinned stupidly at Sammy.

But Sammy was bending over the boy he had seen sucked through the opening, who was lying still on the center rectangle. "He's unconscious. Better get him to a doc," Sammy muttered.

"Aw, Needham'll be okay," Miles shrugged. "Besides, he's just a Doormat."

Sammy felt a flush of anger as he held his throbbing, bloody arm. "Yeah, well, I'm gettin' me to a doc, then." He reached out and yanked a bandanna off of one boy to wrap it around the bleeding wound. "You and your stupid initiations. Help me with this," he told Canton, who assisted him in tying the bandanna over the gash.

"Now," said Sammy, seething, "I'll take care of Kidman for you, but I ain't doing no more of that doorway crap. You give me a number where I can reach you when I'm done."

"Sure," Miles shrugged placidly. He told Sammy the number of the cell phone he carried, adding, "I'll take you to our hole after you do the job. Not before."

"Yeah," grunted Sammy, staggering out into the sunshine. Mounting his bike, he rode up to Preston, then paused to ascertain where the nearest hospital was. Richardson Medical Center was the closest, he reasoned, and turned south.

But Sammy did not reckon with the aftereffects of his initiation. Riding without a jacket in the hot wind and exhaust of summertime traffic, he grew suddenly faint. Before he could safely steer the bike toward the shoulder of the road, he lost consciousness and wiped out.

Marni spent that day doing regular household things —shopping, cleaning, paying bills—but Sammy was always in the back of her mind. She was not surprised that he did not come home for dinner, but she did wish he would at least check in with a quick call. So when the telephone rang about eight o'clock, Marni jumped for it. "Hello?"

"Hello, sweetheart."

"Oh, hi, Daddy," she said, masking her disappointment. "What's new?"

"Well, not much. I was hoping to talk to Sammy some more about that FirstPlace Tower thing, get that cleared up with him," Clayton said amiably.

"Daddy, Sammy's not here. I forgot to call and tell you that Mike put him on another assignment right away," Marni replied.

"I see. Well, then, that must have been him I saw, after all," Clayton mused.

"Did you see Sammy? When?" Marni asked quickly.

"Oh, early this afternoon, in the parking lot of Arapaho Village. I wasn't sure it was him at first, but it looked like that Harley he had at the hospital when Sam was born. He was with a blond woman," Clayton added self-consciously.

"That's another officer he's on the case with," Marni reassured him. "Daddy, he . . . didn't know what kind of hours he'd be working here, but, as soon as he gets this assignment out of the way, I'll have him call you."

"Sure, honey. Do you need anything while Sammy's out of pocket?" the loving dad asked.

"No, Daddy, thanks. I'll let you know if I do." She sounded just as grown-up as she could.

"Okay, Marni. Goodbye."

"'Bye." Marni hung up slowly, feeling a creeping anxiety. She shook her head resolutely. "So he's working with another woman. Big deal. He said he doesn't even like her, so don't you dare get jealous." Her little self-lecture did not relieve her anxiety.

She checked on Sam, sound asleep in his crib, then walked restlessly through the quiet apartment. Unable to shake the apprehension that dogged her, she sat at the kitchen table, put her head in her hands, and prayed for the love of her life. Picturing him as he confidently left this morning, she invoked all God's biggest, baddest angels to accompany him. "It would help if I knew what was going on," she murmured. "If I knew what he was up against. . . ."

She prayed as best she could, then pulled out her Bible to look for some reassurance. Her bookmark had fallen out, but she thought she had been reading in Hebrews somewhere, so she flipped open to read: "Consider him who endured such opposition from sinful men, so that you will not grow weary and lose heart. In your struggle against sin, you have not yet resisted to the point of shedding your blood—"

"Ugh. That's not helpful at all," Marni murmured, searching to read somewhere else. She flipped randomly to Ezekiel, toward the end of the book, where the prophet describes a vision of the Temple: "The man brought me back to the entrance to the temple, and I saw water coming out from under the threshold of the temple toward the east. . . . As the man went eastward with a measuring line in his hand, he measured off a thousand cubits and then led me through water that was ankle-deep. He measured off another thousand cubits and led me through water that was knee-deep. He measured off another thousand and led me through water that was up to the waist. He measured off another thousand, but now it was a river that I could not cross, because the water had risen and was deep enough to swim in—a river that no one could cross. He asked me, 'Son of man, do you see this?'"

A river coming from the Temple, from the presence of God. A supernatural flood of power that neither physical nor spiritual distance could diminish. "No," muttered Marni, shaking her head over the obscure passage. "I don't see anything at all."

eleven

Sammy did not come home at all that night. Marni woke up once or twice to feel his side of the bed empty. In the morning, she fed and dressed Sam as usual, did everything as usual, as though there were nothing to worry about. Sammy had warned her that his hours on this assignment would be irregular. But—not to hear from him at all? She deliberately shook off thoughts of the blond policewoman.

By nine o'clock that morning Marni was calling Mike. "It's Marni," she said. "Mike, I haven't heard from Sammy since he left yesterday morning. It's not like him, not to keep in touch."

"Well, Marni, I understand that this is a pretty sensitive assignment. He probably just has not had a safe opportunity to call. But if you're concerned, you can call Assistant Chief Groebel at the north central substation," Mike said reassuringly.

"I'll do that, Mike. Thanks." Marni hung up and forthwith called the north central station, asking to speak to the assistant chief. When he came on the line, she said, "Chief Groebel, this is Marni Kidman—Sammy

Kidman's wife. I understand that he was sent to your division for a special assignment, but I haven't heard from him since he left home yesterday morning. Um, has —he reported in?"

"Ah, Mrs. Kidman, I'm afraid that the nature of this assignment is highly confidential," Groebel responded.

"Yes, I know, but Mike Masterson is the one who told me to call. Sammy told me something of the assignment before he left—"

"That was unwise. Definitely, the less you know, the better," he said brusquely.

"I understand, but can you at least tell me if he's checked in?" she asked.

"What information I have received indicates that the situation is under control. If there is more you should know, we will contact you," he said, and hung up.

Marni stared at the receiver. "He hung up on me! I don't believe it." Nor did she feel the least bit encouraged. But she did not know what to do.

While Sam played around on the floor, Marni brought in the newspaper and listlessly opened it up. She was too distracted to pay much attention to what she was reading until her eye caught a small article about a vacant house in north Dallas that had been vandalized. The article gave the address, and noted, "Graffiti and blood stains led police to assume it was the site of gang activity, and possibly an occult ritual. The identities of gang members involved have not been established." Marni pored over this. It was not far from the shopping center where her father had seen Sammy.

Blood stains. "Something's gone wrong," she murmured. "I just know it."

Sammy opened his eyes and blearily looked around. He lay in a hospital bed. Sunlight glimmered behind closed blinds. As he started to shift, the door swung open. On impulse, Sammy closed his eyes, pretending to be asleep.

Two people came to stand by his bed. "He's not awake yet," a woman's voice whispered. "You'll just have to wait."

"Yeah, well, you call us as soon as he comes to. No operator's license, riding a Harley that's registered to the DPD—we're gonna have an interesting chat." A Richardson policeman, Sammy surmised.

"You'll have to talk to Dr. Farhoud about that. He's the one who brought him in, and he wanted to talk to him first," the woman said sternly.

"Sure." The officer turned away. "You just make sure we get him next."

They went to the door, opened it, and left. Sammy waited a beat or two, then opened his eyes. He was startled to see another man in a white lab coat standing by the door, whose presence Sammy had not detected. This was obviously Dr. Farhoud—a dark-skinned man of Indian origin with an astute face.

"So, my friend does not wish to wake up to talk to the police," he murmured with a hint of humor as he approached Sammy's bedside. "Because of you, my new Mercedes now has a dented trunk that won't stay shut. When your motorbike went down in front of me, I collected three cars on my trunk rather than hit you. So, will you talk to me?"

A corner of Sammy's mouth turned up. "Thanks, doc," he muttered.

"You are welcome." Dr. Farhoud inclined his head. Then he gently raised Sammy's bandaged forearm. "Twenty stitches," the doctor noted. "From a sharp, cauterized instrument. Bandaged with a dirty bandanna. Would you care to tell me how this happened?"

Sammy shifted uneasily. The doctor assessed him a moment, then said, "The police tell me that there is a house not far from here that was broken into. When I heard that they found blood, I sent someone from my lab to take a sample. It is human blood. And, my friend, it matches your type. Now, I have not told anyone this yet, but if you will not talk to me, I suppose I will have to give the police what information I have and let them talk to you."

"Why are you so interested?" Sammy asked, stalling.

"Because I live here; I have a family, and I do not like the new gang activity I see here. I am not one to sit by and let it continue unchallenged," the doctor replied. It was a gutsy statement, seeing how the doctor did not know the extent of Sammy's involvement in the undesirable activities.

Sammy and Dr. Farhoud studied each other warily. Then Sammy glanced toward the door and said barely above a whisper: "I'm a Dallas cop, on special assignment to infiltrate this gang. I can't talk to the Richardson cops or anyone else yet. What do you know about this group?"

"Very little. Like everyone else, I saw the graffiti that began appearing overnight. There were burglaries around my neighborhood—twice someone attempted to break into this clinic. And over the past two weeks, I have treated three boys for gashes like yours, only on their hands. It was very clearly ritual abuse. I called the police, and they said it was gang activity. But the boys had all given me false names and addresses. I had nothing more to go on until yesterday, when you wiped out in front of me, Mr.—?" the doctor paused pointedly.

Sammy lifted up in bed. "Give me your pen and pad," he gestured. Dr. Farhoud did, and Sammy wrote a telephone number on it. He winced to hold the pen with his right hand. "I can't tell you my name. But I want you to call this number and tell the woman who answers that I'm all right. Then I'll need you to help me get out of here quietly. When this case is wrapped up, I'll come back and fill you in on everything."

Dr. Farhoud looked skeptical. "And who is to pay for your treatment?"

"Call Sergeant Mike Masterson at the Police and Courts Building downtown. He'll take care of it. But you gotta keep it *real quiet,* Doc, or you'll be treating me for a lot more than scrapes and lacerations," Sammy said wryly. It never occurred to Sammy to give the doctor Assistant Chief Groebel's name. Mike was his superior; Mike could be trusted, and that is all Sammy thought of at the moment.

"You are pushing your luck, my friend," the doctor observed.

Sammy shook his head. "Not luck—I've got a very reliable Backup on this one. Just help me get my clothes and get out of here. Do you know what they did with my hog?" he asked hopefully.

"You had livestock with you?" the doctor asked, deadpan.

Sammy laughed. "The Harley, Doc. The motorbike."

"The police impounded it," Dr. Farhoud answered, opening a closet door and bringing out Sammy's jeans and t-shirt. "Wait here," he instructed as he left.

"Dang it," Sammy muttered, shaking out his pants. "I need that hog." He dressed and went back to the closet for his boots. He was a little sore, and had abrasions on his arm from laying down the bike, but overall, he was acutely aware of how blessed he was to walk away from that mishap relatively intact.

Shortly, the doctor had returned with a breakfast tray. Sammy gulped it down, then the doctor leaned out into the hallway and looked before motioning Sammy out. He took Sammy to a back door which opened into a parking lot. "Thanks, Doc. I'll be in touch," Sammy saluted, sprinting away.

"Perhaps you will, perhaps you won't," Dr. Farhoud murmured after Sammy had moved out of earshot. "No matter." He took the number Sammy had written down to his office and shut the door. But before he could place the call, an emergency walked in that the doctor was obliged to treat right away.

Outside, Sammy darted through several parking lots and stopped at a pay phone outside a convenience store. Digging in his jeans pocket, he found that, fortunately, the cops had not cleaned out his little cash looking for an ID, so at least he had some change to call the north central substation and relay a message to Officer McRoy.

Then he went to the alley behind the store to wait, and in a few minutes McRoy drove up in his squad car. "What happened?" McRoy asked as Sammy climbed into the front seat and slumped down. McRoy was a young officer with reddish-blond hair and freckles.

"Aw, I just wiped out on the Harley and spent the night in a clinic," Sammy mumbled. "Several things: you got to get that hog out of the Richardson PD's impound lot. Tell them just enough to keep them off my case. And we gotta kill Kidman."

"Come again?" McRoy said, inclining his head as he turned a corner.

"Miles Craddock wants the cop who testified against his brother knocked off. That's me. So we're going to do that," Sammy said. His eyes narrowed as he considered various methods of doing away with himself.

McRoy took him back to the substation, where they met with Groebel and Canton. She eyed Sammy's disheveled appearance and day-old beard. "Where've you been?" she asked.

"Aw, laid up in a clinic all night. I talked the doctor into letting me slip away, 'cause he's had some previous brushes with this gang. Got to call Marni, in case he doesn't," he mused, but got distracted in laying out the plan for his own demise. Meanwhile, an officer was dispatched to the Richardson Police Department to retrieve the Harley-Davidson with vague explanations.

Then the four discussed how Kidman's murder should take place. "A shooting, definitely," Sammy opined. "Draft somebody to put on a suit, and I'll just pop off a blank at him."

"Where? On the sidewalk in front of the station?" Canton asked derisively.

"Someplace public, sure," Sammy replied. "So there'll be plenty of witnesses that it really happened."

"What kind of witnesses?" McRoy asked quietly. "Who do you want to see a man get shot in cold blood?"

Sammy was stopped dead. Uninitiated bystanders were the most valuable witnesses to something like this. But remembering the trauma inflicted on one such precious witness he had victimized in this manner caused him to flush with shame that he would even consider doing it again. "You're right. That won't work," he muttered.

At that point Groebel suggested, "Let's make this easy. I'll just issue a three-line press release on the death, saying we're investigating and so on and so forth."

So Sammy composed this statement: "Samuel J. Kidman, formerly a detective in the Dallas Police Department, was found dead this morning under suspicious circumstances. As it is being investigated as a homicide, no further details will be released at this time." He allowed, "If you make sure it gets radio airplay, that should do it. But the *Sun-Times* is liable to be suspicious of yet another obituary on me."

To McRoy, Sammy said, "This is all you know: Kidman was shot sometime last night getting out of his car at his apartment. Once in the back of the head, execution style. The bullet was a thirty-eight caliber."

"Right," McRoy nodded shortly.

About the time Sammy reached for Groebel's telephone to call Marni, it rang. Groebel answered it, grunted once or twice, then hung up and told him, "Your bike's down in the lot, but some Richardson officers are on their way up to talk to you. If you're here, I can't really refuse them."

Sammy turned to leave right away. "I'm gone. Just make sure to call my wife and let her know that this news release is just part of my cover."

"Of course," Groebel said.

"I'm going to tell Miles the job's done," Sammy told Canton as he stepped out, allowing her only a nod in response.

When he was gone, Canton turned back to Groebel. "You got his wife's number? I'll call her. I'm kind of curious to talk to her."

"Sure," Groebel said, relieved not to have to talk to the woman again. He retrieved the number from his Caller ID and Canton copied it down to take it to her desk.

She piddled at the desk, shuffling papers, until a fellow officer nearby left the room. Then she picked up the phone and dialed Sammy's home number. It was answered on the first ring by a soft, anxious voice: "Hello!"

"Uh, hi. Is this Sammy's wife?" Canton asked casually.

"Yes, it is." Marni's voice was strained.

"Well, this is Canton Reese. I'm Sammy's partner on his current assignment."

"Yes? Where is he?" Marni asked.

"Ah, he's gone to meet a contact. Listen, he asked me to call to let you know that you're going to hear an official announcement about his death. It's all fabricated. I can't go into the reasons, but the announcement's a ruse," Canton explained.

"I see. I'm glad you called. Sammy's all right, then?" Marni asked guardedly.

"Yeah, he's fine. He couldn't come home last night, because . . ." Canton trailed off, seized by an irresistible temptation. As she considered it, Marni said nothing, waiting to hear more. "Well, you see, my cover's as a prostitute, so we had to convince the gang leader that . . . uh, the bottom line is that he just wasn't able to make it home, but he's okay. He'll call when he can." Canton then quickly hung up.

The guilt that she felt over such misleading statements was overshadowed by the satisfaction of knowing that no matter how strenuously the Great Kidman protested his innocence, his wife would never believe him. Canton had seen divorces over less than that. With a puckered grin, she left her desk.

Marni hung up deliberately. Before she could even formulate an opinion over what she had just heard, the telephone rang again. "Hello," she answered quietly.

"Ah, yes, hello," a voice with an accent began. "This is Dr. Ahmed Farhoud of the North Dallas Emergency Clinic. A man I treated here gave me this phone number this morning, asked me to call and tell you that he is all right."

"Yes? Is he there?" Marni asked, clutching the phone.

"No. He was urgent to leave this morning, and this is the first opportunity I had to call," the doctor replied.

"What happened to him?" Marni asked.

"Yesterday afternoon he had a minor accident on his motorcycle. I was behind him in traffic, so I brought him to my clinic. I treated him for a laceration on his right arm, which required twenty stitches, and released him this morning," the doctor told her.

"He spent the night in your clinic last night?" Marni asked.

"Yes; we held him for observation," the doctor confirmed.

"I see," Marni said, lifting her chin ever so slightly. "Thank you, doctor. I can't thank you enough."

"It will be thanks enough if he succeeds in his assignment," the doctor replied, and Marni wondered how much he knew. "Goodbye, Mrs. Friend."

Marni stared briefly at the phone, then sat down on the couch to think.

Back at the north central substation, Sammy reclaimed the prized Harley-Davidson and drove to a pay telephone outside a convenience store to call Miles. "It's done," Sammy told him in a low voice. "The trash's been taken out."

"Yeah? Already?" Miles wondered skeptically.

"You oughta be hearing about it pretty soon. A clean job, if I say so myself," Sammy replied.

"I'll check with my snitch and see what he's heard," Miles said. "You got a number there? I'll call you."

"Uh, no—I'll have to call you back," Sammy said. Most pay phones didn't ring.

"Okay, call back in ten," Miles said, and hung up. So Sammy went inside the store, bought a soft drink and burrito, and took them back out to lunch on while waiting beside the phone.

As the minutes passed, Sammy mentally retraced his steps thus far. Had he covered his bases sufficiently? Was it safe to trust Dr. Farhoud? Was it prudent to rely on the work Canton had done? Something about this case made him uneasy, and in retrospect, it appeared that

Canton was the weakness. He did not like having to walk into a case trusting someone else's groundwork—too often that meant the floor collapsing out from under him.

Checking his watch, Sammy put in a second call to Miles. "Congratulations," Miles said smoothly. "I hear it was a real professional job. You're in."

"Great," Sammy said, relaxing.

"You gotta get on over to HQ now. We got work to do," Miles said.

"Where?" Sammy asked.

"The Greenleaf Apartments, on Coit and Beltline. Apartment one thirteen. After you knock, you say, 'braindead.' That's our new code word," Miles told him.

"Gotcha. Be right there," Sammy said, and hung up. "My, my, aren't we sailing right along," he muttered as he dialed the north central substation. "Canton Reese," he requested. When told she was out, he left this message: "Tell her Sammy called. I'm going to the Greenleaf Apartments, number one thirteen. She needs to call her contact." That was all he felt safe saying over the telephone.

Sammy turned toward his bike, then stopped. He had just enough money left to make one more call. Returning to the telephone, he dialed another number. It was answered on the first ring: "Hello?"

"Hi, baby," he smiled.

"Sammy!" Marni almost choked. "Are you all right?"

"Sure, baby. Sorry I haven't had a chance to call before now—I've been kinda busy. Did you get the message about my 'death'?" he asked.

"Yes," she said.

"Good. They did something right," he marveled. "Listen, I've only got a minute. I got a foot in the door of the gang's headquarters by knocking off Kidman. I'm going there now."

"Where?" she asked.

"Uh, Greenleaf Apartments, on Coit and Beltline. Apartment one thirteen. Baby, I wanted to tell you not to worry if you don't hear from me for a while. I'll probably hole up with the gang, so I won't be able to check in. But—pray for me. They're into some really bizarre stuff," he muttered, glancing around.

"All right," she said tensely.

"Gotta run. I love you, baby."

"I love you, Sammy," she whispered. She held the phone to her ear long after the click and the dial tone, feeling her insides coil in sudden apprehension.

After that conversation, Sammy felt better. He considered lifting another motorcycle jacket from the substation's equipment room, but decided he had better head for the apartments Miles had mentioned. "Just knowing where their headquarters is will help Groebel's people keep tabs on them. But let's see what more we can come up with," Sammy mused.

At the north central substation, Canton returned to her desk and picked up the message left by the officer who had taken Sammy's call. "The Greentree Apartments," she noted. Looking them up in her directory, she found these apartments to be way down past LBJ Freeway. "That's strange," she murmured. "Why would they meet so far out of their territory?"

At this time Sammy was pulling into the Greenleaf

Apartments parking lot. After a quick canvass, he found number 113 and knocked. "What?" a voice called from within.

"Braindead," Sammy said at the door.

It was opened to him. Miles and Jobs were there, as well as six or eight other youths. Sammy briefly noticed that these boys all looked bigger and older than the ones he had seen earlier. There wasn't a one smaller than himself. They gathered, smiling, around a single empty chair.

"You done real good, knocking off Kidman," Miles told Sammy, patting him on the back. "So have a seat and we'll finish the initiation."

"C'mon, gimme a break. What more do you expect?" Sammy groused. He somewhat unwillingly yielded to Miles' hand on his back, steering him toward the chair.

"This'll be a breeze," Miles assured him. Sammy sat in the chair and crossed his arms indifferently. Inside, he was churning. He did not like the looks on their faces.

Miles gave a nod and the two youths on either side of Sammy grabbed his arms. "Hey! What gives?" Sammy said angrily as they forced his arms through the back slats of the chair and handcuffed his wrists.

"It's part of the initiation," Miles said casually. Another boy knelt and duct-taped Sammy's ankles to the legs of the chair. He was now thoroughly immobilized. "See," Miles continued, leaning forward, "we figure a cop rates a special kind of initiation."

Sammy glared at him. "You're crazy."

Miles laughed. "Crazy, maybe, but not stupid. You didn't knock Kidman off, 'cause you're him!"

twelve

Sammy maintained his glare while the bottom of his stomach dropped out. "Are you *nuts?*"

"You're nuts, if you thought I wouldn't find out!" Miles shouted. With all pretense abandoned, he was free to let his anger explode. He balled up his fist and struck Sammy in the face so hard that he almost passed out.

"You're dead," Miles promised, and Sammy believed him. As the boys clustered around him pulling out blackjacks and brass knuckles, Sammy closed his eyes to breathe a prayer for the composure to face death by beating. Marni and Sam flashed before his eyes, and he added a prayer for their sustenance after he was gone.

"Wait," Jobs said, reaching out a hand to Miles' shoulder. "We gotta do this smart."

"What're you talking about?" Miles turned on him. Wanting blood on his fists, Miles could hardly be persuaded to listen.

"Think, man! Stop and think! He's a plant! If we off him, they'll know who did it! It'll take them half a minute to come after us!" Jobs shouted. The other boys backed off slightly.

"So we dump the body where they won't find it," Miles countered.

Jobs shook his head impatiently. "But what if they do? We gotta do this right, man!"

"How?" Miles demanded.

"Lemme think," Jobs demanded, pacing in front of Sammy. "They know he's with us. A cop, with us. You cops think you're untouchable, don't you? That you can do anything 'in the line of duty'—we get arrested and you get a medal, all for doing the same thing! You weren't above sleeping with Angie, were ya?" he shouted, and Sammy watched him stonily.

Then Jobs' fury suddenly abated, and a leer spread on his face. "But sometimes you get caught. Remember those two cops arrested last year for selling coke?" Jobs asked Miles, who grinned and nodded. "Well, we got us a smack addict, here. He's gonna die of an overdose."

After a moment's reflection, Miles decided, "That'll be easy." He jerked his head at one boy, who ran to another room. In a few minutes he came back out with an armload of syringes, tubing, and plastic bags of white powder. Sammy turned his head away, looking at the drawn shades of the window.

"Now listen," Jobs said seriously, "we can't kill him with one fix—that's just as plain as blowin' him away. We gotta take him up to an OD gradual-like. Get him hooked and keep him pumped up for a few days. Then the tests they do will show he's an addict. They'll figure he got in over his head and went bad, and they won't be able to pin anything on us."

Miles groaned, "You know how much smack that'll take? How much it'll *cost*?"

"What's it worth to you to kill him without goin' up on death row yourself?" Jobs asked.

Impulsive, thick-skulled Miles thought it over, then reluctantly nodded, "Right. You're smart, Jobs. This'll get you up to Doorman, for sure." Turning to Sammy, he added as a benediction: "This is for Ben, cop."

Jobs melted down the powder in a spoon over the burner and loaded a syringe. Sammy stared at the closed window. *Canton knows I'm here. But so does their plant, and it's not McRoy. I don't know who tipped them off about me,* he thought calmly. *But—Marni knows I'm here, too.* He lifted his eyes in the barest glimmer of hope, one not even strong enough to make a prayer.

Then he winced at the needle jabbing into his arm, and as the smothering caresses of the drug took effect, he remembered, *I told her not to worry if she didn't hear from me for a while. . . .* And then he faded away.

That Tuesday was another regular day for Marni. She felt better, so much better after hearing from Sammy that she called Kerry Pruett to offer assistance in planning the Dallas Police Department's annual family picnic, scheduled for the weekend of July 17.

There was not that much work involved, as each family brought their own food, but Marni did want to help get materials together for the games. That included the softball team Sammy played on. He was their first baseman/power hitter/strikeout king, and relished his star status with adolescent vanity.

So Marni made one trip to a feed store to get burlap bags for the sack races and another trip to a party store to get hypoallergenic paints for face painting. She made lists and phone calls and kept profitably busy until dinner time. Then, as she fed Sam and made a light supper for herself, loneliness for Sammy began to creep in. Still, she did not feel his absence too terribly until she had tucked baby Sam into bed for the evening. Then the quiet of the apartment became oppressive.

To drive the quiet away, Marni put on a CD, but that was a mistake. Hearing music reminded her of how much Sammy loved music and loved to hold her on the dance floor. She turned it off.

Then she decided to sit down and pray for him, which was an even worse mistake. The moment she opened her heart to the Lord and said Sammy's name, apprehension roared up inside her like a smoldering cinder bursting into flame. As much as Marni prayed, the disquiet was not allayed. She finally gave up and went to bed tired and distraught.

The following morning Marni resolved to put aside these foolish fears and go about her business. So she resolutely thrust thoughts of Sammy out of her mind and took care of her housewifely duties. Those times during the day when he would not go quietly, she paused and prayed for him. But each time she did seemed to open the door to fresh fears and irrational thoughts.

Late that afternoon she considered calling someone at the department, but squelched that idea immediately. Mike did not know what Sammy was doing or where; Groebel would not tell her anything even if he knew; and Canton Reese lied to her about him. "You'll just have to wait for him to call," she told herself sternly. "You're just feeling jealous and left out. Now stop being a shrew and trust your husband."

But finding some peace to sleep that night was a blind chase. Marni prayed futile prayers and tucked Sam and herself in bed, then she lay wide awake and stared into the darkness. A faceless horror loomed just beyond her sight; the harder she tried to sleep, the more she heard the blood rushing past her ears, sounding like a marching army. Her prayers for enlightenment went unanswered, and all she could do was writhe on a bed of needles until she finally fell asleep from exhaustion.

Thursday morning she groggily came to at Sam's peeved, insistent cries. It was about an hour later than his usual 6:30 wake-up time. Moaning, Marni shook off the rumpled satin sheets and staggered into the nursery to take care of her son.

The day was hellish. Marni grew increasingly distracted, miserable, and confused. She tried to work on lists for the picnic but found herself going over the same three items repeatedly. She changed Sam's diaper three times in an hour and then panicked when she forget where she had laid him. (She found him in his crib.) She called Kerry and forgot what she wanted to tell her.

By one o'clock, a steady pain had lodged in her stomach. Marni assumed it was floating anxiety until she realized that she had not eaten anything since breakfast. So she fixed a sandwich with lots of lettuce and mustard, the way Sammy liked it, before realizing that she did not like sandwiches that way. Then she put her head down on the counter and cried in frustration and helplessness.

But not even tears helped. The tension continued to wind inside her unmercifully, inexorably. By mid-afternoon Marni was pacing the apartment in a near-frenzy. Then she stopped in the middle of the living room and shouted, "All right, God! I can't stand any more of this! You've got to tell me what to do! *Tell me what to do!"*

There was instant peace. "I'm supposed to do something," Marni realized. She held her breath, waiting, listening.

The telephone rang. Marni looked at it, then went over and calmly picked it up. "Hello."

"Uh, hello. Marni?"

"Yes. Is this Canton Reese?" Marni asked.

"Uh, yeah. I was wondering if you'd heard from Sammy," Canton said in a deliberately offhand manner.

"No, not for several days," Marni answered quietly. "What's wrong?"

"Oh, nothing. Nothing. I just—wondered if he'd called you. Okay. No problem. We'll get on it," Canton said distractedly, and hung up.

Marni hung up slowly. "She doesn't know where he is. She's his partner, and she doesn't know what's happened to him." Intently, Marni focused on something in her memory. "He said he was going to the Greenleaf Apartments, on Coit and Beltline. Apartment one-thirteen," she said softly. She started to call Canton right back, then stopped. "She lied to me," Marni murmured. "She lied to me once already."

Marni replaced the receiver, looking at it as if peering through to the other end of the line. Then she picked it up and dialed. "Hi, Mom," she said brightly. "I've got a little something to take care of, and I was wondering if you could watch Sam for a while this afternoon. . . . Can you? Great, thanks. I'll be by in just a minute." She packed his bag and took the baby to her mother's with cheerful thanks, though she did not tell Pam what it was that needed attending.

Arriving home, Marni shut the door behind her and went up to her closet. "She said she was posing as a prostitute," Marni murmured. She dug through her closet until she found a leather outfit Sammy had bought her at an outlet store, one of his rare impetuous purchases.

"July is a miserable time to be wearing leather," she muttered, wriggling into a short skirt. To her immense relief, it still fit. Marni completed the outfit with a halter-type t-shirt, spike heels, lots of jewelry and heavy makeup. By the time she climbed into her Miata to go look for the Greenleaf Apartments, it was closing in on five o'clock.

Twenty-five minutes later, she was pulling into the parking lot of the low-rent apartments, which were old and poorly maintained. As Marni searched around for number 113, her thoughts were running feverishly: *I have no idea what I'm going to say. What if they're not here? What if they* are *here? You brought me here. You've got to help me find out what they did with him.*

Eyeing the door of apartment one-thirteen, Marni pulled out a stale stick of gum and began chewing it. Then she took a deep breath and rang the doorbell. "What?" somebody shouted from inside.

"Is this the party?" Marni asked languidly through the door.

Several seconds later the door was cautiously opened, and a teenaged boy peered out. "What?"

"I said, is this the party?" She popped her gum.

He looked her up and down appreciatively. "It is for you. Come on in."

Marni did, glancing around at the dirty, scarcely furnished living room. "Where is everybody?" she asked. One other boy came out from a bedroom.

"We got enough for a party," leered the boy who had opened the door. "What's your name?"

"Misty," Marni replied, chewing her gum. "Who are you, cutie?"

"I'm Rank and this is Buzzard," he said, nodding toward the boy who had come out. "Who told you there was a party here?"

"Some guy I met down at the Quik Stop. He was cute, and he said there was, like, stuff here, ya know," she said, slurring her words in cool youth style. Marni knew no gang party would be complete without drugs.

"That woulda been Goober," Rank said knowingly to Buzzard, who eyed Marni suspiciously. "He's always poppin' off to impress the girls. Sorry, baby," Rank said to Marni, "the only stuff we got here is for a job."

"What job?" she asked curiously.

"Shut up, stupid," Buzzard upbraided Rank. Buzzard looked a little older and a little smarter than his buddy, but Marni was working hard on them both. He turned to her and asked, "What's the password?"

Marni stared at him a moment as she worked the gum. There was no use pretending she knew anything about a password. So she walked up to within inches of Buzzard's scruffy face and murmured, "Do I look like I need a password, sweetie?"

Rank shoved Buzzard on the shoulder. "See? If she was from the cops, they'd 'a' given her the password!" Rank argued. Marni did not understand his reasoning, but in light of this evidence, Buzzard weakened.

Pressing her advantage, Marni leaned up against Rank and began toying with the greasy brown curls hanging down around his ears. She guessed why he was named "Rank," and it wasn't because of his position on the organizational chart. She murmured into his ear, "I'm *really* fond of guys who can get me what I like, ya know?"

Rank knew. Buzzard knew. They exchanged glances, then Rank said, "Well—lemme show you what we got workin'." He went to a door and opened it. Marni followed him.

As she looked into the bedroom, her heart lodged in her throat to see Sammy lying on a dirty bed. He looked bad—unconscious and gray, with parched lips and needle marks dotting his arms. "Who's that?" she asked idly.

"It's a cop," Rank grinned. "We're givin' him a little goin' away party." Buzzard came in, watching Marni's reaction.

"Oh. Good for you," Marni said. She went over and picked up Sammy's wrist to feel for a pulse. It was slow and weak, but it was there. "He's dead. Whatcha gonna do with him now?" she wondered.

"Dead! Uh oh. He went down quicker than he was supposed to," Rank said, looking at Buzzard.

Marni could not afford to let them examine this situation too thoroughly. "You know, the guy I met at the Quik Stop was telling a bunch of people to come party. I don't know who all you're gonna have show up in a minute." She deliberately tossed Sammy's hand back down to the bed.

Rank and Buzzard stared at each other. "That loony

fart! What are we gonna do?" Rank asked desperately.

"We gotta dump him now," Buzzard said, leaning over to pick up the body. "Gimme a hand."

Lest they handle him enough to find a pulse, Marni warned them, "There's a traffic cop sitting just out of sight of the door, watching Arapaho." Rank froze on his way around the bed.

"That's not a traffic cop!" Buzzard exploded in fear. "They're watching us!"

"We're gonna get caught with a dead cop on our hands!" Rank breathed, white in the face.

"Okay now, listen, guys," Marni said authoritatively. "They don't know me. Let me just take this guy out to my car like he's drunk, you know, and if anybody asks I'll tell them he's my boyfriend. Then I'll dump him out of the way somewhere."

"Why would you risk doin' that?" Buzzard asked, at once hopeful and skeptical.

"I'm doing it so you'd owe me a *favor,* sweetie," Marni said with a soft voice and hard eyes. "When I come back, I want stuff and I want lots of it. Like, are you hearing me?"

"Yeah, baby," Buzzard nodded. "I hear you."

"Good. Now open the door," Marni said, lifting Sammy's ravaged arm over her shoulder.

"Lemme help you," Buzzard said, reaching for the body.

"Just—clear the way to the door, sweetie," Marni grunted, lugging Sammy up to rest his weight on her back. They stood aside obediently as she dragged Sammy's solid one hundred seventy pounds of dead weight to her car, tottering on her spike heels.

She loaded him in the passenger seat, fastening the seatbelt around him, then sat behind the wheel and started the car. She pulled out onto Coit and drove with glazed eyes six blocks, then had to pull over at a gas station. She was shaking so hard she could hardly steer.

"Sammy," she whimpered, clutching his limp hand to feel for the pulse again. "I have to get him to a hospital," she whispered. "Where . . . ?" She put her head down on the steering wheel to think, and suddenly recalled Dr. Farhoud of the—the—

"What was it?" She looked up intently over the wheel. "The North Dallas Emergency Clinic." Then she saw that without realizing it, she had pulled up directly in front of a pay telephone. The directory sat on a shelf under the phone.

Marni jumped out of the car and yanked out the directory. She looked up the clinic's address and found it was just a few blocks away. With focused resolve, she jumped back into the car and threaded her way through rush-hour traffic to the clinic. She parked directly in front of the door and ran in to seize the nurse on duty. "Get Dr. Farhoud—please—I have a very sick man in my car—someone he knows—"

Sammy was brought in on a stretcher as Dr. Farhoud was paged. While several attendants laid the patient on an examining table, another young doctor asked brusquely, "What all's he been shooting up?"

Marni literally grabbed the six-foot doctor and shook him. "This is my husband! He's an undercover cop, and they were trying to kill him! I don't know what all they pumped into him!"

"Okay ma'am; it's okay, don't worry," he said

hastily, then ordered an intravenous solution and blood tests. Marni stayed right by Sammy's side, holding his unresponsive hand while the preliminaries were administered. Afterwards, they moved him to a bed in a private room of the clinic.

She helped the nurse undress him, then Marni took the damp washcloth herself to begin bathing him. Stoically washing sweat and grime from his bearded face, she bit back tears on seeing the large black bruise that covered one cheek. She washed his neck and shoulders, then turned to rinse the washcloth in the shallow pan of warm water on the table beside her.

"Don't forget the ears, Mama," he mumbled, and she whirled around to see his groggy half-smile. She could not get out a word—just collapsed onto his chest. Sammy brought up an arm laden with tubes to rest on her back. He glanced around at his surroundings, then murmured, "Who found me?"

"I did," she lifted up to whisper. "Your woman partner called to ask if I'd heard from you, and I knew something was wrong. I went to the apartment you told me about, and I found you there." She strained to keep her voice under control.

He frowned disconcertedly. "What's today?"

"Thursday, my friend," answered Dr. Farhoud from the doorway. Marni turned, and she and Sammy watched as the doctor closed the door behind him. "And you must be Mrs. Friend," he said to Marni.

"My name is Marni," she smiled weakly. "Marni Friend."

With a wry smile at her, Dr. Farhoud came to Sammy's bedside. His eye took on a critical cast. "It's

Thursday evening, and you have been fed a steady diet of heroin for some time. Do you know how long?"

Sammy muttered, "I went to the apartment on Tuesday, right after I called Marni. But somebody at the department tipped them off about me. Miles knew who I was the minute I walked in." As his mind gradually began to clear, he gripped Marni in sudden alarm. "You got me out? How?"

"By pretending I was looking for a party." Marni related how she had maneuvered him out of the apartment under the noses of the two gang members and Sammy closed his eyes.

"Marni, that was dangerous. Don't *ever* try that again," he scolded her.

"You're welcome," she said, peeved. "I'll remember that the next time you get in trouble."

"Another thing: why can't you dress like that when we go out?" he demanded, surveying her party outfit.

Marni opened her mouth as Dr. Farhoud asked, "But why did you not call the police?"

"I didn't trust them," Marni said darkly. "Your new partner tried to make me think you had spent the night with her Monday when you were actually here," she told Sammy.

He laid his clouded head back on the pillow, thinking out loud, "She called you to see if you had heard from me?"

"Today," Marni nodded. "That's how I knew something was wrong."

"But . . . I called her before I called you, and left the same message for her that I told you. She should have known where I was," he mused.

Marni asked suddenly, "Did she tell you a code word that they were supposedly using? Because Buzzard asked me if I knew the password—as it turned out, they were looking for a password that would have told them I'd been in touch with the police."

Sammy forced his stuporous mind to concentrate. "They do have a contact in the department, and it's not the guy Canton told me it was. It's a real live informer. He not only told them Kidman's death was faked, but that I was him. I've got to find out who that is," he said, starting to raise up.

"Sammy." Marni put her hands on his solid shoulders and pushed back gently. In his weakened condition, he yielded. "Your cover's blown. And when they find out that nobody in the gang told me about any party, mine will be, too. You've got them for attempted murder of a police officer. Isn't that enough? What more can you do?"

"I can uncover their stooge in the department and make his life hell," Sammy said, lifting up against her hands.

But then Dr. Farhoud pulled up restraints from the sides of the bed and began wrapping them around Sammy's wrists. "I think not, my friend," he said.

thirteen

Sammy and Marni stared at the doctor. "Why not? What are you doing?" Sammy demanded.

"Restraining you. Once you start withdrawal, it will be very difficult to restrain you without injury," Dr. Farhoud said gravely.

Sammy lay back with a moan and Marni asked, "Withdrawal? Like an addict?"

"We will hope that it won't be as severe as that experienced by a long-time user, but with as much as you have mainlined in the past two days, there is certain to be some discomfort, Sammy." The doctor pointedly used his name. "Would you prefer that we ease you down with methadone?"

"No," Sammy said. "We'll go cold turkey."

"Then I will remember that, despite what you tell me later," Dr. Farhoud said dryly. "You should rest if you can, because it will come over you sometime between now and tomorrow morning."

In spite of the fact that Sammy was growing very hungry—he couldn't remember being given anything to eat at the Greenleaf apartment—Dr. Farhoud would not let him have more than diluted juice and a few dry crackers. Marni was incensed, but Sammy understood. "You ever seen a smack addict undergo withdrawal?" he asked her.

Marni sat beside his bed, holding his hand under the restraining cuff. "No," she replied.

He looked up at the ceiling. "They turn inside out. It's almost like a horror movie—their bodies would turn inside out, if they could." Marni gripped his fingers and laid her head on his chest. "Now, this is torture," he observed, and she looked up. "My nose itches." She scratched it gently for him. "Other side," he corrected, and she got that side for him, too.

Evening fell and Sammy dozed with the head of his bed slightly elevated for comfort. A male nurse named Farley—tall, gangly, with a ponytail—brought in a cot for Marni to sleep on. She washed off most of the makeup and removed the heavy jewelry, but before lying down, she went out into the bright hallway and found a telephone.

She dialed her parents' number. "Hi, Mom," she said quietly. "I wanted to let you know that . . . Sammy's been injured. He's in the hospital now. No, Mom, listen —he's going to be all right, but I have to stay with him a little while. I can't tell you where, and if anyone calls you to ask about him, you don't know anything. You haven't heard anything from him. Mom, that includes anyone from the department. I'll—have to explain it all to you later. Okay. I will. Love you, too." Marni hung up and returned to Sammy's darkened room.

By the thin strip of light from the hallway, she studied his face. Even strung out and unkempt, he still looked winsome as a sleeping child. "Oh, Sammy," Marni whispered, leaning her head beside his on the pillow. "Why do you love a job that gets you beat up so much?" Regarding his arm with the needle marks and stitches, she winced.

By this time, he was resting so soundly that Marni kicked off the uncomfortable spike heels and stretched out on the cot. She immediately fell asleep and did not stir for the next five hours.

The change in Sammy's breathing woke her. He began panting and moaning softly in his sleep. Clicking on the bedside light, Marni slid off the cot to check him. He was sweating profusely, stirring restlessly. Then all at once he relaxed and slipped back into sleep. Marni washed the sweat away with a cool cloth and watched him. When he continued to lie still she turned off the light and lay back down, almost daring to hope that the withdrawal would not be as rough as Dr. Farhoud feared.

Some time later a sudden crash woke her. Marni bolted up in confusion, then gazed at Sammy's shadowy form writhing on the bed. In the dimness of the unlit room, she first thought she was having a nightmare.

In spite of the restraints on his wrists and ankles, he had slammed back on the bed so hard that he broke the lifting mechanism which raised the head of the bed, and it now lay flat. "Marni—" he gasped, retched, and coiled.

"I'm here," she said, holding his clawing fingers. But his grip was so tight she had to pull her fingers free before he broke her hand.

He flung his head to one side and arched in agony. Trembling, Marni pushed the call button. "He's going into withdrawal. Get Dr. Farhoud!" she pleaded into the intercom.

"Gotcha," Farley replied, and in a moment entered the room. When he turned on the light Marni drew in a quick breath. There was blood smeared across Sammy's face and the top of the sheet. The pillow was on the floor. "Great," the nurse muttered.

He bracketed Sammy's face between his hands and said, "Listen, pal. Listen! Don't chew your tongue! Understand? Keep your tongue in the back of your mouth!"

Breathing hard, Sammy nodded. Marni asked as calmly as possible, "Can't you help him?"

"Nah. Anything I put in his mouth is liable to make him suffocate when he vomits. He's just gotta remember to keep his tongue back out of the way," Farley said, surveying the patient. Still, he rolled up a washcloth and tried inserting that between Sammy's teeth while keeping his own fingers out of harm's way. Sammy resisted the aid. After some tense struggling between the strong nurse and the delirious patient, the cloth was in place.

Sammy jerked his head and promptly spat it out. "Gimme methadone," he breathed before twisting up in another spasm of pain.

"We gotta see what the doc says about that, guy," the nurse replied. He told Marni: "Dr. Farhoud left instructions to page him when withdrawal set in. He's on his way."

"Thank you," Marni whispered, helplessly watching Sammy thrash on his bed of fire. He would work himself to exhaustion and lay quivering until the torment became unbearable, then lash out again, straining against the leather restraints.

During one particularly severe convulsion, Sammy flexed until the restraint on his right ankle snapped. "Dadgum. I'd like to see how much weight he can dead lift," Farley remarked, then went out to fetch another restraint.

At that point Dr. Farhoud arrived. Marni was so glad to see him, she almost hugged him. "Doctor, please do something," she begged.

Looking rather tired and rumpled himself, the doctor quickly examined his patient. He looked in Sammy's eyes and mouth, removed the IV to prevent further injury, and held Sammy's leg down while Farley fastened another restraint on it. Finally Dr. Farhoud said to Marni, "This must be very frightening to you, but he is coming along fine."

This did not sit well with Sammy. "I wan' the methadone now," he grunted, tossing his head.

Dr. Farhoud sighed. "When your mind was clearer, you told me you did not want it. I'm afraid I agree that this is the best way."

Spitting slurred invectives, Sammy balled his fists and pulled so hard against the wrist restraints that for a moment Marni feared he would break those as well. Then he collapsed and moaned thickly, "Mar'i, help me."

"I'm doing all I can," she whispered, bathing his face with the cool cloth. Shuddering, he gazed at her reproachfully, then jerked away and retched over and over again. Wiping his face with a wet cloth, Marni understood what he meant about turning inside out.

This nightmare lasted for several more hours as morning broke and the day staff came on duty. Dr. Farhoud was called out occasionally to attend other patients, but Marni never left Sammy's side, nor stopped praying.

Finally, the attacks began to subside. Delivered from extreme pain to just extreme discomfort, Sammy collapsed into tormented sleep. Dr. Farhoud was relieved to see that. "The worst is over," he told Marni, "though the effects will linger days, perhaps weeks." He swabbed Sammy's lacerated tongue with a diluted solution of hydrogen peroxide followed by a topical anesthetic, then left both the patient and his wife to rest.

When Marni awoke late in the morning, Sammy was still asleep, sprawled across the bed on his stomach. The wrist and ankle restraints had been removed. She got up for a washcloth and pan of warm water. As she began washing him tenderly, he opened his eyes. "Am I s'ill 'live?" he mumbled.

"Still kicking," she confirmed, leaning over his shoulder to kiss his cheek. "How do you feel?"

"Uhhglmmm. You know shose carcasses you see hanging up in thuh mea' market freezers?" he mumbled around his swollen tongue. "Tha's me, third from th' end. I'm hungry." He lifted up shakily. Smiling in relief, Marni pressed the call button to ask for breakfast.

A short time later she was brought a tray, but all Sammy got was a bland vanilla shake. "Wha', iz he running a diet clinic here?" Sammy grumbled. Still, he found his tongue too sore to even drink the shake without a straw. And any exertion caused his tired, achy muscles to tremble.

After breakfast, Sammy lay back with his eyes closed under Marni's soothing washcloth. Dr. Farhoud came in, and she discreetly pulled the sheet up over her husband. "Well, now. Are we through with our little tantrum?" the doctor asked.

Sammy's eyes opened to mere slits. "Come jus' a l'il bit closer, doc," he invited darkly.

"Yes, I've seen what kind of damage you can do," Dr. Farhoud said, picking up the broken leather restraint from the trash can. Sammy eyed it bemusedly. "But I have other concerns. Someone called this morning from the police department, supposedly, asking if we had treated a man of your description."

"For heroin addiction?" Marni asked.

"For anything. I told them, no," the doctor said shortly.

"Di' they give a name?" Sammy asked, swallowing the pain to speak clearly.

"It was a Lieutenant Haskell, if I heard correctly," Dr. Farhoud said. Sammy shook his head briefly. "Yet, he sounded very young to me. I am not a reliable judge of voices, but, he sounded young," Dr. Farhoud mused.

"So it could be a gang member checking up to see what happened to Sammy," Marni observed.

"I felt so, yes," the doctor admitted.

"Could be someone from th' department tha' I dunno," Sammy said around his sore tongue. "Or could be th' gang's plant. I'm . . . wonderin' why you came got me and Ca'ton didn't," he said, looking up at Marni.

She explained again, "When she called me, I got the definite impression that she didn't know where you were. That's why I went looking for you."

"Then she didn't get th' message. It mus' have been intercepted," Sammy said.

"By whom?" Marni asked.

"Tha's what I have to find out," Sammy stated, rolling his tongue gingerly.

"How?" she asked.

He contemplatively bunched the pillow under his head. "Lemme think abou' that."

Dr. Farhoud prepared a swab and applied it to Sammy's tongue again while the patient made disgusted faces. After spitting in the trash can, Sammy began to rise from the bed. "I need to make a call, Doc."

"I'll bring you a telephone," Dr. Farhoud said.

"No. It can't be a cell phone," Sammy objected. "Those are too easy to tap."

"Then use the one in my office," Dr. Farhoud said, opening the door and pointing down the hall.

Marni tied Sammy's hospital gown back in place and he leaned on her to climb down from the bed. He paused. "Di' I thank you for bailing me out?"

"No, you ingrate," she said lovingly.

"Oh," he said, and she pursed her lips as she walked him down the hall to Dr. Farhoud's office. Sammy sat in the doctor's leather chair to dial while Marni shut the door. Rocking back in the chair, he scratched his hair and waited with the receiver at his ear.

"Masterson," the line was answered.

"Hello, you flea-bitten, scum-sucking sewer dweller," Sammy said clearly, and Marni silently applauded this heroic exertion.

There was a moment of silence. "Will you hold, please?" Mike said in a stilted voice, and Sammy heard the creak of a chair and the closing of a door. Mike came back on the line, whispering, "Where the hell are you? Do you know there's a department-wide manhunt going on for you right now?"

"Really? I didn't know you cared," Sammy sneered, then turned serious: "Someone at the north ce'tral station se' me up, ol' buddy. You'd 'a' found my body in the gutter by now if my *real* partner hadn't come for me." He then gave Mike a rundown of the past three days—concisely, as it still hurt to talk.

Mike exhaled heavily. "That's bad news. What kind of support do you want, Sambo?"

"First, a surveillance unit at Greenleaf Apartments. I kinda doubt they'll still be there, once they figure out Marni's con, but—we may get lucky. Don't have our guys move in yet. I wanna catch their plant," Sammy said. "Oh—and see if you can find the hog. It should still be there, unless they filched it."

"Right. And where will you be?" Mike asked.

"Marni and I are holed up at the North Dallas Emergency Clinic. Dr. Ahmad Farhoud is the senior physician—did he call you?" Sammy asked.

"Yeah, several days ago—wait a minute. That was *you* he was talking about?" Mike exclaimed.

"Who'd you think?" Sammy exclaimed. "Whu—never mind. Did someone from the north central station call downtown this morning? A Lieutenant Haskell?"

"I don't know, since I'm not in charge of this operation," Mike said, sounding peeved. "I don't know any Haskell."

"Neither do I. But it don't really matter—ever'body up there is suspect until I find out who the plant is,"

Sammy muttered. He paused, and Marni could see the wheels turning. "Mike, I'm . . . gonna try to shake down the gang."

Mike balked, "Sammy, I won't tell you not to, but that tactic has a tendency to spin out of control."

"I know, I know. But it's the best way I can think of to expose their plant. You jus' cover my rear with the department," Sammy said, then looked behind him at the gaping hospital gown.

"Consider it covered. Keep me apprised," Mike ordered.

"Right." Sammy hung up smiling. "He'll never let them fire me again. He can't live without me, I make him look so good."

Marni leaned down on the desk. "Okay, hot shot, what do we do now?"

Sammy eyed her in the clingy t-shirt and leather skirt. "We attack you." He raised up to kiss her, but flinched when their mouths made contact.

Marni backed off to look at his tongue. "Poor thing," she sympathized.

Sinking back into the leather chair, Sammy pulled her down on his lap with a sigh. "Okay, well, next thing we do is get us both some fresh clothes—just jeans and tees. But don't go back to the apartment; it's liable to be watched. Head out to one of the malls and put it on your charge card. And *please* don't get me those skimpy little briefs. I'll croak if I see any of those again."

Getting up, Marni made sure she was out of his reach before observing, "Oh, but they photograph so nicely—" She barely escaped out the door before he could grab her.

In slightly more than an hour Marni was back with her purchases. Sammy, of course, defied Dr. Farhoud's orders to rest and instead began dressing. Marni saw that he was still pale and shaky, but she knew it was pointless to point that out to him.

When they were dressed, Sammy and Marni sat once again in Dr. Farhoud's office with the door shut. "Take notes, baby," he instructed. "You're about to learn a double-double cross." With a fresh dose of topical anesthetic on his tongue, his speech was quite clear— only a shade thicker than usual.

Marni perched on the desk attentively as he picked up the telephone and dialed. "Canton Reese," he requested.

"Reese," she answered her line.

"Hello, partner," Sammy said mildly.

"Sammy?" she asked in a low voice. "What happened to you? Where have you been?"

"I got waylaid for a little while, baby. Didn't you get my message?" he asked.

She confirmed, "Yes. I went right to one-thirteen at the Greentree Apartments, and the people there didn't know anything—"

"Greenleaf," Sammy interrupted. "I was at the Greenleaf Apartments, Canton."

"The message I got said 'Greentree,'" she insisted.

Sammy shrugged off the apparent misunderstanding to ask the crucial question in an offhand manner: "Never mind, it was no big deal. Have you been in touch with Jobs?"

"Not for a few days. He's not answering his phone," she said tensely.

Sammy hesitated. This could indicate her innocence in the matter—*if* she was telling the truth. Cop to cop, he had to give her the benefit of the doubt. "Well, you might better back off. Somebody blew my cover, and the gang found me out."

"What?" she gasped.

"It appears they have an informant in the department other than McRoy, which means I was right in the beginning when I said they already knew who you were," Sammy told her.

"But—why would they go along? Why would they let me in their meetings?" she asked dismally.

"Baby, you were seeing and hearing just what they wanted you to. Why, I don't know, but it sure wasn't for your health. You've been really lucky that they hadn't acted on your presence earlier—you can't push it now. As senior partner, I'm aborting this operation," Sammy said.

"All that work down the drain," Canton groaned.

"Just consider it schooling. I'm going back to the Big Building Downtown to submit a wrap-up to my boss. Pleasure working with you, Ms. Reese," he said aloofly, with a glance up at Marni.

"I'm sorry it didn't pan out," Canton said miserably.

"That happens, sometimes. I'm just glad nobody got hurt. *Ciao.*" Sammy hung up. "She's either honest or a better actress than I thought," he told Marni, who nodded. "Now for the really interesting part."

"Are you calling the gang?" Marni asked.

"Yup."

"Sammy, Caller ID will show the name of the clinic," she said anxiously.

"Won't matter now," he asserted. He picked up Dr. Farhoud's telephone and made another call. "Yeah?" a voice answered.

"Missing any bodies?" Sammy asked sarcastically.

There was a brief silence, then Miles demanded, "Who is this?"

"Who've you tried to waste lately?" Sammy returned. "You picked the wrong cop to mess with, pal —I don't mind playing outside the rules. I've got you and all your flunkies on an attempted capital murder charge. It's a sure conviction and probably a medal for me."

"So whaddyou want?" Miles asked tensely.

"Twenty thou," Sammy replied coolly.

"You're crazy!" Miles exploded. "We don't got that kind of dough!"

"Then keep somebody on watch wherever you sleep tonight, 'cause there'll be a dragnet out for you guys. Cops get kind of touchy when weasels like you start messin' with one of their own," Sammy said.

"Wait, now, wait. Let's talk," Miles urged.

"I'm listening," Sammy said languidly.

"We don't have that much cash on hand. But we can give you a percentage of each job," Miles offered.

Sammy laughed, "What, a dollar-fifty a week? Forget it. It's got to be pretty substantial to pass up the satisfaction I'd get seeing you fry."

Miles was approaching desperation, but still reluctant to play his ace, which Sammy figured to be the plant. "Let's meet and talk it out," he suggested.

"And give you another shot at doing me in? How stupid do you think I am?" Sammy asked hotly.

"Okay, we'll use a go-between," Miles offered. *You're getting warm,* Sammy thought. "Angie. We'll send Angie back and forth," said Miles.

No! Sammy almost groaned audibly. He had not given Miles enough credit: Canton was the perfect choice for a go-between from any angle—what man could refuse Angie? Then again, if Miles knew her as Canton as well, she could provide supposedly damning evidence to Internal Affairs about this shakedown attempt. Sammy had to come up with a believable objection to force Miles into using his police contact.

He opened his mouth. "No. Not Angie."

"Why not?" Miles asked.

Sammy carefully deliberated his answer. He had ordered Canton off the case. Could he be sure she would comply? She had better, he decided. "Because," Sammy replied, "she's a cop."

fourteen

Miles did not say anything for a moment. Then, "You're lying."

"Even if I were," Sammy acknowledged, "I still wouldn't use Angie." *Thoroughly confused yet?* Sammy thought sarcastically.

He said nothing further to interrupt Miles' creeping train of thought. Sammy wanted Miles to reach his own conclusions that: (a) he could not use a gang member as go-between—it had to be an outsider, and (b) using a friendly cop whom Sammy did not know could be just as advantageous to the gang as using Canton.

Finally Miles allowed, "I know a guy who works at a gas station. His name is—Butch. Gimme a number and I'll have him call you to set up a meeting."

"Not likely," Sammy sneered. "You give me his last name and the station he works at. If he checks out, I'll give you the go-ahead."

Reluctantly, Miles said, "Uh, Harrell. Butch Harrell. He works at the Texaco on the corner of Greenville and Forest Lane."

"I'll get back with you," Sammy said, and hung up.

He stood to quickly kiss Marni. "I'm going to check out one Butch Harrell, who allegedly works at the Texaco on the corner of Greenville and Forest Lane," Sammy said. One's partner should know one's whereabouts at all times. "I should be right back. I gotta take your car, so don't go anywhere."

She nodded, handing him her keys. "You will fill it up, then, won't you?"

He rolled his eyes. "Sure. Why not? Gimme your credit card, then." She just gave him her wallet.

Exiting the clinic into the hot sunshine, Sammy had to pause to shake off some dizziness. He still felt drained and queasy, and his tongue throbbed, but he wasn't about to let a little discomfort get in the way of completing an assignment.

As he got into Marni's car and drove toward the service station, he thought about Canton. Under any other circumstances, he would have told her he was continuing the operation without her, but—he just didn't trust her enough to do that now.

"You're afraid of her," Sammy muttered to himself. Unflattering, but true. Her effect on Miles, Jobs, and even himself was volatile. Throw a sexy woman into an unstable situation and you couldn't predict what would happen. The fact that she also tried to make Marni think he had slept with her incensed him. "Well, for your own sake, Canton, do what you're told and stay out of it," he murmured as he pulled into the service station.

He filled the tank, then walked to the window to pay. Because he wanted to talk to a live person, he ignored the credit-card reader on the pump. Swallowing the pain in his tongue, he smiled at the attendant, whose name patch read, "Jack." "Hey, I heard an old buddy of mine works here—Butch Harrell. Know him?" He withdrew the credit card and placed it in the tray underneath the bulletproof glass.

"Butch?" repeated Jack, taking up the credit card. "Yeah, Butch works here, but he don't come in till tomorrow. We're open Saturday and Sunday, with the long holiday weekend, and nobody but nobody wanted to come in this weekend, but on the Fourth you always got a lot of travel, and the boss says we'll be open, so we'll be open, and we had to draw straws and Butch lost. Driver's license?"

Sammy opened up Marni's wallet and held her driver's license up to the window. "I'm wondering if it's the same guy I knew—tall and skinny, with red hair and freckles?"

"Well, Butch is tall, all right, 'bout six-three, but his hair ain't red, just brown and frizzy, bad hair, and he don't got freckles, just zits," the attendant clarified. He glanced at the driver's license, then ran the credit card through his scanner.

"Must not be the same guy," Sammy said, disappointed. "Is he about thirty?"

"Oh, no. Butch is just twenty-two," Jack corrected, shoving the receipt back through the window for Sammy to sign.

"Not the same Butch I knew," Sammy said, illegibly signing the slip. "Well, thanks anyway." He took the receipt, waving, and the attendant waved back.

He left there with a good physical description of Butch Harrell, then stopped at a pay phone down the street to call Mike and have him run a check on the guy.

Sammy stayed on the line until Mike returned to tell him that the Butch Harrell who worked at the Texaco had no criminal record, only one speeding ticket.

Sammy then detailed his plan to Mike, adding, "I've told Canton Reese to abort the assignment, but a little imp on my shoulder is whispering that she might not. If she doesn't stay out of it, she's going to get hurt."

"I'll verify the discontinuation with Groebel. That's about all we can do, short of suspending her," Mike said.

"That'll do, then," Sammy said. "Oh—you will see that Dr. Farhoud gets paid for his services, woncha?"

"Sure," Mike growled. "Along with this invoice for —one hundred twenty-seven and ninety-six cents from Dwight. Now why the hell did you stick me with this instead of Groebel?"

"Because I love you," Sammy said warmly. "Incidentally, have you checked out the good doctor?"

"Right after he first called. He's clean, so far as we know," Mike said.

"You're a good man," Sammy said approvingly. "*Ciao.*"

He then called Miles. "Okay," Sammy said, "We'll use Butch. You tell him to meet me in one hour at the northeast edge of Churchill Park. Our code word will be *incandescent.*" And then he hung up. "Let's see Butch use that in a casual sentence," he said with dark satisfaction.

In an hour Sammy was sitting on a bench in the northeast corner of the park. He'd brought a book which he pretended to be reading under his dark glasses while he actually surveilled the park. There was nothing but wide-open spaces all around him. A few people were scattered around the park, but without a pool nearby, it was just too hot for most folks.

Sammy waited only a few minutes before a guy walking a dog strolled by. He glanced nonchalantly at Sammy and asked, "Wouldn't it be easier to read that under an incandescent light?"

Sammy scrutinized the speaker. He was in his mid-twenties, with dark wavy hair and a healthy tan. He was no taller than five foot ten. Therefore, Sammy judged that this was not the genuine Butch Harrell. Moreover, he wore a dress shirt with the sleeves rolled up and slacks—to the park! Sammy took one look at his posture and determined that he was wired for sound.

"Maybe," Sammy replied laconically.

"Butch" sat on the bench beside Sammy. "Miles sent me," he said in a low voice, although there was no one else around.

"Good for you," Sammy said plainly. He wanted to make sure his voice was clear on the tape.

"So what is it you want?" Butch asked, louder.

Sammy closed his book. "To put Miles away for a thousand years," he replied, smiling.

Butch looked disconcerted while Sammy studied him, memorizing every contour of his face. "But—I thought you two were going to . . . work something out."

"You trying to bribe me?" Sammy asked in righteous indignation. "Do you know that I'm an officer of the law?"

"Uh, no—I mean, yeah, but—" Butch stammered. "You asked for this meeting to talk about what you'd take for not arresting Miles."

Sammy shook his head in condescending pity. If

Butch here was trying to get something incriminating on Sammy, he just blew it. "Let me tell you something, pal. Miles is the kind of rodent that'll chew you up and spit you out when he's done with you. If I were you, I wouldn't risk anything to do him any favors. Understand?"

Butch looked at Sammy with an expression approaching consternation. Clearly, he did not know what to think. "'Scuse me. I think there's been a mistake," he said, getting up and tugging at the panting dog on the leash. He walked off quickly, looking back once or twice to make sure that Sammy—or somebody —wasn't following him.

But he needn't have been concerned about that. Sammy idly got up and took Marni's car to the nearest pay phone, where he called Mike. "Hello, lacunose face," Sammy greeted him.

"Do you study the dictionary to come up with these, or what?" Mike asked irritably.

"You'd better be nice to me, or I won't tell you what I found out," Sammy threatened.

"It had better be good. Groebel went into orbit when I told him you aborted the operation. He's almost mad enough to go to the chief about it. Sambo, my life is interesting enough without your shenanigans," Mike informed him.

"Just tell me that you told him to take Canton off it," Sammy said.

"Yes, I told him," Mike confirmed.

"Good. Now this: I believe I just met Miles' stooge in the department. I need you to round up photos of all male personnel in the north central bureau."

"Great. Groebel will be happy to help us out there," Mike said sarcastically.

"Don't drop my name in this request, Mike—the guy was wired. Miles took the bait and half the fishing pole. All I have to do now is identify the guy I just met," Sammy said.

Mike was silent a few seconds. "Sammy, you don't think there's a cover-up in north central, do you?" he asked in genuine concern.

Sammy hesitated. With one crooked cop, that was always a possibility. "No. But until we know who this is, we can't make any assumptions. Just find a way to make Groebel think the photos are for special recognition, or something."

"Yeah," Mike said unhappily. "Okay, Sambo. I'll buzz you at the clinic when they're ready. Keep me posted."

Sammy hung up and drove straight to a fast-food place where he ordered a double-decker hamburger. Waiting in the restaurant, he grew self-conscious at the sidelong stares from other patrons and restaurant workers. He folded his arms to hide the needle marks and casually covered his bruised cheek with one hand. When his burger was ready, he took it out to the car.

He sat in the driver's seat with the door open, unwrapped the burger and chomped down. Then a girl's voice said, "Why doncha eat inside where it's cool?"

Sammy looked up at a young girl in tight shorts and heavy makeup. "'Cause I don't like being stared at," he said thickly and took another bite. When some salt on the patty reached his tongue, he almost arched up out of the seat. Add to that some rising tension and discomfort, and Sammy began to fear a relapse into withdrawal.

Oblivious of his distress, the girl said, "Some people like attention," thrusting out her hips for emphasis.

Sammy glanced up in general dismay. He was in no condition to preach, and she wouldn't have listened if he did. Sighing, he took off his sunglasses and propped his arm on the steering wheel so that the fresh needle tracks were in plain view. "Hop in, baby," he said with an evil leer. "Just make sure nobody'll miss you for a *long time*." He made his voice as hateful as he could, considering that she was so young.

Putting the flirtation on hold, she stared at him as the indecision in her eyes welled up into healthy, overdue fear. Then she backed away and ran into the restaurant. Sammy wadded up the rest of the hamburger and threw it away, leaning over to shut the car door. "And don't approach strange men," he grunted, driving away before anybody from the restaurant could come out and get Marni's license-plate number.

He managed to make it to Dr. Farhoud's clinic, where Marni was waiting to help him back to his room with clean sheets on the bed. "No, no, not again," he moaned, collapsing to the bed. "Please, God, no—" as the trembling crept over him. But the symptoms never progressed further than that, and when they eased, he fell directly to sleep.

Sammy awoke later in the afternoon and just lay there a while. He turned his head to see Marni asleep on the cot nearby, and he smiled. He had regained his appetite, but was disinclined to get up for something to eat. Right now all he wanted to do was lie there and relish feeling no pain.

He looked over again at Marni in shorts and t-shirt. She had kicked off her sandals to lie down, looking so girlish and . . . and. . . . Sammy suddenly slipped off the bed and knelt beside the cot. Carefully, so as not to waken her, he loosened her clothing and kissed her. Marni stirred and Sammy climbed on board.

A few minutes later the door opened and Farley, back on duty, stuck his head in. "Hey! You're feeling better. There's a call for you in Dr. Farhoud's office," he said matter-of-factly, and then withdrew.

Marni blushed crimson under Sammy and he grinned at her. "Sorry. It's a side effect of feeling good again." They got up and pulled themselves back together, then went to the doctor's office to take the call.

"Yo," Sammy said into the receiver.

"All right, Sambo, the portfolio you want is here downtown. Slide by to see Sergeant Purifoy. He's expecting you," said Mike.

"What a guy," Sammy said appreciatively. Mike grumbled something in return. As Sammy hung up, he began to tell Marni, "I'm going—"

"So am I," she interrupted. "I'm tired of hanging around here, and now that you fixed it so that I'm embarrassed, too, you have to take me with you."

"Reason enough," Sammy mumbled with an abashed grin. He left a brief note on Dr. Farhoud's desk before they went out to her car. "Forgot to ask Mike if they found my bike," he muttered, opening the door for her.

"*Your* bike?" she quizzed.

"You know," he said, and she did. Men developed emotional attachments to machines easier than to people, sometimes. Sammy stopped at another fast-food place for a less greasy sandwich, which he ate without a trace of queasiness.

Thirty minutes later when they arrived at the Big Building Downtown, they slipped in a back door and took the stairs to Sergeant Purifoy's office. He greeted them with a handshake and pointed Sammy to a loose-leaf notebook containing photographs of all the personnel at the north central substation. Sammy sat down to look through it confidently, but after he had combed it twice, his self-assurance dissolved.

"He's not in here," he finally confessed to Marni. "Dang! I just know he's a cop. And I'm sure he was wired."

He handed the book back only to discover that Purifoy had collected albums of all department personnel. So Sammy perused the book of northeast substation employees. Not finding what he wanted there either, he combed the books on all the other bureaus, even downtown, and still came up empty.

"Maybe he's with another department," Marni offered. "Or maybe he was with the DPD, but got fired."

"Yeah," Sammy grudgingly admitted, "that's likely —especially the part about getting fired. But that doesn't explain why he would be wired."

"Sammy," Marni began hesitantly, "are you *sure*—?"

"Yes," he said adamantly. "He was wired. I've seen it enough. I'm sure."

"Maybe Miles just wanted to hear what you had to say," she proposed.

"I'm sure he did, but anything he'd want to hear, he'd want to use," Sammy muttered. Marni nodded quietly.

Sammy thanked Sergeant Purifoy and they drove

back to Dr. Farhoud's clinic. Having gone for the day, the doctor left instructions that Sammy was to have free run of the clinic and access to whatever he needed—also, that his presence was to be kept confidential. So while Marni called her parents from Dr. Farhoud's office to reassure them of Sammy's improvement, Sammy cracked the blinds to stare out at the five o'clock traffic.

When Marni hung up the telephone, Sammy let the blinds down and sat with a troubled sigh. She leaned her chin in her palm and watched him. "I'm stymied," he admitted. "I banked everything on being able to identify Miles' go-between as a cop. It looks like Miles has more brains than I gave him credit for. I don't know where to go from here." He looked down at the floor, unwilling to face the possibility of being outmaneuvered by the gang.

"You still have them on solid charges of attempted capital murder," Marni pointed out.

"Yeah, but with their informant intact, they'll get word of warrants and make themselves scarce for as long as necessary. There's—something more that needs to be resolved, but I can't see my way clear to know what," he muttered disjointedly.

Marni studied a cluster of framed diplomas on Dr. Farhoud's wall. "You told me when you called last Tuesday that the gang was into something bizarre. What were you talking about?"

Sammy looked up. "They call themselves the Doors. They seem to think they can conjure up doorways to—I don't know, a supernatural realm or something. I did see some strange things. After thinking about it, though, I believe I was hallucinating due to blood loss." Marni's brows lifted and Sammy described the weird experience in the vacant house which led to his motorcycle accident and meeting with Dr. Farhoud.

Marni listened with chills running down her spine. When he was done, she said, "Sammy, they may have actually tapped into something dangerous."

"What, *The Exorcist* kind of stuff? C'mon, Marni, they're not sophisticated enough to understand all that. They're just a bunch of kids," Sammy protested. In spite of his own experiences, he seemed unwilling to allow for the supernatural at work here.

"They don't need to understand it. We understand very little about prayer, but we've seen what it can do. It's true in the other direction. They don't even have to take it seriously to get hooked—it's different, it's exciting, and they can do it believing they're in control," Marni said.

Sammy regarded her. "So, what are you saying?"

"I don't know," she hedged. "It just seems that perhaps you're not focusing on the real threat here."

"What's that?" he asked quietly. Marni shrugged and looked away. She hated to preach at him. She was afraid he might see her as a nag or a self-righteous prig. "I'm just about desperate, Marni," he added.

"If they're soliciting spiritual help, you should, too," she said abruptly.

He grinned knowingly. "You're saying that I need to pray about it." She eyed him as he pulled up a chair to the desk. "I know that," he admitted. "I just always tend to feel like I should handle it on my own without bothering God."

Taking her hand in both of his, he placed his elbows on the desk and rested his head on their hands. "All right, God, here I am again. By the way, thank you for my partner. Thanks for sending her to rescue me and straighten me out. Thanks for such a foxy nag." He opened one eye to look at her but Marni kept her eyes closed even while she pursed her lips.

"Anyway, God, she's right. I have this situation that I don't know how to handle and I can't just leave it hanging as is. You've helped us before in really amazing ways, and I need Your help again. I don't even know what to pray. Show me how to proceed on this assignment. Show me who this informant is and—and—demonstrate Your authority over the 'powers and principalities.' In Jesus' name, Amen."

Sammy opened his eyes and Marni regarded his faint half-smile. He suddenly got another idea that caused the blue of his eyes to take on an electric quality. He picked up the telephone and dialed. When he said, "Hello, maggot," she wasn't sure whether he was talking to Mike or Miles. He continued: "Getting cute, aren't we? I didn't like the flunky you sent. He smelled bad."

Miles protested, "I don't know what you mean, man. You agreed to Butch. But hey—it's cool. We got somebody else you'll like better."

Miles went off the line and a moment later Sammy heard: "Sammy—they've got me. They're going to kill me if you don't—" It was Canton. Her voice abruptly broke off.

"That's right." Miles came back on the line with a note of satisfaction. "Thanks for the tip, pal. I checked her out and what do you know, she *is* a cop. So Jobs called her up and one-two-three, she's with me. You want her back, you come get her. She'll be on the bench at Churchill Park at nine o'clock tonight. See ya!" he chortled, and hung up in Sammy's ear.

Sammy pensively replaced the receiver. "They have Canton," he told Marni. "Miles told me to come get her at Churchill Park tonight at nine."

"That's brazen," she murmured. "How does he know you won't arrive with a fleet of squad cars?"

"I don't know how he knows, but he's right," Sammy replied, stroking his bristly face. The situation had now gone from grim to galling. Being outsmarted by a juvenile gang was bad enough, but forfeiting his partner to dimwitted Miles was mortifying. While he reflected on this, his conscience berated him: *I blew it, telling him she was a cop. I'm directly responsible for placing a fellow cop's life in jeopardy just to jumpstart a dead operation.*

He suddenly remembered Pam's dream, about it being Tuesday and his trying to make it Thursday. *That's right—that's me. Always trying to force the issue, always trying to make things happen.*

"What are you going to do now?" Marni asked, watching his silence.

"If it's the last thing I live to do, I'm gonna find out who that informant is and blow him away," Sammy replied.

fifteen

Sammy and Marni discussed alternatives for quite some time, until he finally conceded, "I'm going to have to go to Groebel for undercover support. Me and my brilliant ideas. The park is such a great location, no one can hide anywhere nearby. No trees for a hundred yards around. And we can't put cops disguised as park maintenance out there at nine o'clock at night. The best we can do is put somebody with binoculars on Breckenridge or Helsem. But if something goes haywire, they'd be too far away to do much but pick up the pieces."

He drew in a sigh and Marni was silent. "When will I ever learn?" he went on, unable to stop flailing himself. "I always have to be Supercop, doing it all by myself. I should have cooperated more with Canton. I never should have continued the operation without telling her."

Marni stirred slightly. "Hindsight is great, except that it's not very helpful now. If you want to catch Groebel today, we'd better get out there soon."

Sammy nodded and rose from the chair, extending his hand to put it at Marni's back as they walked out to her car. She sat in the passenger seat while he got behind the wheel of the Miata.

It was not far to the north central substation, but Sammy did not appear too eager to get there. They came upon a railroad crossing which had just lowered its barricades and started flashing its lights. Second in line behind the barricades, Sammy inhaled and waited patiently.

The train chugged down the tracks, then slowed ever so gradually and came to a complete stop. Minutes dragged by and it stayed stopped. Cars began piling up in deep lines. Sammy rose in his seat to try to see the cause of the delay. He could not, because the problem was somewhere at the front of the train while the caboose was—maddeningly—just entering the crossing.

"How long have we been here?" he asked, looking at his watch.

"About five minutes," she guessed.

"They'd better move it," he grumbled.

Still they remained stopped, pinned in front and back. Cars far down the line somewhere began honking. Sammy gritted his teeth. "That'll help get the train moving. Honk at it," he said sarcastically.

Ten minutes later they were still sitting in a sea of cars with restless drivers stretching back to infinity. "That does it. Get behind the wheel," uttered Sammy, hopping out. "They can't block any street for more than twenty minutes. I'm going to kick somebody's tail." And he began heading toward the engine far down the track.

About the time he was three cars down the track, the train began moving and suddenly the crossing was clear. Sammy had to dance to get back to the Miata as impatient drivers whizzed around him. Marni edged forward slowly, allowing the driver behind her to vent his frustration via the horn until Sammy was safely in the Miata's passenger seat. Then she took off, following his directions to the north central substation.

Five minutes later she pulled up to the front of the substation and parked along the street. Sammy and Marni got out of the car, turning up the front walk as a man exited the building and walked quickly around them. Head down, Sammy opened the door that was just now wafting shut.

Slowly he raised his head, a glassy look in his eyes. Then he darted back outside and peered down the sidewalk. Puzzled, Marni followed. He stared an instant, then started down the sidewalk at a run. He stopped, looked around, went a few paces farther and looked in all directions. Marni watched from the front of the substation.

He hurried back to where she stood and pulled her inside. Then he demanded of the desk clerk: "The cop who just left—dressed in—ah—khaki shorts and a—a plaid shirt—who is he?"

The uniformed officer cocked a lazy brow at him. "No cop just left."

"The guy with brown hair—about five-ten, dressed in shorts, who just left!" Sammy clarified urgently.

"Oh, you must mean Blanton," the officer said.

"Blanton? Blanton who?" Sammy demanded.

"Blanton Reese. What's your problem, guy?" the officer wondered.

"Reese? Any relation to Canton Reese?" Sammy asked.

"Yeah. It's her brother. Boy, are you bright or what?" the officer replied disparagingly, picking up his ringing telephone.

Sammy and Marni stared at each other, then he took her arm and urged her back out to the car. They sat, and Sammy looked around disconcertedly, almost as if not knowing where he was. "Was that him? Butch, from the park?" she asked in a tense whisper.

"Yes," he said. "I'm sure of it." He wiped his face in a nervous gesture.

"Does that mean *Canton* is the informant?" she asked.

He shook his head uncertainly. "I—I don't know. It could mean that, or that her brother double-crossed her —I don't know." He sat in the car chewing his lip, then got out suddenly and went back into the building with Marni on his heels.

Sammy and Marni went to the investigators' bureau in the back of the building. No one else was here right now. Casually, Sammy sat at Canton's desk and began going through it. Marni stood watch nearby. Suddenly he stilled and picked up a scrap of paper. Marni leaned over his shoulder to see what it was: a telephone number. He laid it carefully aside as he continued to rummage through her desk.

Then he stood, his eyes sweeping the room as if it were enemy territory. He moved from behind the desk and hustled Marni back out to the car. She sat, waiting for him to download his information. "That phone number," he said quietly, watching the rearview mirror, "was Miles' private number. Canton had told me that she had to go through Jobs to reach Miles."

"Then she is in with Miles," Marni said.

"Yes," he nodded slowly. "I believe it's safe to say that she is with Miles voluntarily." He sat immobile, breathing through slightly parted lips, gazing into a maze of deceptions. Then he abruptly jumped out of the car again. Marni, breathing exasperation, followed as usual.

Sammy went back in to ask the desk clerk, "Is Lieutenant Peters still in? Can you buzz him for me?"

"I'll see," the officer said, picking up his telephone. He dialed and spoke into the receiver, then handed it to Sammy.

"Lieutenant Peters?" Sammy asked.

"Yes. Who's speaking?" said a deep, authoritative voice.

"This is Sammy Kidman—Canton Reese's partner on this special gang assignment. I'm—trying to piece together some information we've come up with, and I need to know who recommended me for this assignment."

"Well, let's see. Once we determined to make the gang the focus of a special investigation, I believe it was Canton herself who mentioned your name. We were originally going with someone from our division, of course, but I understand she was impressed with the undercover work you'd done in the past, and thought you could teach her something. I felt the person we had already tapped was capable, but, well, Canton usually gets her way," Peters confessed.

"In the six months that Canton has been working this gang, has she made any substantive arrests?" Sammy asked.

"Well, no, not as yet, because this is mostly fact-gathering, you understand," the lieutenant hedged uneasily.

"I see. Thanks, Lieutenant," Sammy said, and slowly hung up the telephone. Once again he headed outside to the car, and Marni threw up her hands as she followed.

"Spill it, buster," she ordered.

He looked up at her with an affectionate, slightly troubled expression. "Lieutenant Peters said that Canton selected me to be her partner on this assignment. That's contrary to what Mike told me he'd heard. It's sure contrary to what she led me to believe—she told me she'd originally asked for Geoff. So why would she tell Peters to get me, and then lie about it . . . ?" He went silent, drumming his fingers noiselessly on the steering wheel.

"Suppose," he began, "suppose Canton makes contact with the gang through her burglary investigations, and attempts to get in. Suppose she's successful—so successful that the gang leader falls in love with her . . . and she with him. Then suppose he tells her about his brother being sent down the river by this hotshot undercover cop and she says, 'Why, I can serve him right up to you on a platter.'" Sammy eyed Marni, who had stopped breathing. "Is that scenario credible?" he asked.

"Too credible," she breathed. "That means this is all one big setup. You go to that park and they'll just blow you away!" she said passionately.

"Maybe. Depends on how we work it," he murmured, looking across the asphalt shimmering in the late afternoon heat. A moment later he observed, "That train held us up just long enough so that I'd see Blanton

Reese coming out." She nodded in pensive agreement. "Otherwise I'd 'a' gone on in, flayed myself in front of Groebel, then showed up at the park as cop *a la flambé*."

In spite of herself Marni smiled, and Sammy's face suddenly lit up. "Of *course!*" he exclaimed, striking his forehead. "This is the Fourth of July weekend!"

"Yes," Marni said slowly, wondering how his synapses made these bizarre connections.

"Okay, baby," said the hotshot, self-confident cop. "We've got a lot of work to do. Here's our plan. . . ."

At 8:58 that evening, Sammy drove up to Churchill Park in Marni's Miata. Sunset had taken place barely twenty minutes before, and streaks of orange still glowed on the western horizon like embers which heated the night air to a sultry eighty-five degrees.

Unarmed and unwired, Sammy stepped out of the Miata and glanced around. Not a figure in sight. He ambled over to the bench, sat, and folded his arms. A slight breeze stirred the warm air around. Unconsciously, Sammy touched the stitched gash on his right arm, which was healing nicely but still sore.

A motorcycle passed by on the street behind him. Without turning to look, Sammy surmised that he had been spotted by the gang's lookout. Sure enough, in a few moments an entourage of cars and motorcycles, led by a Pathfinder, pulled up beside the Miata. Sammy looked over his shoulder.

Miles, dragging Canton, climbed out of the Pathfinder with Jobs and a few other boys. More gang members disembarked from the other vehicles—about twenty in all. *A good haul,* Sammy mused, smiling. He stood as they approached and encircled him.

"Pat him down," Miles uttered, and Jobs stepped forward to search Sammy thoroughly. Sammy submitted passively, and a few minutes later Jobs backed up with a short nod at Miles.

Grinning in his slack-jawed way, Miles observed, "Man, you're cocky, ain't you? What would you do if I told you we decided we'd rather kill you than give up this here lady cop?"

Canton started and moaned, "No—please—I can't endure any more. Sammy, help me, please!" In her short skirt and tight top, with her blond hair mussed in the twilight, she was the picture of the princess in distress. It was calculated to bring out the knight in any man.

"What do you want for releasing Canton?" Sammy asked.

"First of all, complete immunity. Second, you recant your testimony that convicted Ben. And third, a nice round figure—like about twenty thousand dollars," Miles said with a leer.

"How about the sun and the moon thrown in?" Sammy asked sardonically, and Canton began to cry.

"If you think your life is worth it," Miles shrugged, and the boys tightened their ring around Sammy.

"Kill me if you like," Sammy said with composure. "That'll just upgrade the charges from attempted capital murder to capital murder. You're all under arrest. You too, Canton."

"Sammy?" she gasped in disbelief.

Sammy went on impassively, "You have the right to remain silent. If you choose to speak, anything you say can and will be used against you—"

The boys interrupted with gleeful howls of laughter, one of them thrusting the bat he held into Sammy's lower back. "Shut up!" Miles shouted, and they stilled. "You're crazy," he snapped at Sammy.

"—will be used against you in a court of law," Sammy continued. "You have the right—"

"Enough, already!" Miles shouted. "I know all that! What makes you think you can arrest us all by yourself?"

"What makes you think I'm all by myself?" Sammy asked with curled lip.

The boys began scanning the park. Even in the darkness, they could see no one between themselves and the trees, several hundred yards away. "He's bluffing," one boy finally said, and the others agreed.

Canton, however, had other concerns. "Sammy, why are you talking about arresting me?" she asked pleadingly. To Sammy's mind, that reaction in itself was damning. Accusing an honest cop of complicity provoked outrage, not hurt feelings.

"I found Blanton," he told her. "I offered him the opportunity to sit down and chat with Groebel, Peters and myself. He spilled his guts. It's over, Canton. The D.A. is swearing out a warrant for your arrest right now. And if I die tonight . . . well, you know what kind of trial an ex-cop can expect for the murder of her partner."

At once hysterical, Canton spun to grab Miles' t-shirt. "You can't kill him! What he's saying is true! Don't kill him, Miles!"

"All right, woman!" Miles shouted, knocking her away. Crying fitfully, she collapsed into Jobs. Miles pointed a shaky finger at Sammy. "You haven't won by a long shot, scuzzball. All this hangs on you testifying against us. You forget who we are? You been to the *Doors,* man. We're going to take you back to 'em, only this time you're going through. And by the time we're done with you, you won't know which end to sit in that witness chair!" He gestured to his cronies, who brought out their mystical paraphernalia. Undaunted, Sammy looked past them to the trees.

Canton stopped crying to watch Fos mark out rectangles on the ground with white powder–eight of them, one inside the other—and set up the candle. "What are you going do to him?" she asked anxiously.

"He's too uptight—got too much on his mind. So we're gonna make him a happy camper like Needham," Miles said, nodding. Several of the boys pushed forward a young man who smiled vacuously, looking around without the least hint as to what was going on. He was the one whom Sammy had seen sucked through the Doorways in the vacant house.

"He won't remember anything?" Canton asked hopefully.

"He won't remember there was anything to remember," Miles grinned as Fos stepped back from his completed preparations.

"Then all I have to do is discredit what Blanton told them," she murmured, thinking.

For the first time tonight, Sammy grew uneasy. He did not care for a replay of the events in the vacant house, regardless of their cause. He watched the trees intently. Then he mentally thumped himself. He was looking in the wrong direction for backup. Redirecting his attention skyward, he focused his imagination on a

Man slain from the foundation of the world.

Miles lit the candle and knelt before it. The boys behind Sammy forced him down on the other side, pushing his face into the dirt. But they could not block his inner vision. Miles began his incantations. The words were strange, rhythmic, and hypnotic. Unfortunately, Sammy was diverted in listening to them. Suddenly he felt peculiar, as if something were tugging at his insides. It was very like the feeling of trying to turn inside out during withdrawal.

Looking at the ground, Sammy saw the rectangles instantly telescope in a realm of space which disregarded the distinction between air and ground. He felt something attempting to suck his very soul from his body, and one by one the Doors, starting with the farthest, smallest rectangle demarcated by the white lines, began to fly open. The horror of that invisible something approaching through the Doors left Sammy gasping helplessly.

He closed his eyes and barely whispered the start of a prayer. At once a breath of wind came up which ruffled their hair and extinguished the candle. That light wind also appeared to slam the Doors shut until they collapsed into mere lines on the ground. Everything returned to normal. Muttering expletives, Miles stopped and relit the candle.

They heard a loud popping in the distance. "What was that?" someone exclaimed as they all looked around. The hands were relaxed from Sammy's neck so that he could look up. From just in front of the trees they saw a bottle rocket launch and explode in a shower of colored sparks.

"Cool," a boy said.

"Somebody celebrating the Fourth," another muttered, watching to see what else would go up.

"Pay attention. We got work to do here," Miles scolded. He knelt again and Sammy's forehead was shoved back down to the ground. Miles paused to check the wind, but all was still, so he relit the candle and started the incantations over.

He did not even get as far as the first time. Immediately a stronger gust not only put the candle out, but knocked it over. Then from in front of the trees came the *boom-boom-boom* of a Roman candle shooting into the sky. Several of the boys looked over with interest. "That was a good one," noted one boy.

"Was it closer?" another asked.

"Shut up and get over here!" Miles shouted, aggrieved. "You all stand around me so the wind can't blow out the candle. We can't do the ritual without it."

As he relit the candle in the sudden calm, several more fireworks, palms, went off in quick succession. The group of people shooting them moved steadily away from the trees into the open space closer to the gang, who could hear their laughter and exclamations over the displays. A few boys in the gang, especially the younger ones, seemed more interested in the fireworks than in the nonaction going on around the candle. Once Miles got it relit, the feeble little flame looked pathetic in comparison to the brilliant rockets lighting up the sky.

"Okay. Get close, now," Miles instructed. Neither he nor Jobs noticed the one boy who slipped away to join the rocketeers.

The boys formed a tight cluster as Miles began

chanting the spell for the third time. Two things then happened in quick succession: first, a particularly large rocket exploded above them, and everyone who was clustered around Sammy turned to look. Even he was able to raise his face from the dirt to the sky, and his jaw dropped in wonder.

As the willow shell exploded, it seemed to turn the surrounding night sky green while the descending stars took on the shape of rubber chickens hurtling earthward. Sammy blinked rapidly, seeing the chickens from the underwear in that despicable photo shoot.

But attached to that wilting memory was a promise: that in all his disjointed experiences, in his fumblings and humiliations and dangers, the wisdom of God was an infallible cover, available for the asking. That was his security and the ultimate backdrop of his life. This realization caused an uprush of joy that made all this business with the Doors look so stupid, Sammy doubled up in helpless laughter.

Miles had turned on him furiously when the second thing happened: from behind Sammy a fierce wind lit into the group. Like a whirlwind, it kicked up the dirt in their faces until they were cringing, hiding their eyes. Several boys fell down and began crawling away. Miles was knocked flat on his back, writhing with the pain of the dirt blown into his eyes. Canton crouched, covering her head with her arms as her hair whipped wildly around.

Sammy saw all of this. Although he had hit the ground at the first blast of wind, when he chanced to look up, he found his sight unthreatened. It was as though the wind was being generated directly behind him, blowing everything away from him. Had his hair been as long as he usually wore it, it would have lashed his eyes painfully, but now it merely parted in a neat line along the back of his head.

The rocketeers, having drawn much closer, suddenly sprang toward the prone gang. In the milliseconds between their sudden movement and the voiced command, the wind abruptly died. With guns drawn from a crouch, the rocketeers covered the gang members and Pruett shouted, "PO-leece! Toss down your weapons and spread on the ground!"—an unnecessary order, as they were all flattened anyway.

When Sammy got up, Marni ran over to throw her arms around his neck. "Are you all right?" she whispered anxiously.

"Yeah," he said, squeezing her, then he stared down at the ground. There was no trace of the rectangles remaining. They had been so thoroughly obliterated that four inches of topsoil had been gouged out along with them. Sammy glanced heavenward. "You made Your point," he muttered wryly.

"What?" Marni said.

Pruett came up to them while an officer from the north central substation handcuffed Canton. In great distress, she gazed at Sammy, who returned the look. "Why'd you do it, Canton? Why'd you set me up?" he asked quietly.

"You wouldn't understand," she moaned, then turned away with the officer.

Sammy turned his attention to Pruett. "You took your sweet time getting the pyrotechnics going, pal. Didja forget the matches?" Sammy asked scathingly.

"Shooting off low explosives is an art, Sambo," Dave replied haughtily. "We certainly expected that you were professional enough to keep your own hide intact until we had maneuvered in for the assist."

"They couldn't get the launcher to stand up until somebody finally realized they had it upside down," Marni whispered.

"Really?" Sammy grinned, his arm around her. "I can't *wait* to read about that in your report."

Pruett looked uncomfortable. "Not really worth mentioning."

"You bet it is. I'll mention it plenty. Unless—" Sammy hesitated for emphasis, and Dave eyed him suspiciously. "Unless I *never* see or hear anything about a certain newspaper ad again," Sammy finished.

Dave appeared crushed. "Spoilsport."

Police cruisers began arriving to take the gang members into custody. Sammy noticed one young boy clinging to an officer's hand. The boy was not cuffed, nor did it appear he would be. The officer with him paused by Sammy and Pruett. "I know Chad here. I'm takin' him home."

Sammy eyed the boy and Pruett explained, "This kid ran over to us and told us there was a cop about to get wasted. We told him to stay back and watch the show." He patted the boy's shoulder.

Sammy was still studying him. Discerning his features by the occasional sidelight from a flashlight was difficult, but he finally recognized the boy as the one he'd grabbed to prevent his being sucked through the Doors in the vacant house. Sammy suddenly smiled and nodded at him, and the boy responded with a tentative smile before being escorted to a patrol car.

Looking up, Sammy watched Miles, Jobs and the others being loaded into a transport van. Then he saw Lieutenant Peters coming over from where Canton sat, head down, in a cruiser.

"Well, Kidman," Peters began reluctantly, "I didn't believe one word you said this afternoon, especially when Blanton denied it down the line. You were lucky that Masterson had the guts to back you, else we never would have run this cockamamie scheme. But Canton's spilling it all out. It's just about what you said. She says she just fell in love—she did it all for love." He seemed chagrined to say it.

Sammy murmured, "What you do for love is useless unless you understand where it came from to start with. I mean, He set the standard." Sammy glanced up at the sky, then down at Marni, still tucked in his arm. "And she said *I* wouldn't understand."

As he walked Marni to the Miata, he murmured, "It's been days since I've seen Sam . . . how cranky will he be tomorrow if we wake him for a little while tonight?"

sixteen

Sammy lay on his back with his eyes closed while Sam, bouncing on rubbery legs, alternately beat and drooled on his chest. Sammy took it with aplomb, listening as Marni, sitting on the blanket beside him, told Pam and Clayton all about the gang assignment.

He could not help smiling as he detected the minor (unconscious) colorations she put on the narrative to make him look ever the hero. But he said nothing until Sam grabbed a fistful of chest hair under Sammy's tank top and yanked.

Sammy sat up with a yelp, scooping up the mischief machine and pleading, "Sam, that's ATTACHED"— while Marni was relating how bravely he had endured withdrawal.

Pam smiled as she reached over and plucked her grandson from Sammy's hands. "C'm here, kissyface. Let's not inflict any more pain on your poor ol' daddy." So saying, she glanced at Sammy's solid arms. In the two weeks since the assignment's completion, the needle marks had healed, but the two-inch scar on his forearm remained. Pam concealed the worried expression on her face by smothering baby Sam with kisses. He squealed and cackled.

Clayton leaned over to the cooler and brought out another soft drink. Opening it, he glanced around at the scores of other families on blankets and lawn chairs. Kids were everywhere, eschewing the organized games for tossing projectiles and running in circles to exhaustion. A few dogs jumped and barked among them, happily greeting the occupants of every blanket.

"A department-wide picnic," Clayton mused. "Good idea. I'm glad to meet so many of the people you work with. There is a strong sense of camaraderie," he observed.

"Yeah," Sammy muttered, lying back down and squinting up at the spreading oak branches high overhead. There was something about trees that took the bite out of summer. Even in mid-July, it was pleasant resting in the shade of one of these old folks. Natural air conditioning.

"By the way, I don't believe I told you the latest about FirstPlace Bank Tower. At the last board meeting, we viewed the film from the camera in the security room which showed your—encounter with Ms. Bancroft," Clayton said.

Sammy looked over from behind his sunglasses. His father-in-law continued, "The upshot is, she has been fired, but the board agreed you were still in a good position to sue. They asked me to re-extend the offer as security chief to you at a guaranteed salary of ninety thousand a year, plus benefits."

Marni and Pam quickly looked at Sammy. He began slowly, "I'd be crazy not to accept that—"

"But he can't. Thanks for the offer, Daddy, but he can't accept," Marni said cheerfully.

"Why not, dear?" Pam asked with a touch of irritation.

"Because I won't let him. He's doing what he needs to be doing, and he's earning plenty to support us," Marni said, wiping drool from Sam's chin with a napkin. Pam looked down and bit her tongue to keep from interjecting an unsolicited opinion.

Sammy sat up on his elbow and took off his sunglasses to regard his wife. There was surprise and gratitude in his eyes. "I guess I understand that," Clayton reluctantly allowed, "though certain aspects of his job give your mother and me gray hairs."

"Tell me about it!" Marni said with feeling. "But then, you don't see all the people he helps. The gang has been broken up, and a lot of the boys have gone into special youth programs. Dr. Farhoud sponsors three of those boys in rehabilitation himself."

"What about the lady cop who double-crossed you?" Clayton asked. "You know, when I saw you two in the parking lot, I knew there was trouble. You looked about ready to dump her then and there."

Sammy smiled thinly. "And I didn't know the half of it at the time. Canton is up on a slew of charges, but the worst part of it is the black eye she gave her whole station. I almost feel sorry for her." Marni glanced away with pursed lips and Sammy hastened to add, "She was just in the wrong line of work—she didn't have the mental toughness to take the pressure. Lucky for me, I have a partner who does." He reached over to touch Marni's fingers. Pam smiled in private resignation.

"Know what I can't figure out?" Marni suddenly asked Sammy. "Why did Canton call me when you were being held at the Greenleaf Apartments? Didn't she know where you were?"

"Actually, she didn't," Sammy replied, replacing his shades. "That little fact saved her from the charge of accessory to attempted capital murder. They found the message I had phoned in to her, and it actually said 'Greentree Apartments.' When she never heard from me and started trying to track me down, she called Miles, and left his number sitting out on her desk. He told her I was with them, but he didn't tell her what they were doing to me—they both swore to that. He didn't want her involved. But he did want to know if I had told anyone else where I was going, and that's why she called you." He tilted his head toward Marni.

"Now, with his previous convictions," Sammy resumed, stretching lazily, "Miles will be looking at a mandatory life sentence."

"With the doors behind him slammed shut in deep echo," Marni murmured, and Sammy looked over with a crooked smile.

"Then, you won't have any more special gang work?" Pam asked hopefully.

"Not unless Mike assigns it. Whatever gang activity remains in the north central area will be handled by the regular gang unit. They're competent, and they didn't appreciate my incursion onto their turf. Me, I'm happy to get back to the grungy, bottom-of-the-barrel assignments that crop up at TAS," Sammy said in transparent contentment.

Pam sighed very slightly. "I do wish that community

college job had panned out," she said wistfully.

Sammy adjusted his sunglasses. "That's not entirely dead in the water. The executive director talked me into teaching a couple of special Saturday sessions. Should be interesting. He's a real mover and shaker—a guy after my own heart."

At that point Dave Pruett's eleven-year-old son, Chris, came running up. "Sambo! They're ready to start the game! Come on! They need you!"

Grunting in gratification, Sammy hopped up and grabbed his cap and softball glove. He started to trot importantly after Chris, then stopped and turned, hands on his hips. "Isn't *anybody* in my family supportive enough to come watch me play?" he asked, affronted.

The people on the blanket exchanged quick grins, and Pam began to pack leftovers in the basket. "Wouldn't miss it for the world, my darling peacock," Marni said, standing with Sam.

"Sammy, *come on!*" Chris exclaimed impatiently as the guys waved him over. And the peacock strutted onto the field.

Clayton brought the blanket closer to the diamond, where they sat to watch the game. Sammy's team, The Clock Cleaners, was playing a team from the southeast bureau, The Rock Bottoms. They were allegedly the toughest team in the department. The Clock Cleaners won the toss, and Sammy headed the lineup.

He stepped up to the plate, taking a few practice swings. Sleek and muscular, he crouched in a serious stance awaiting the pitch. His wife smiled tightly to hear a woman nearby ask, "Who's the studmuffin at bat?" Marni wasn't telling.

Sammy jumped on the first pitch and cracked it just over the shortstop's head. He missed it, and Sammy took off for first base. A fielder's error allowed him a stand-up double. Hands on hips, he stood on second base popping his gum in a too-cool manner, acknowledging the applause with the quick flash of a grin.

Marni continued applauding as Dave Pruett stepped up to the plate. Chris was jumping up and down in his show of support. Marni smiled at him and waved at Chris' mother, Kerry, seated in a lawn chair. Pruett took a more cerebral approach to batting than Sammy, which usually resulted in a hit or a walk after a three-two count. His distracting ploys drove opposing pitchers crazy, and numerous suggestions were made from the infield as the pitcher worked up to a full count.

While the pitcher and catcher discussed strategy, Marni watched Sammy. He was glancing along the sidelines when suddenly he paused and yanked off his sunglasses. He was staring at someone just past first base. Curious, Marni looked down the baseline and saw a blond woman lift her hand in a subdued greeting to him.

Marni looked back at Sammy, who replaced his sunglasses and turned his attention back to the game. But he had lost his cocky attitude. He kept glancing toward the blond woman, and Marni felt her insides freeze up.

As the pitcher prepared to deliver on the full count, Sammy took a large lead off second base. Pruett cracked a sound shot down the third-base line and Sammy hardly looked before tearing around third for home. He slid into home base—a painful proposition in shorts—and limped off to cheers after scoring the first run.

Bypassing his family on the blanket, he walked right over to the blond woman, who clasped his face in her hands and kissed him. Sammy held her and kissed her in return. "That must be his wife. The good ones are always married," said the anonymous admirer near Marni, whose face was burning. First Canton, and now this woman—where were these blondes coming from? Marni began to feel an irrational hatred of blondes.

A moment later Sammy turned, urging the woman to accompany him. He began bringing her toward his family seated along the baseline. Marni fought the urge to jump up and run away. Seeing the two approach, Clayton and Pam, holding Sam, stood. After a moment of reluctance, Marni did, too.

Sammy changed course in the middle of a sentence: "—these are my in-laws, Clayton and Pam Taylor; my son, Sam, and my wife, Marni." They extended hands to the woman, who had gossamer blond hair and the delicate, flawless face of a fairy queen, wary in the land of mortals. Marni felt clumsy and coarse shaking her hand. Sammy began to introduce her: "This is my—"

"Old friend," she interrupted. "DeAnn Cedrano. It's so nice to meet you," she said to Marni. "I hadn't seen Sammy in years, and had no idea whether he was still with the department or not. Oh, Sammy, your baby is— adorable. It's amazing how much he looks like you. You look happier than I've ever seen you. Well, got to run. My husband's going to wonder what happened to me. Good to see you, Sammy. 'Bye, now." She waved and turned to walk off with a quick, bouncy stride. Sammy watched her go a moment, then shrugged and rejoined the game.

"Lovely girl," Pam remarked as they settled back down on the blanket. "It says a lot about Sammy that his old girlfriends think so highly of him."

Marni nodded pensively. "I agree." Especially since that was his ex-wife.

They continued to watch the game, but Marni saw nothing further than DeAnn's face imprinted on her memory. Marni recognized her from a picture she had found in one of Sammy's old record albums. DeAnn looked just like the kind of woman a man like Sammy should marry—beautiful, fragile and childlike even in her thirties. That Marni was about ten years younger was little consolation—DeAnn looked all of twenty-five.

Sam began fussing and wailing. Marni lifted him to her shoulder. "I think he needs to nap," she murmured, rocking him.

"Let us take him home and put him down. You and Sammy can come for him after his game," Pam urged.

"Are you sure?" Marni asked hesitantly.

"Sure. You know he'll go right to sleep as soon as he gets in the car seat," Pam said, taking him from Marni's shoulder. Sam yawned and began howling. Sammy glanced over from his position at first base.

"Okay. Thanks, Mom," Marni relented. Clayton took up his diaper bag and leaned over to kiss her. "'Bye, Daddy."

"See you later, sweetie. We're real proud of your old man, Marni," he added.

"Thanks, Daddy. Me, too," she smiled as they departed with their grandson.

Marni leaned back on the blanket to watch Sammy play. He was seriously into the game, his eyes riveted on the Rock Bottoms' batter. Pruett's pitch came sailing over the plate; the batter swung and made mighty contact. The ball came out in a straight line over the infield. Sammy sprang up and snagged the ball in midflight four feet over his head then wheeled to fire the ball to Robeson on second base, who picked off the runner.

It was a typically brilliant Sammy-type move. The spectators went crazy. Marni looked around at the enthusiastic crowd. Everybody loves a showboat, and Sammy played the part grandly. In character, he ignored all the adoration, only casting a glance over his shoulder at Marni. He did a doubletake when he saw her sitting still. She quickly brought her hands together to clap like everybody else, and he turned back to the game, satisfied.

Marni watched him: The studmuffin. The star. The risk-taker and the ground-shaker. Then Marni looked at herself next to him and saw an indistinct figure in the shadows. Just a wife.

Reflecting on this, she grew disturbed. When had she relinquished everything to become an extension of him? Was this what marriage was all about—her living vicariously in his shadow, applauding him, rescuing him, focusing all her energy on him and his son? Was she nothing but a baby-maker and caretaker?

Marni wrestled unhappily with this as she watched the two teams thrash it out. They had gathered quite a crowd, as it was a close, exciting game, with many spectacular plays and long hits.

While Sammy kept his eyes on a pop-up, waving away his teammates, Marni was thinking, *This is scary.*

Apart from him, who am I? He caught it, of course.

The game ended with a narrow, one-run victory for the Clock Cleaners. The two teams filed past each other to shake hands, then a happy, exhausted ballplayer came over to collapse on Marni's blanket and rifle the cooler for a soft drink. He pulled out the last one, then upended the cooler to douse himself with ice water. Marni sat back laughing as he shook his head, showering her with beads of water from his black hair.

Wet and grinning, Sammy flopped back contentedly in her lap. "Where'd everybody go? They missed a great game."

Stroking his hair, Marni replied, "Sam got tired and fussy, so they took him home with them for a nap."

Nodding, Sammy raised up slightly to pop the top on the can and take a swig. "Yeah, I heard him. Your parents are great, Marni. I couldn't ask for better in-laws. They're so supportive."

"Yes, they sure are," she murmured. And she thought of her mother, who had relinquished her position at the art museum in order to stay home and raise her only child. Pam had always told her that although it was often difficult and lonely, it was the best decision she'd ever made.

Pam, who had spent her life denying herself for the sake of her husband and child, was nothing of a martyr. She was intelligent, beautiful, interesting, fun and rather unpredictable. She found everything she desired from life in her painting, her volunteer work, and a family who adored her.

Look to the rock from which you were cut and to the quarry from which you were hewn; look to Abraham, your father, and to Sarah, who gave you birth. The verse from Isaiah came to Marni's mind with startling clarity. Yes—look to the example her mother set in her faithfulness. Look at the profit from her life. If Marni was unsure of what role she should play, all she had to do was look to her origins for a pattern.

"I hope DeAnn showing up like that didn't bother you," Sammy said from her lap.

"No, it didn't," Marni lied.

"That was a shocker. It's been—" he counted on his fingers. "It's been nine years since I'd last seen her. She said she and her husband just moved to Plano from Houston. They were passing by the park; she saw the picnic and stopped to see if I was here. I'm surprised she'd go to the trouble."

He paused to greet somebody who came over to congratulate him on the game, then he lay back happily in her lap and closed his eyes. "She's—very beautiful," Marni observed.

"Huh?" Sammy squinted up at her. "Oh, DeAnn. I guess. Not nearly as beautiful as you." He kissed her hand and pressed it against his face.

"C'mon, Sammy; she's gorgeous." Marni pulled her hand away, taking offense at what she perceived as a white lie.

He looked at her, then raised up on his elbow. "Sometimes I forget you're so young until I have to explain things to you that everybody else knows. Because DeAnn's got a pretty face doesn't make her beautiful. She's totally self-absorbed and hasn't got a shred of love in her for me or anybody else. Sure, I was young and selfish too, but I tried to be good to her. And when our baby died, she turned on me like a—a rattlesnake. By the time she was through ripping into me, I was impotent."

He considered something. "You know, for a long time I thought it was Meredith's death that made me that way, but now I realize it was DeAnn's *reaction* that did it. Marni, you don't appreciate the power you have as my wife—you can destroy me or make me invincible. You'll never know how grateful I am for the strength you give me. It's a cliché, I guess, but only because it's so true: I'm nothing without your love and support. I couldn't make it without you." Sammy's blue eyes glowed like neon.

Marni absorbed this, then leaned over to kiss him. He placed his hand at the back of her head to press her face tightly to his. "Well," she murmured, "it's a tough job, but somebody's got to do it."

"Thank you," he whispered, encircling her with his arms.

At the Big Building the following Monday, Sammy had begun to settle into his between-assignments routine of working Auto Theft when he was called by a colleague from Capers (the Crimes Against Persons Bureau). The weekend had been a busy one for the criminal element, producing a spate of reports, including numerous robberies. These received top priority, and when there were too many for the Crimes Against Persons Bureau to investigate adequately, other experienced detectives were enlisted to take the overflow. So Sammy and Dave Pruett were both detailed to Capers for the day.

Sammy spent much of the morning on the telephone tracking down a witness to a carjacking. He was finally able to get an address, and hung up as he wrote down the information. Immediately his telephone rang again, and he plucked it up. "Kidman."

"Hi, Sammy," said a soft voice.

He paused, lifting up from the pile of papers scattered across his desk. "Hello, DeAnn," he said levelly. Pruett, at his desk, glanced back at Sammy over his shoulder.

"You always hated desk work—said you wanted to be on the street forever," she observed in her breathy voice.

"You do what the job requires," he shrugged. "Uh, what can I do for you?"

"Oh, it's been so long. I thought we should have lunch and talk about old times," DeAnn suggested with a slight laugh.

Sammy lowered his head and scratched his eyebrow. Marni's reaction when they had talked about DeAnn sprang to mind as a clear warning. "Uhhh, DeAnn, I'm —pretty busy. I probably won't take time off for lunch today."

"Tomorrow, then?" she asked lightly.

"If anything, tomorrow's going to be worse than today. Besides, I don't really know what we'd have to talk about. You're married, and I'm married, and . . . life goes on. Let's just—wish each other well and leave it at that," he said. Pruett didn't turn around, but Sammy knew he was listening.

In the ensuing silence, DeAnn inhaled. "I didn't realize it would be so easy for you to forget Meredith."

Sammy's gut coiled. "I haven't forgotten her. I think about her all the time. But you and me getting together is not going to bring her back."

DeAnn started crying, and Sammy leaned back in his chair, rolling his eyes. She pleaded, "How can you be so heartless? Are you forgetting all the pain I suffered—the emergency Caesarean and the—"

"I remember!" Sammy shouted, and Pruett quickly looked back. Lowering his voice, Sammy said, "I remember, but there's no point in rehashing all that ten years later. If you're still having trouble dealing with it, you need to go talk to somebody about it. But not me. I'm not going to be any help to you at all, DeAnn."

"You certainly weren't any help then, either," she said coldly. "You wouldn't even give me the chance for another baby." She hung up before Sammy could reply.

Jaw tensed, Sammy replaced the receiver. Then he stood, saying, "Let's go, Pruett. I got a witness to the Grand Am hi-jacking."

Nodding, Pruett took up his sports coat and accompanied him down in the elevator. He glanced at Sammy's rigid face, but said nothing until they got out to his Mustang in the white-hot parking lot. Sitting in the passenger seat while Sammy cranked up the engine, Dave asked, "Was that your ex?"

"Yeah," Sammy muttered, turning the wheel to back out of the tight space. "Did you ever meet DeAnn?"

"No. Was she at the game Saturday?" Dave asked.

"Yeah. First time in nine years I've seen or heard from her, now all the sudden she wants to go out to lunch. Go figure," Sammy muttered. Pruett nodded silently.

They arrived at the target address and spoke with the man who had witnessed the carjacking. It had been a rather brutal affair—two men had approached the Grand Am at a stop sign, jerked the driver from behind the wheel, and had driven off over him. But first they had relieved him of a diamond-studded Masonic ring, worth somewhere in the neighborhood of eight thousand dollars. The victim was presently in the hospital with two broken legs. The Grand Am had been recovered, stripped. Sammy and Pruett were now working on apprehending the perpetrators.

"Let me see if I've got this: the first guy was Caucasian, twenty to twenty-five, five-foot-nine, one-hundred-fifty pounds, long brown ponytail—d'you think you remember enough to give a description to our artist?" Sammy asked. It did not fit the description of any known cons from the area who had recently been paroled.

The witness, a retiree, sat back in his easy chair. "Sonny, I never got closer than twenty feet away. You won't catch me trying to play the hero—not with scum like that," he declared.

"Yes, well, could you identify him in a lineup?" Sammy asked.

"Not a chance," he said firmly.

"Well—" Sammy returned in disappointment to his notepad. "Suspect number two: Caucasian, twenty to twenty-five, five-foot-nine, one-hundred-fifty pounds– can you remember anything more distinctive about him?"

"He wore a green cap." Shifting in his chair, he shouted, "Maude! Where's my lemonade?"

"Coming, dear." His wife entered with a tray of three tall glasses, which she set down on the table beside them. "I thought these gentlemen might like some," she added, smiling.

"Thank you, Mrs. Darby." Sammy accepted a glass and took a perfunctory sip. Pruett thanked her and downed his entire glass. "What, like a baseball cap?" Sammy asked.

"Yep," Mr. Darby said, settling back with his drink. "Wore it backwards on his head, like they do now."

"Was there a logo or anything on it?" Sammy asked.

"No. It was just green," Darby said.

Sammy looked down at his notepad and scratched his eyebrow. His beeper suddenly went off. He glanced down at it and frowned. "May I use your telephone?" he asked Darby, who jerked his head toward the kitchen. Sammy got up and went to the kitchen, where Mrs. Darby was preparing lunch.

"Would you care for a sandwich?" she asked brightly.

Sammy hesitated. She was at work on a big hero-type sandwich with deli meats and tomato slices on a toasted bun that smelled fresh-baked. "No, thank you. It looks great, but I can't take the time right now. May I use your telephone?" he asked.

"Certainly. Right behind you," she nodded.

He turned to the wall phone at his shoulder and pulled out his phone card to dial the unfamiliar number from his beeper. He had to use the card because the number had a Houston area code. It rang, and—"Hello," a soft voice answered.

Sammy drooped. Now he knew who had been

calling his home from Houston. "DeAnn, why are you still using your Houston cell?—never mind. What is it?"

"I did what you suggested. I've made an appointment with a grief counselor for two o'clock today," she said coolly.

"Great. I'm glad. I hope you get it all worked out. Goodbye," Sammy said.

"Wait! You need his address," DeAnn said.

"No, I don't," Sammy disagreed.

"You do. He said you need to come, as well," DeAnn told him.

"No way. This is your problem. I've got plenty of my own," Sammy said, looking down at his notepad.

"Sammy, you have to come. He said he needed to talk with both of us," DeAnn insisted tearfully.

"You just call him back and explain that I couldn't take the time," Sammy said, and hung up.

He went back to the den where Darby sat in his chair watching a game show on television. Sammy stared at his notepad, trying to recapture his train of thought. "Mr. Darby—"

"Maude!" he hollered. "Where's my sandwich?" Pruett began to rock in his chair and then stood up, a barely restrained smile playing on his face.

"Here it is, dear." Mrs. Darby came in with a nicely garnished sandwich.

"I don't see anything else we need at present. Thank you for your help, Mr. Darby. If you do remember anything else, please give Detective Kidman or myself a call," Pruett said, placing a business card on the table beside the easy chair. Darby grunted.

Sammy sighed and nodded. He hated to let go of

their only lead in the case, but. . . . He and Pruett headed out to his car. "Do me a favor," Sammy muttered. "If I ever start treating Marni like that, give me a good, swift kick in the rear."

"Let me go get my roach-killers on. Kerry says you order Marni around like a geisha girl," Dave replied. Sammy looked up, startled.

"Oh, officers!" Mrs. Darby came out of the house waving, and Sammy got out of the car to meet her on the front walk. She handed him two brown paper sacks. Sammy opened one to find a loaded hero sandwich and a napkin. "Since you didn't have time to sit down and eat, I thought you'd like to take a sandwich with you," she explained.

Sammy cleared his throat and humbly said, "Thank you very much, Mrs. Darby."

seventeen

Sammy sat at his desk typing out a summary of Mr. Darby's comments. The half-eaten sandwich lay atop yet another report. He took a bite of sandwich and finished the last line, yanking the paper from the carriage. His telephone rang. He picked up the receiver and mumbled, "Kihnmum."

A pause. "Is this Detective Kidman?" asked a man with a professional voice.

Sammy cleared his mouth. "Yes, it is."

"Detective Kidman, this is Dr. Graham Haliburton. I am Ms. Cedrano's grief counselor. She tells me that you refuse to come in for counseling."

"That's right," Sammy said, picking through the papers on his desk for a clean sheet.

"I must emphasize how important your cooperation is to Ms. Cedrano's healing," Dr. Haliburton said. "In order for her to reach acceptance, she must work through the stages of grief with the person who was part of the initial crisis."

Sammy looked up at the wall with steely blue eyes. "Look, uh, Dr. Haliburton, I don't know exactly what

DeAnn wants out of this, but she's doing a number on you. Before Saturday, I had not seen or heard from her for nine years, and now all of a sudden she needs me to come to counseling with her? Get real."

"It sounds as though your denial of the grieving process requires professional attention," the doctor observed.

"I didn't ask for your opinion," Sammy retorted.

Dr. Haliburton paused. "Who is your supervisor?"

"Sergeant Mike Masterson. Would you like his telephone number?" Sammy asked.

"Yes. I would like to alert him to the fact that your hostility and lack of cooperation indicate the advisability of psychological testing of your fitness to be a police officer," Dr. Haliburton said.

Sammy blinked. After a moment, he mumbled, "I'll be at your office at two."

"Thank you," the doctor acknowledged. He gave Sammy the address—the thirty-first floor of the FirstPlace Bank Tower—and hung up.

"I should've known he'd be located at The Money Place," Sammy muttered darkly.

At two o'clock he was trotting warily through the FirstPlace lobby to the elevators. He saw Allison Pinella coming off an elevator and quickly averted his face, only to brush against Ms. Bancroft's secretary. Muttering apologies, he sidled onto an elevator. A girl he had seen in Ms. Pinella's waiting room stared hard at him. "Haven't I seen you before?"

"No," he said, raising a hand to cover the lower half of his face.

The girl turned to her companion to quietly insist, "I

know I've seen him in print." While he rode up to the thirty-first floor gritting his teeth, everyone on the elevator studied him.

When the doors slid open at his stop, he quickly disembarked and found the counselor's suite. "I'm Sammy Kidman and I've got exactly thirty minutes," he informed the receptionist. Eyeing him with offended brow, she buzzed the doctor.

Sammy was shown into a lush interior office, heavy on the wood paneling and plants. He shook hands with Dr. Haliburton, who looked exactly like what Sammy imagined Sigmund Freud must have looked like. DeAnn was already sitting across from the doctor's desk. "Detective Kidman, please have a seat." Dr. Haliburton gestured to the vacant leather chair beside DeAnn. Sammy plopped onto the seat without looking at her.

"Now," Dr. Haliburton drew his chair up to his desk and folded his hands. "Ms. Cedrano, why don't we begin with an account of your marriage?"

"I've got thirty minutes," Sammy warned him, glancing at his watch.

"I understand. We need to be brief, Ms. Cedrano," the doctor said gently.

"Well," she began, twisting her hands together, "Sammy and I met at the University of Texas, where he was majoring in sociology—"

"Criminal justice," corrected Sammy.

"—and I was a theater major. He was just so—good-looking, and all my friends were after him, but I felt that he really drank too much. He wouldn't leave me alone, though, so finally I told him he'd have to marry me to get what he wanted," she said. Sammy rolled his eyes.

"We got married in our junior year, and Sammy decided he wanted a baby right away," DeAnn continued.

"We talked about that before we got married. I told you I wanted a baby and you agreed," Sammy said.

"Please don't interrupt, Mr. Kidman," the doctor said. "Go on, Ms. Cedrano."

"I got pregnant barely a month after we were married, and had to drop out of school. That was so hard," she said, biting back tears.

"At the time, you were glad. Your grades weren't all that great," Sammy interjected.

"Mr. Kidman," the counselor reminded him.

"The pregnancy was very difficult for me. And then the day she was born—the ultrasound tests showed problems—they put me under and did an emergency Caesarean—" DeAnn put her face in one hand and began to cry.

Sammy sighed, then reached over and took her hand. "Our daughter was born with hydrocephalus. She lived about six hours. We—weren't prepared for anything like that. It tore us up."

"I see. And what was your reaction, Mr. Kidman?" the doctor asked.

"I just told you. I was devastated," Sammy replied with drawn brows.

"But what was your reaction to your wife?" Dr. Haliburton asked.

"I tried to comfort her as best I could. What do you say?" Sammy asked.

"You never shed a tear," DeAnn flung at him accusingly as she withdrew her hand.

"I didn't know how to cry, DeAnn," Sammy said in a low voice. "That didn't mean I wasn't hurting."

"And after that, he refused to have sex with me at all. He wouldn't even try!" DeAnn said indignantly.

"I *couldn't,* DeAnn; I was impotent. But I didn't wait ten years to get help for my problems!" he shot back.

She broke into fresh tears and the doctor admonished, "Recriminations are not helpful, Mr. Kidman."

"Do you mind assigning us the same set of rules, doc?" Sammy asked irately.

"And what were your feelings toward your husband, Ms. Cedrano?" the doctor asked.

"I hated him," she replied, and Sammy nodded slightly. "But I stayed with him another two years, trying to make our marriage work."

"Punishing me to within an inch of my life," Sammy amended.

Ignoring him, the doctor asked, "Did you ever talk with him about your child's death?"

"I tried to, but he wouldn't talk about it," she said.

Sammy nodded. "That's true."

"So what would you like to say to him about it now?" the doctor asked.

DeAnn turned passionately to Sammy. "I hate you for shutting me out and abandoning me during the worst time of my life. You were cold and indifferent. You spent all your time partying or at work. You kissed me only when you had to and you wouldn't hold me at all. You treated me like defective goods because I had delivered a defective baby. Emotionally, you discarded me like a piece of trash!"

Sammy gazed at her. Dr. Haliburton allowed a few seconds of reflective silence to pass, then turned to him. "Your turn, Mr. Kidman. What would you like to say to Ms. Cedrano?"

Sammy swallowed and said, "I'm sorry, DeAnn." That's all. No excuses, no self-justification, no counter blaming, just a helpless admission of guilt.

There followed a long moment as they stared at each other. The grief, the silence, the animosity—it all washed up like long-discarded garbage on the shore. Then DeAnn lowered her face to cry quietly and Sammy looked away. Dr. Haliburton blinked several times, but otherwise his face was impassive.

Finally the doctor cleared his throat and said, "Well, I suppose that provides some closure as to your relationship at the time. You may leave, Mr. Kidman. I will continue the session with Ms. Cedrano alone."

Nodding, Sammy stood and walked out. He took the elevator down and went to his car. It was a blindingly hot day. He paused to remove his coat and lay it on the seat, then he cranked up the engine and backed out.

Driving out of downtown, Sammy picked up his car phone and dialed with his thumb. "Pruett," it was answered.

"Guy, give me the address of that Grand Am jacking again. I'm gonna go knock on some doors around there," Sammy said.

"Right. It was—" Pruett paused as he dug through papers on his desk. "The intersection of Burrows and West Claiborne."

"West Claiborne. Thanks," Sammy said, and hung up.

He drove to the intersection and parked along the street. It was an older, slightly run-down neighborhood. Replacing his coat, he walked up to the first house on the east side of Burrows nearest the intersection and rang the doorbell. After a few minutes an elderly lady with a cane opened the door slightly and peered out suspiciously over a door chain.

"Ma'am, my name's Sammy Kidman. I'm a detective with the police department." Sammy held his badge up to the door crack. "Last Saturday, around nine o'clock at night, there was an incident at this intersection where two men hijacked a red Grand Am and ran over the driver. I'm wondering if you or anyone in this house may have seen that happen?"

"No," she said, and shut the door. Sammy withdrew down the sidewalk and went to ask the same question at the next house, and the next, and the next. In the event that someone in the neighborhood was out and around that night, Sammy canvassed houses clear down the block to the next intersection—ten houses. At several doors his knock went unanswered; those who did come to the door to hear him out claimed to know nothing.

When Sammy reached the end of that block, he went back to the West Claiborne intersection and started canvassing the east side of Burrows south of Claiborne. He walked, and talked to people, listening carefully to their replies, but there was something vaguely detached about his manner. In between visits he wiped sweat from his face and neck until his handkerchief was sodden. "Gotta be over a hundred today," he muttered.

An hour and a half later he was covering the houses on the north side of West Claiborne. A grandmotherly-type woman answered his knock at her door and invited him in. "Would you like some iced tea?" she asked.

"Thank you, ma'am, that would be greatly appreciated," Sammy said. His coat felt about ten pounds heavier than it had been that morning.

As he stepped inside, Sammy glanced around the tidy front room of her home. A teenager watching television lolled in a chair in front of a window air conditioner. He glanced up when Sammy came in. Sammy looked at his green baseball cap, worn backwards.

"Here you are." The woman returned with a tall, cold glass of iced tea, which Sammy accepted with gratitude.

After chugging half of it, Sammy began his spiel: "Ma'am, last Saturday night around nine o'clock, there was an incident at the corner of Burrows and Claiborne here in which two men hijacked a car out from under the driver and then ran over him. I would like to know if you or anyone in your house may have seen it happen."

"Goodness, I didn't. Did you see anything, Charles? But you weren't here, were you? My grandson Charles," she told Sammy.

Charles looked languidly over. "The Grand Am? That was Bodunk," the boy said.

Sammy startled. "Bodunk? Bodunk who? Did you see him do it?"

"Nah, I was out at the Headless Barbies concert then. He was just braggin' about it all weekend. He's such a twerp," Charles said derisively.

"Why didn't you call us?" Sammy demanded.

"Hey, man, I didn't hear nothin' else about it, so I

thought he was just blowin' wind," Charles said defensively.

Sammy flipped open his notepad. "What's his full name?"

"Terence Leroy Black," said Charles. "Bodunk."

"What's his address?" Sammy demanded.

"Oh, he's staying at his girlfriend's apartment. One sixteen at the Trail's End," Charles replied.

"You got a picture of this Bodunk?" Sammy asked.

Sighing at all these demands, Charles got up heavily and went to a back room. In a few minutes he returned with a snapshot. Pointing to one of three boys in the picture, he said, "That's Bodunk."

Sammy took the photo, a reasonably clear shot which matched the description Darby had given him, and scribbled on the back of it. "Now, did Bodunk say anything about an accomplice? Who helped him take this car?"

"He said it was somebody called Zebroid. But I don't know him, man," Charles replied.

Knowing that he could be buying a pack of lies, Sammy asked, "One more question, Charles: How long is Bodunk's hair?"

"Oh, it's extensive, man. You can't tell from the picture, 'cause he wears it pulled back," Charles replied.

Sammy gave him a quick, canny smile. "Thank you," he said, pocketing the picture and heading out to his car.

He called Pruett with the information he had just gathered. After taking it all down, Pruett said, "Get out there and I'll meet you in an hour with a warrant."

"Do it," Sammy confirmed.

He drove to the Trail's End apartments and parked on the street in sight of number 116. Then he sat and waited, watching the door.

Five o'clock rolled around, and people started coming home. Sammy watched a girl pull into the parking lot in an older Chevy. She unlocked the door to 116 and went in. A few moments later she came back out, shouting angrily over her shoulder at someone inside the apartment. Sammy observed as she got into her car and peeled out of the lot. He continued to watch the apartment.

About forty minutes later Pruett arrived, armed with an arrest warrant for one Terence Leroy Black. Sammy got out of his car to meet him. "He's there," Sammy nodded toward the apartment.

"Let's go," Pruett invited with curled lip.

They approached the apartment door. Pruett drew his gun and flattened himself on the right side of the door while Sammy knocked from the left. When the door opened a crack, Sammy kicked it wide open and they sprang inside with guns drawn. "PO-lice!" Sammy shouted. (Not "puh-LEESE," as most people said, but an authoritative "PO-leese!" so that there was no question that it was a statement and not a request.)

The man inside jumped back and threw his hands into the air. "Don't shoot, man! Don't shoot!" His long brown ponytail hung over one shoulder. Sammy reached forward cautiously to pat him down. He extracted a pistol from the suspect's belt and a wallet from his back jeans pocket. After looking at his driver's license, Sammy nodded.

Pruett produced the arrest warrant while Sammy

turned Bodunk around to cuff him. "Check it out," Sammy said, holding up Bodunk's hand, adorned with a diamond-studded Masonic ring.

Pruett nodded. "Excellent. You're under arrest for aggravated robbery and assault with a deadly weapon. You have the right to remain silent. . . ." As he recited the Miranda warnings with the relish of an Academy Award presenter, Bodunk slumped in resignation.

It took another hour to get Bodunk processed in and a photo lineup delivered to the victim in the hospital, who had no trouble at all selecting Bodunk's picture from the lineup. Sammy then confided to Bodunk that he was sure this whole thing was Zebroid's idea, and that Bodunk was just basically in the wrong place at the wrong time, but they couldn't do a thing about it because they didn't know Zebroid's real name and address. So it was a crying shame that poor ol' Bodunk would have to go down alone on charges that rightfully belonged to Zebroid.

Bodunk then looked to save his own skin by giving them all the information they needed to arrest Zebroid, which they did. (Regrettably, Sammy neglected to clarify to Mr. Black—Bodunk—that he would be facing the same charges whether Zebroid was ever apprehended or not.) What with picking up the accomplice, notifying the federal authorities of the arrests, and completing all the required paperwork, it was eight-thirty before Sammy dragged himself home that night.

When he opened his apartment door, Sam lifted up sleepily from his blanket on the floor. Ella was playing on the stereo and the aroma of barbecued chicken wafted from the kitchen, where Marni had kept supper waiting for him. In shorts and her tight Juju's t-shirt, she came to greet him with a smile and a kiss. "Hi, Sammy. Hungry?"

His eyes began to water. "Marni, I love you, and not just because you gave me Sam. Even if there had been anything wrong with him, I would still love you and stay by you. I know I've been taking you for granted, and I'm sorry; I'll try to be better about listening to you and not treating you like my own personal maid. You're the most important person in my life, and God reminded me that I need to treat you that way. Please bear with me— I'm better than I used to be, and I really, really love you."

Marni listened open-mouthed. "I love you, Sammy. What, have you been sitting around lashing yourself all day long? You don't want to get fired again."

He bent to pick up Sam. "Not to worry; I got a few things done at work. But I have been thinking about you all day, yes. And yes, I'd love a plate of that chicken. Thank you, baby."

(The story continues in *Sammy: On Vacation*)

Books by Robin Hardy

The Streiker Saga
Streiker's Bride
Streiker: The Killdeer
Streiker's Morning Sun

The Annals of Lystra
Chataine's Guardian
Stone of Help
Liberation of Lystra
(first published as *High Lord of Lystra*)

The Latter Annals of Lystra
Nicole of Prie Mer
Ares of Westford
Prisoners of Hope
Road of Vanishing
Dead Man's Token
Games of God and Men
In Extremis
All Mirrors and All Suns
The Laughing Side of the World

The Sammy Series
Sammy: Dallas Detective
Sammy: Women Troubles
Sammy: Working for a Living
Sammy: On Vacation
Sammy: Little Misunderstandings
Sammy: Ghosts
Sammy: Arenamania
Sammy: In Principle
(continued on next page)

Sammy: Grave Agreement
Sammy: Love Shouldn't Hurt
Sammy: The Consolation of Bucephalus

The Idecis
Unknown Name, Unknown Number: A Wimsey Reade Mystery
Padre and its sequel *His Strange Ways*

Edited by Robin Hardy

Sifted But Saved: Classic Devotions by W.W. Melton

Made in the USA
Columbia, SC
07 December 2020